IN THE MADNESS OF TIME

Ian Macpherson

This paperback was first published in 2024 by
Gnarled Tree Press
an imprint of Cloudberry Books, Glasgow

The right of Ian Macpherson to be identified as the author of this book has been asserted in accordance with Section 77 of the Copyrights and Patents Act 1988.

All rights reserved, including the right to reproduce this book in any form whatsoever without the express written permission of the publisher. For more information and permissions contact
Cloudberrybooks@gmail.com

Author website: IanMacpherson.net

British Library Cataloguing-in-Publication Data
A catalogue for this book is available on request from the British Library.

This book is a work of fiction. Any references to historical events, real people or real places are used fictitiously. Other names, characters, places, events are products of the author's imagination, and any resemblance to actual events or places or persons, living or dead, is entirely coincidental.

ISBN 978-0-9569056-3-5

All moral rights of the author reserved.

Typesetting & Cover Design by Cloudberry Books

Ian Macpherson's One-Man Shows at Edinburgh Fringe

Other People   Calton Studios   1988
'It is hilarious; but it is also rich Dublin social history, incisive and instructive, as well as universal in its wit and wisdom. The man is an entire city on the move.'
Owen Dudley Edwards, The Scotsman
'Even his silences are funny'
Edinburgh Evening News

The Chair   Assembly Rooms   2001
'A small tragic masterpiece, but you would hardly have known it to hear the laughter from the audience'
The Scotsman

The Joy of Death   Pleasance   2002
'A mini-masterpiece'
Scotland on Sunday
'Best laugh I've had in nine years'
Man

Macpherson's Lament   The Stand   2003
'As James Joyce remarked of Flann O'Brien, he might equally have said of Ian Macpherson: "That's a real writer with the true comic spirit." Joyce wrote that the Irish sea's snot-green waters would be the future bards' inspiration and Macpherson hysterically proves him correct. His deadpan manipulation of English is a joy to the ear. If you fancy previews of undoubtedly great fiction to come, join Ian Macpherson in this entertaining lament.'
Jay Richardson, The Scotsman

Macpherson's Lament   The Stand   2003
'Macpherson presents a world decked out in vibrant colours and grotesque absurdity. His Dublin is decked out with soul-smashing Lady Chatterlys and homeless Madonnas, its streets course with a distorted sense of religion, found in bookshops or shown on TV. There is no salvation but to laugh.'
Fest

The Everlasting Book Launch   The Assembly Rooms 2015
'Droll, deadpan and devastatingly funny. We are instantly drawn into the sheer absurdity of his crazy, unique world. A master comedian at the top of his game.'
Arnold Brown

Ian Macpherson's Stand Up

'The Godfather of leftfield Irish comedy'
Hot Press

'The Comedians' Comedian'
Irish Times

'One of the most creative and intelligent comedians I've ever seen.'
The Guardian

'The Comedians' Comedian's Comedian'
Harry Hill

'Pre-dating and pre-empting all contemporary Irish comics, and the originator of the most influential joke of all time, Ian Macpherson is the Newgrange Megalithic Passage Tomb of stand-up comedy.'
Stewart Lee

'The evening belonged to Ian Macpherson – a self-effacing master of immaculate one-liners.'
Guardian

'(His) somewhat morose aspect conceals much that is not morose'
Alasdair Gray

'In spite of my best efforts, Ian was always the perfect gentleman.'
Gayle Tuesday

Ian Macpherson's Novels

Sloot

'The comic energy of voice and character is given genuine weight by the sense of mortality that pervades; add a meta magnificence and you get a wonderfully funny novel bathed in a melancholic Clontarf garden light that shines, ultimately, with life and art.'
Irish Times

'Perfect for fans of comedic detective metafiction; if Thomas Pynchon and Flann O'Brien had collaborated, they might well have come up with a novel like Sloot.'
Jane Harris

Hewbris

'Very smart, very funny lunacy'
Irish Times

The Autobiography of Ireland's Greatest Living Genius
Deep Probings & Posterity Now

'The Spinal Tap of Irish Literature. The funniest book I've ever read.'
Brian Boyd, Irish Times

'Comedy's answer to James Joyce'
BBC Radio 4

'*Fiachra MacFiach, Genius, bursts from the womb clutching a slim volume, his mission to storm the citadel of poetry. Deep Probings will destroy you: it is fiercely, resentfully and damagingly funny.*'
Lucy Ellmann

'*A deft satire about a self-absorbed poet, which felt far closer to Swift or Voltaire than alternative comedy.*
The Guardian

Late Again!

'*A bittersweet but charming book for children about a daydreaming dad on a cross country dash to keep a date with his estranged daughter. Its plot twists should appeal especially to kids from broken homes, but its surreal twists and melancholic sense of fun will delight adults of all ages.*'
The Guardian

The Book of Blaise

'*Kick Myles na gCopaleen into the next century and you'd get something like Ian Macpherson - the same eye for absurdity, the same ear for wordplay*'
David Robinson: Literary Editor – The Scotsman

'*The Book of Blaise is the unapologetically personal account of one man's struggle with the superiority of women, specifically his wife Blaise. It's the funniest book I've read since… his last one.*'
Northwords Now

In the Madness of Time

"*Crazy. Dangerous. Hilarious. Do not fucking read.*'
Ali Whitelock

IN THE MADNESS OF TIME

Ian Macpherson

'All will be revealed,' she said, *'in the madness of time.'*

To Magi Gibson
&
all like-minded women

1

According to my therapist, I suffer from high self-esteem.

That line came to me as I opened the living-room shutters on a glorious Edinburgh morning. Sunshine streamed in like nature's spotlight. I was lost, for a moment, in a reverie of the past. Me onstage at the festival, oh, years ago now. I shook myself out of it, and went to wake Blaise.

Easing the bedroom door open I whispered into the semi-darkness. 'Are you asleep?' Blaise shuffled under the covers. 'Mnnng'. I took that as a yes. Her head was visible just above the duvet, framed by her lovely hands. My heart did that skip-a-beat thing. I hadn't seen her face for some time. Since the previous night, to be precise. And gazing on it slumbering so peacefully gave me an excellent idea. Blaise's latest slim volume, *The Crone Diaries*, had just been published. There was a nice little independent bookshop nearby. I'd leave her to sleep on for a while, check if they had it in stock and report back. So I closed the bedroom door quietly, pulled on my light summer jacket, and headed for the outside world.

I bounced down the spiral stone staircase of the flat we'd be calling home for the next few weeks. Tiny turret windows, perfect for defending the place with a bow and arrow, or am I harking back to a kinder, gentler age? Possibly. I slipped the arrow back into its imaginary quiver, headed out the main door and Oh! The Grassmarket. Tall centuries-old buildings with distinctive crow-step gables. Colourful cafés and bars reflecting modern times and, looming up behind, the rear view of Edinburgh Castle.

The Grassmarket itself is a modest square in the heart of the Old Town, steeped in Scottish history. Public hangings, ancient inscriptions over the doorways – *Blissit be God for Al his Giftis*. These days, however, it throbs and bustles with the present. Early morning still, but the square was already teeming with life. Flagstones being washed, rolls being delivered to a tiny café close by. I breathed in the city-scented air, turned right and strode off towards the narrow Cowgate and on to Nicholson Street, past the towering Surgeon's Hall with its six Greek pillars and its grisly history, down a small side street and there it was. *Qwe(e)rtyuiop Books*. Intriguing name. Which, from a marketing point of view, is pretty clever. It draws you in. Not that I needed drawing. I was going in anyway. So in I went.

It was, in a good way, a pretty modest space. Just two small rooms joined by an open partition. And wall to wall, table to groaning table, books.

Behind a counter, to the left of the entrance, a young woman sat reading. I glanced at the cover. *Orlanda* by Virgil Woolf. Nearby, a tall, slightly-built young man cradled a pile of paperbacks while he scanned the shelves for more. You'd think he'd be like the tables, groaning under the weight, but no. Straight-backed in his neatly cut jacket and neatly cut jeans.

I managed to locate the poetry section pretty easily. No sign of *The Crone Diaries*. I was wondering about asking at the counter when I realised the young guy was staring at me. In a pretty overt way, to be honest. He could have been looking past me at the bookshelves, of course, but when I moved, his eyes moved. The bookshelves stayed where they were.

He moved tentatively closer, still cradling his bundle, and peered directly at me. 'It is you, isn't it?'

'It is indeed,' I said. 'Who else?'

'*The Joy of Death*, right?'

Oh. Right. A one-man show I'd performed at the fringe some years back.

'Recognition at last,' I replied.

He hugged his pile of books closer and almost danced with excitement. 'I knew it. Oh my *gosh*! I'm literally *speechless*. I *loved it loved it loved it*.'

This was – well, let's say it was the last thing I was expecting. He must have been half my age. I toyed with the word *humbled* but decided against. Two reasons. I hate the word. And why lie?

'So what are you doing in Edinburgh?' he said, almost caressing me now with his books.

I took a discreet step back. 'Cat-sitting,' I said. He seemed disappointed. Wrong answer. 'Actually it's just a short break.'

'Fantastic!' He balanced his books on top of another pile of books on a display table. 'You don't know who I am, do you?'

'No,' I said, 'but you know who I am. And that's the important thing.'

He didn't laugh, just seemed to weigh it up. 'Torquil Pittock,' he said at last, beaming at me. The young woman looked up momentarily from her book as if the name meant something to her.

'Wow!' I said. '*The* Torquil Pittock?'

'Well, yes,' he said, straightening up even straighter.

'Double wow!' I paused for a beat. 'Who's Torquil Pittock?'

He beamed approvingly. 'Genius!' He took his books over to the counter. 'Look, how can I get hold of you? I mean, like, maybe I could have your number?'

Bit forward? Having said that, there was nothing threatening about him. Besides, a fan was a fan. And fans, at this stage in my career, were pretty conspicuous by their absence. So I gave him the number.

Should I be worried though, I wondered, as he tapped it into his mobile.

A fan, after all, could sometimes be more than a fan.

Back at the flat I found Blaise up and dressed, sitting by the living-room window, engrossed in a book. She blew me a silent kiss. It was going to be that sort of break. Calm. Peaceful.

And, yes, meditative. We'd had a pretty hectic year. As I said, Blaise's latest poetry collection, *The Crone Diaries*, was out in the world. I'd just finished *Hewbris*, the follow-up to my post-postmodern crime anti-thriller *Sloot*. Only a few days ago, we'd been looking forward to a three-week break on a lighthouse in the far north of Scotland. A kind of second honeymoon. Just the two of us. No Internet signal. No phone. In the end, no break. The lighthouse, they informed us at the last minute, had been double-booked. Pretty infuriating, as you can imagine. Then this urgent request had come in. Could we do a month-long cat-sit for Blaise's old university friend, Fraser? His flat, his cat. Why not, we thought. Not exactly the away-from-it-all break we'd been hoping for, but it had its positive side. Bumping into old friends from my festival days. The odd coffee out. Oh, and Blaise was keen to locate the grave of her great-aunt Isabella, a feminist before the term existed, apparently. And that was it. An excellent rent-free base for four weeks in Edinburgh, and all we had to do was feed Freya. Perfect.

My reverie was interrupted by a loud ping from Blaise's mobile. She glanced at the screen. Important ping. She was on it. Total concentration. Freya, I noticed, a green-eyed fluffy ball of black fur, was glowering at me from the corner. I mean, what is it with cats? I hardly knew the blessed thing, so why the glower? I pushed my chair out from the table and patted my lap. No response. Freya stayed rooted to the spot. Glowering. Four weeks of this? I could take it. I went into what the Scots call a dwam, my mind flitting back to the bookshop and the strange young man, Torquil Pittock. He seemed to think he was someone, and for all I knew maybe he was. This was Edinburgh at festival time. Everyone thinks they're someone, and some of them possibly are. Bumping into him had been a nice little ego fillip if I'm being honest. I was about to relive the experience when Blaise set her mobile down on the windowsill, killing the dwam.

'That was Karima. She says hi. In Urdu.' Blaise smiled one of her amused for a reason smiles. 'So,' she said. 'What's happening?'

'A walk, maybe?' I said. 'A la Recherche du Grave Perdu? I thought we might start at Greyfriars Kirkyard.'

'Sounds good. But before that.' She narrowed her eyes. 'What were you just thinking?'

'Sorry?'

'You know what it's like when you – no, maybe you don't.'

'Okay,' I said. 'I popped into a little bookshop just off Chambers Street earlier, thought I'd check if they had any *Crone Diaries* in –'

'*Qwe(e)rtyuiop Books*,' said Blaise. 'Don't tell me. They didn't. Go on.'

'– when I was accosted by a fan.'

'Ah! That would explain the smile.'

'He'd seen *The Joy of Death*. Positively gushed!'

'Lovely. And?'

'That's it. Gushed. Exit me.'

'I see. Did you get his name?'

'Torquil.'

Blaise nodded. 'Torquil.'

'Exactly. Torquil – something. Pittock. Torquil Pittock.'

Her eyebrows shot up. 'Really?'

'Yes. Really. Why?'

'Oh, just – he could be *another* Torquil Pittock, I suppose.'

'What? You don't know him, do you?' I asked.

'Not know, exactly,' said Blaise. 'Know of. He runs *Le Salon Littéraire*. Very influential in certain circles. But never mind that now. I seem to recall some mention of a walk?' As Blaise grabbed her bag and popped her mobile in, Freya mngiaowed loudly. Blaise gave me a suspicious look. 'You did remember to feed her, didn't you?'

Ah. That would explain the glower. 'Not,' I replied sheepishly, 'as such.'

'Good start,' said Blaise. 'Four blissful weeks. One dead cat.'

She went over to the kitchen, grabbed a tin of cat-food from the nearest cupboard, prised it open and scooped the contents into Freya's bowl. Freya purred loudly, rubbed up against Blaise and started happily gobbling it down, tail erect, her rear end pointed, reprovingly I felt, at me.

*

We were halfway down the spiral stairs, when my mobile rang. 'I'll get it later,' I said. 'Won't be anything important.' We'd just stepped into the street and closed the main door when it rang again.

'Better take it,' said Blaise. 'Just in case.'

I glanced at the screen. Number unknown. 'Hello?'

'*Hi!*'

That was it.

'Hi yourself,' I said.

'Can we meet? Like, asap!'

Ah. I'd just placed the voice. 'Thing is, Torquil,' I said, 'I'm a bit tied up at the moment –' Blaise waved a hand. 'Ah. I think I'm just about to be untied.' A pause at the other end. Possibly shock. 'Figure of speech, Torquil,' I said. 'How about *The Naked Munch*?'

I could see it right across the street from where I stood.

'Perfect,' said Torquil. 'Let's say fifteen? Twenty tops.'

'Okay. See you there.' I pocketed the mobile as we started walking again.

'I was half-expecting something like this,' said Blaise.

'Like what?'

'You? Edinburgh? Festival-time? It was never going to be a quiet retreat, was it?' she smiled.

Me. Edinburgh. Festival time. She certainly had a point. 'Tell you what,' I said, 'let's stick to the original plan. I'll call him back. Cancel. Today is just for us.'

Blaise thought about this. 'Better idea,' she said. 'I was going to drop into the National Library at some point anyway. Pick up a couple of books I need for my Women's Library talk next week. So how about I do that now, you have a little bonding session with your new fan, I pop back and rescue you.'

'Promise?'

'Promise. Now fly to him. Fly to him!' Blaise likes to have fun with old rom-com groaners but this, I felt, was in poor taste.

'As well you know,' I said, 'there's only one man for me and he's a woman.'

Blaise put her arms around me and pulled me close. 'Do I know him?' she whispered, I'm tempted to say, huskily.

'You know him very well,' I said, 'but not, I like to think, as well as I do.'

'I wouldn't bet on that,' she laughed, disengaging.

Maybe she was right. Maybe this break wasn't going to be as quiet as we'd planned. I watched her go, then headed across the road.

2

The celebrated *Naked Munch*. Home to the legendary *Sewer* magazine in the late fifties, now a trendy bistro, its large front window plastered with posters for arts and book events. In pride of place, a blown-up replica of the very first *Sewer* magazine cover. Or was it? Hold on. Same retro artwork, but no, not a magazine cover at all but a poster for a forthcoming event.

Sewer Relaunch
with
Very Special Guest

I took a mental note of the date. Thursday, August 21st. Brilliant. We were still in town. This was a definite must, a chance to connect with a mythical artistic age. But who would the special guest be? Ginsberg? Ferlinghetti? Some beat-up old beat? Or maybe they were going for the next generation of cool. Toby Smyrke? "The novel is dead. I should know – I killed it." He didn't say the last bit. I'm saying it on his behalf. Toby, an alumnus of all the best educational establishments, author of some of the most incomprehensible – sorry – *lauded* novels in the English language. Very Special Guest? It probably had to be Smyrke. I grimaced mentally, opened the *Naked Munch* door and headed inside.

The interior was bigger than I'd expected. Busy, but not too busy. I wandered over to a long wooden table laden with an eclectic mix of old copies of *Sewer* amidst a display of Frida Kahlo dolls, brightly coloured bead necklaces and ornamental hash pipes. At least, I assumed they were ornamental. A young man stood behind the *Sewer* table with faux-hippy hair, matching straggly beard, loon pants – loon pants! – and a neatly ironed

Fuck The Cops t-shirt.

But where to sit? I chose an empty table near the door. Two chairs. One from an Edwardian sitting room, the other one of those narrow wooden jobs with a very high back. Presbyterian Chic? I chose the well-upholstered Edwardian and made myself at home. While waiting I checked Torquil out online. Ah, now this was interesting. He'd just published a memoir. At his age?! I was about to delve further when –

Enter Torquil. I waved, he spotted me immediately and strode over. If anything he was taller than I'd remembered. Still too young for a memoir, though. He sat down in the high-backed chair and beamed down at me.

'So,' I said, 'what are you having?'

'Can we skip the drink?' he said, leaning eagerly forward in his chair. 'I am so, so busy.'

'But not too busy to meet me?' I asked.

He leaned even closer and lowered his voice. '*Book Snuff*,' he breathed.

I was confused. *Book Snuff* was one of my little jeu d'esprits. A mock pitch for a radio series. I'd stuck the blurb for it on my website a year or two previously then pretty much left it to itself.

'Sorry?' I said.

'You heard. Two words. *Love it love it love it.*' He paused for a happy sigh. '*Le Salon Littéraire*,' he continued. 'I've got to have it for the last night of our festival run. Great website, by the way. Love the images. You are so – God, what's the word – photo*gen*ic.'

'Oh well, you know,' I said. 'Great photographer.' Blaise had taken them all with her mobile. They'd never got that sort of response before. But *Book Snuff*. Could Torquil really be interested? For the last night? Essentially, it's a subversion of the panel show format. Authors slug it out to win the fabulous prize   a posthumous book deal. I'd sent it to a couple of producers at the BBC. Sheer mischief on my part. Naturally, they turned it down.

'You were saying,' I said. '*Book Snuff.*'

'Exactly. It's an awesome concept. Original and edgy. Perfect for The Grand Finale! All we have to do is book the authors, then you turn up on the night and do your amazing compère-type thing. I mean, you are *so funny.*'

I'd have to say I was totally thrown by this. I'd never thought of *Book Snuff* actually happening outside the dark recesses of my head. At the same time…

'Sounds tantalising,' I said. 'Slight complication, though.'

'Other commitments,' said Torquil with an exasperated sigh. 'I know. A man of your talents? You must be *inundated*.'

I hadn't been inundated for some time, but I wasn't telling Torquil that.

'Tell you what,' I said. 'I'll have to run it past my people.' For my people read Blaise, but you have to play the game. At which point, however, my performer's ego kicked in. 'Having said that, I'm sure we can work something out.'

Torquil *phew*ed. 'That is *such* a re*lief*,' he said. 'Everything is falling into place. Oh, and maybe I will have that drink. Lemon tea would be perfect.'

While he dived on his mobile, I went up to the counter and took my place in the queue. As I waited I took out my own mobile to check what I'd said about *Book Snuff* on my website.

BOOK SNUFF*

Writers! Ever thought you'd sell more books if you were dead? Well, now's your chance. *Book Snuff* – an innovative and daring new panel game in front of a live audience – is the ultimate Great Career Move. Pit yourself against your arch-rivals in a winner-takes-all scenario.

What you pitch:
- A one-paragraph blurb of the book you'd like to be remembered by
- A short extract in the style of yourself

- The ideal setting for your own posthumous book launch
- Original ideas for your – also posthumous – bespoke marketing campaign

In a further attempt to market you we'll also shamelessly exploit one of the following:
- Your most humiliating rejection slips
- Your best sex scene – with ambient soundscapes courtesy of the *Book Snuff* quadrophonic sound effects department
- Your mother's teenage diary

What you get:
- A posthumous publishing deal with *Snuff Books*
- The chance to present your own obituary to a sympathetic audience
- A lifetime supply of Euthanasia Kits

Finally, you get to choose the manner of your own death, the wording on your tombstone, and the book you'd like to be buried with. You've already got the *Bible*, the *Torah*, the *Bhagavad Gita*, the *Book of Mormon*, the *Tibetan Book of the Dead* and the *Koran*.

* *Book Snuff* was originally devised as a panel game in 1920 by emerging author Virginia Woolf in an ill-fated attempt to murder fellow author James Joyce. She was furious with Joyce, it seems, for being even more impenetrable than she was. The plan backfired when she ended up winning the first grand finale herself. Her career hasn't looked back since. Winners of subsequent finals include Ernest Hemingway, Sylvia Plath, Richard Brautigan, Anne Sexton, Hunter S. Thompson and Yukio Mishima.

Little Known Fact: Ms. Woolf, or Miss Woolf as she was known in those days, offered *Book Snuff* to the BBC Home Service. She was turned down on the grounds that the BBC didn't exist at the time.

All blackly comic, and I hadn't seriously intended it for performance; but maybe, with a bit of work, it would provide the framework for a panel show. Three authors with a book to promote, me to compère. Choose the right guests, set them off, what could possibly go wrong?

I'd just started to check my biography was up to date when –

'I'll try that again. Can I help you?'

'I'm terribly sorry,' I said, holding out the mobile to the young woman behind the counter. 'My website. Just checking the *About Me* page.'

She had the good grace to laugh. 'Welcome to Edinburgh.'

Back in my seat with the drinks, Torquil got straight down to business.

'I was thinking about possible writers,' he said. 'But just to be clear.' He looked momentarily troubled. 'The winner doesn't *actually* die?'

'Course not,' I said. 'They win the Edinburgh heat. We then take the show to New York, Sydney, Kuala Lumpur and so on. So there's never an outright winner.'

'Oh, good,' he said. 'It might be a bit of an ask getting it past Health and Safety.'

'Relax,' I said. 'It's all good clean fun. A chance for writers to be creative and playful. Oh, and sell books. So, *Book Snuff* at *Le Salon Littéraire*. Tell me more.'

'No, no – first, you tell me all about yourself. Spare nothing. I want to know *everything*.' He sipped his lemon tea, his long fingers delicately holding the small china cup, his gaze intent. And strangely discomfiting.

I've edited the next few pages. Save them for the memoirs. But, and this surprised me, Torquil proved a very good listener. I'd just got to the part where I devote my life to the comic muse – 'That is so, so *riv*eting' – when the cafe door opened and in came Blaise. She grabbed a wicker chair en passant and plonked it at the table in front of a startled Torquil.

'Blaise Torquil, Torquil Blaise,' I said. 'Blaise is my – ' I was about to say wife, but something stopped me. 'Torquil wants me to do *Book Snuff* at his gig. Last night of the festival.'

Blaise looked temporarily thrown. 'Oh. Right.'

For his part, Torquil seemed suddenly fascinated by the menu.

Back to Blaise. 'Okay then,' I said. 'Can I get you a drink?'

'I'll sort that,' she said. 'You know I like a good queue.'

As she headed off to join it, I tried to make out what she was thinking from her back.

No luck. Ah, well. Just me and Torquil again.

'I've had a think about the line-up,' he said, popping the menu back behind the sugar bowl. 'How about Toby Smyrke?'

'Seriously?' I said. 'Have you read his book?'

'Which one?'

I meant the new one, *word*, but any would do. Before I could answer, Torquil was back in. 'I've read them all. Reviewed most of them in the *LRB*. He's hot.'

'Hot is good,' I said. I patted my pockets for my notebook. Last pocket. Always last pocket. 'We'll stick him on the shortlist. Anyone else?'

He reeled off some names. All of them well-known, all of them in town for readings or shows or generally just to be seen. Shortlist, shortlist, shortlist. I was just giving them the once over when Blaise arrived with a latte and sat back down.

'Torquil has some excellent ideas for the *Book Snuff* line-up,' I said. 'I've jotted them down for consideration.'

She slid the notebook over and studied the page. 'Interesting list,' she said. 'Lots of – what's the word I'm looking for? Help me out here.'

I glanced at the names. Nothing suggested itself immediately.

'Men,' she said. 'Might be an idea to include a, you know, *woman*?'

Torquil picked the notebook up and pretended to examine it in detail. 'How about Robin/Robyn? They'd be great, yeh?'

Blaise almost splattered the table with her coffee. A sudden sneeze? Uncontrollable mirth? Or outrage? Hard to tell. It took her a few moments to compose herself.

She smiled at Torquil.

'Sorry,' she said. 'Hay fever. You were saying?'

'How about Robin/Robyn?' I repeated on Torquil's behalf. 'They'd be great.'

'Well,' said Blaise, 'they'd certainly up the numbers.' She turned to Torquil, and smiled. 'Have you maybe thought about Karima Lucknawi? Could be a great fit.'

'Karim Alucknawi?' He frowned for a moment as if riffling through a file drawer in his head. 'Not sure I've heard of him.'

'Ka-ri-ma,' Blaise corrected him, emphasising each syllable. 'Luck-na-wi. Fabulous talent. We both love her stuff.'

'We certainly do,' I said. 'Hilarious comic novelist. Karima would be a perfect choice.'

'Brilliant titles,' said Blaise, counting them off on her fingers. '*The Property Chain (My Father's Daughter, My Husband's Wife)*. Great sequel too. *Arranged Divorce*.'

'Not to mention my particular favourite,' I pretty well gushed. '*The Patriarch's Protuberance*.'

'Penis,' said Blaise. '*The Patriarch's Penis*. We're all adults here.' She turned to Torquil. 'Her take on Gogol's *The Nose*.'

We were on a bit of a roll and Torquil, to be honest, looked borderline shell-shocked. Facial subtext? Robin/Robyn - yes, Karima with an "a" – no way. I decided to help him out.

'Sadly, however,' I said, 'Karima's in Rawalpindi –'

'At present,' Blaise interjected. 'But the excellent news is that she flies over for the last day of the festival. Afternoon event. She'll be free for *Book Snuff* in the evening. I'm sure she'd love to do it.'

Torquil looked troubled. 'Let me have a think about that, yeh?' he said, fixing me with a brooding look and handing me back the notebook. 'Obviously,' he said, 'this initial list is just off the top of my head. Anyway, got to go.' He pushed his chair back and stood up. 'Oh, and I'll need a tagline. For the website.'

Blaise glanced at her mobile. 'Bloody hell. Six missed calls.' She stood up abruptly. 'I'd better deal with this. Could take a while. Tell you what. You finish your coffee, I'll see you back at the flat. Great talking to you, Torquil.' An enigmatic smile aimed straight, I felt, at me, and she was off.

Torquil watched her go, an odd look on his face. He waited till the door had swung shut behind her and turned back to me.

'Best get the initial blurb up today,' he said. 'Just the basics. We can announce the line-up later as we get the acts booked. So. *Book Snuff* at Le Salon Littéraire.'

I put his strange behaviour around Blaise to one side and concentrated on the job in hand. The thought that *Book Snuff* might become a reality – and at the Edinburgh Festival – excited me. Who knew what other doors it might open?

'How about *Book Snuff – The Ultimate Great Career Move*?'

'Sweet.' He tapped it into his phone. 'This is going to be awesome!' He gave me the full beam treatment – 'Go Team Us!' – and headed for the exit.

'You know what they say,' I shouted after him. 'A dead writer is a happy writer.'

A passing customer seemed to agree with me. Late fiftyish. Crumpled suit. Dark, unkempt hair. Slightly hungover look. He gave me a lopsided grin in passing. The "nice one" grin.

I was intending quickly finishing my coffee and heading back to the flat, but crumpled suit man intrigued me. He seemed totally out of place. And from the looks of him this was a liquid lunch man. You might get a bottle of Czechoslovakian craft beer in a miniature bottle at *The Naked Munch*, but a pint of heavy? I very much doubted it. Sure enough, he didn't go to the counter, but straight to the *Sewer* table where – to my astonishment - he flashed a police badge. The kid in loon pants, not to mention the *Fuck the Cops* t-shirt, blinked at the badge. I could see his terrified Adam's apple, bouncing in his throat like a trapped budgie. He tried to cover the t-shirt message by awkwardly scratching his left ear with his right hand.

The cop indicated the poster in the window. 'Okay, sonny. Who's the special guest?'

Not the t-shirt then. Or, come to think of it, the hash pipes. The kid's Adam's apple, however, still looked pretty upset.

'We're – we're not supposed to –'

The cop moved closer and shushed him gently. 'Let me rephrase that, comrade. So who's the special guest?'

'It's – it's supposed to be –' the boy's Adam's apple did one enormous leap for freedom, so I didn't catch the strangulated name. The cop, however, did.

'See?' he said. 'That wasn't so hard now, was it? Hit me with a ticket.'

Sewer magazine, though. The cop didn't look the type. Oddly enough I gave the magazine a mention in my recent podcast, *Hardly a Fit Subject for Levity*. I've recorded twelve episodes so far, all focused on me, my three imaginary, nonagenarian aunts, and a shed. I often feel they write themselves, like voices inside my head. In episode two, the three aunts remember an historic visit to Edinburgh.

> *'Of course, you weren't around for our last trip to that most illustrious of cities. The late fifties, Een.'*
>
> *'We had a modest involvement, as we recall, wit* Sewer *magazine.'*
>
> *'The title is based on a quote by Oscar Wilde's mammy. "We are all in the sewer, but some of us are swimming against the tide". Oscar cleaned it up later for the English market. Sorry, where were we?'*
>
> 'You were in the sewer, ladies. Swimming.'

> *'Oh, very good. Anyway, the place was bursting wit genius.'*
> *'Ginsberg, to name but Ginsberg.'*
> *'He was trying his hand at the limerick. Someting about tree dry-dugged old shrews from Dublin. Trute is, Een, we spurned him. He swore off the ladies after that.'*
> *'His limerick, as we recall, expanded into a howl of rage. First performed at Edinburgh's legendary vegan restaurong, The Naked Munch.'*

As I came back to the present I became aware the cop was standing at my table, staring down at me. Bit unnerving. He was grinning again.

'You can always find a copper when you don't need one,' he said. 'Thought I'd get that in first, Sir. Only I couldn't help overhearing your conversation earlier with the tall young arty type. *Book Snuff*, eh? Bit of an author, then, are we?'

Well, that was a relief. You never knew with these people.

'Yes,' I said. 'Heard of *Sloot*?' Long shot, but I thought I'd give it a try.

'No,' he said. 'Heard of the DCI Fulton Strang series?'

I shook my head. 'Can't say I have.'

He grinned again. 'I didn't write it, Sir. I lived it. But back to *Book Snuff*. Bit risky?'

'Not at all,' I said. I located the web page on my mobile and held it up.

He waved at the empty chairs.

'Mind if I –'

He glanced at Torquil's straight-backed chair then, choosing Blaise's, he lowered his bulk into it. As he read the *Book Snuff* blurb, he nodded his head every so often. Muttered the odd comment. 'Old Hunter S, eh?' He eventually put it down. 'Excellent stuff,' he said. 'But here's me with my DI's hat on. With a title like that, it's sure to end in murder.'

'Oh, I don't think so,' I said. 'It's fiction, right?'

That lopsided grin again. In close-up. 'This is Edinburgh,' he said. 'Trust me.'

He squeezed my shoulder, stood up and headed for the door.

3

I had a lot to think about as I left the *Naked Munch*. Apart, that is, from murder. Blaise, for instance. I suspected she wasn't entirely happy with the prospect of *Book Snuff*, and I thought I knew why. This was supposed to be a break. Together time. An event is never just the one evening. Let's just say I tend to get a bit intense, particularly in the lead-up. And then there's all the organising stuff. It always ends up more work than you expect. If I'm the emcee I need to be involved in choosing and approaching authors, a pretty time-consuming task in itself. Blaise hadn't actually said anything against me doing *Book Snuff* when she joined us in the *Naked Munch*, and her suggesting Karima as one of the authors seemed like an endorsement of the idea. But was it?

I found Blaise in the bedroom when I got back. On her mobile. Deep in conversation. In the kitchen, Freya stood with her front paws on the table, her back paws on a chair as if expecting to be served. Self-anthropomorphism?

'One way to find out, Een.'

That was the three aunts. I probably shouldn't have mentioned them in the first place. Let me put it this way: they seem to have taken up permanent residence. Disembodied voices in the head? Is that normal? Having said that, they were right. I'd got off to a bad start forgetting to feed Freya, I needed to make amends.

While I feed the cat and wait for Blaise to finish her call, perhaps this is a good time to fill you in on Fraser's living room stroke kitchen? At the kitchen end, a sturdy pine table with four matching chairs and a window overlooking back gardens crowded with small trees and shrubs. The kitchen units are topped by oak worktops, with an ancient coffee grinder displayed like an antique work of art. While at the living room end, a deep pile rug in warm reds and golds covers the polished wooden floorboards. Under the window looking down on the Grassmarket sits a big comfy sofa with an abundance of squishy cushions.

Books over a sideboard set against the far wall. In front of the books, a framed photograph. Older man, younger woman. On the opposite wall a large print, *The Tussle for the Keg*, depicting a couple of wild-eyed inebriates, kilted, squaring up on a rugged mountainside over a whisky cask. On closer inspection I'd noticed two discreet arrows. One labelled "Morag", the other "Me". Not, I suspected, part of the original artwork. Yet adding a note of humour distinctly lacking in the faces of the ferocious protagonists, both of them clearly male.

Also on the sideboard sat a bronze statue of the President of the United States in the shape of a cosh. With hand-grip. Another note of humour? Difficult to tell. I hadn't met Fraser. I picked it up and slapped it absently against my palm, at which point Blaise entered the room, still on her mobile.

'I'm sure he won't mind,' she said, finger-fluttering in my direction. 'See you tomorrow then.'

Who won't mind? More importantly, what won't they mind?

Blaise quickly pocketed her phone. 'Well,' she said, avoiding eye contact by opening and closing kitchen cupboards as if looking for something. 'Your new friend Torquil certainly seems keen on *Book Snuff*. All you need is the writers. Hardly a problem I would have thought. Edinburgh in August. The place will be full of them. Well *done*.'

What? I hadn't expected this. Well done?! There was something about her tone. Not to mention the avoidance of eye contact. As if –

Hold on. My grip tightened on the president. Possibly an animal instinct. I put him back in place and moved away from the sideboard.

'Who won't mind?' I said. 'What won't they mind? As in "I'm sure he won't mind, see you tomorrow."'

'Ah,' said Blaise. There followed a pause. A long pause. She was weighing her response carefully. 'You know Fraser's study?'

'The room with the desk and the bookshelves?' I asked.

'And the sofa bed –'

'Indeed,' I said. 'The study with the desk and the bookshelves and, as you rightly point out, the sofa bed. The study we agreed not to use while we're here?'

Blaise said nothing. Silence. Back to me. 'Let me guess where you're going with this,' I said. 'Someone is coming to Edinburgh. "Why not stay with us?" "Oh, I couldn't possibly." Cut to "Oh, I'm sure he won't mind. See you tomorrow then." So, who exactly are we talking about?'

Blaise breathed audibly in. The brace yourself breath. 'Ashley Burnet?'

'Ashley Burnet.' I repeated the name. Without the question mark. 'What? As in?'

Blaise breathed, equally audibly, out. 'As in.'

'Ashley Burnet, eh? Don't tell me. You agree to me doing *Book Snuff*, but deep down you're seething. And this is your terrible revenge.'

I meant it as a joke, but immediately regretted saying it. Blaise looked genuinely upset. I had to think quickly. 'Tell you what, though,' I said. 'Great set-up for a three-hander play. Happy couple. House guest from hell. Double suicide. I mean come on, she can't be that bad.'

'Oh yes she can,' sighed Blaise. 'Oh yes she very definitely can.'

I'd never met Blaise's old friend, Ashley, but I knew her by reputation.

A feminist firebrand. Where Ashley Burnet went, trouble inevitably followed.

'Relax, Een. The worst is yet to come.'

Another invasion of the head from my three interior aunts. Having said that, they were probably right again, but I couldn't bear to see Blaise suffering.

'Ashley too shall pass,' I said.

> *'Nice try, Een, wit your beautiful Persian quote which suggests the impermulence of all tings.'*
>
> *'But consider this: The Persians never encountered Ashley Burnet.'*

'How long,' I asked, 'is she staying?'

Blaise brightened visibly. 'Just a couple of days,' she said. 'Oh, and she's travelling incognito. All the way from Australia. No-one will even know she's here.'

'What? Beard? Glasses? Call me Bernice? Sounds like fun. Besides,' I said, 'she's probably totally different in private.'

'What? Like *demure*? *Quiet*? *Reserved*?' Blaise almost choked on a laugh. 'I really don't think so. Now, about Isabella. Could we maybe leave her till tomorrow. We'll need to stock up.'

Neat change of subject.

'Fine,' I said. 'She's not going anywhere.'

Not that we knew where she was now, but wherever it was she'd been there for a hundred and fifty years, approx. Another day here or there was no great inconvenience.

4

What is it with women and shopping? For women, read Blaise. We soon ended up with two heavy bags and enough frozen stuff to feed Ashley if she stayed till Christmas.

We were heading back to the flat, me on Sherpa duties heaving the two overflowing bags, when Blaise 'just remembered'. She 'just remembers' on a regular basis when we're out shopping. Same procedure every time. She halts in mid-stride or mid-sentence and out it comes. And here, on this occasion, it came.

'Ah, just remembered,' she said. 'One last stop.' Thing is, I never know what it is till we get to it. At which point it seems preordained.

Cut to the local pharmacy. Me holding a basket full of "women's things" in the central aisle while Blaise stands at the counter talking to the pharmacist about "other women's things".

'Will you look who it is!' a deep disembodied voice boomed from somewhere close by.

I recognised it immediately. And sure enough a head bobbed out from behind the Durex stand to join it. Robin/Robyn! As mentioned by Torquil Pittock. I'd worked a lot with Robin during the early days of my standup career. Since then he'd gone stratospheric. TV. International tours. Robin-related merchandise. No such distractions for me –

'You being an artist of the spoken word, Een, and not in trall to the blandishments of fame.'

– so our paths had long since diverged.

Robin joined me in the central aisle and peered into my "women's things" basket.

'Interesting!' he proclaimed approvingly. 'Good to see. But where have you *been?*'

I was about to answer when a thrusting young fan nudged between us, holding out a pen and show flyer for Robin to sign. Robin, striking as ever in a bespoke three-piece fine tweed suit with matching sculpted beard, took both with an ease born of practice, signed the flyer on the young fan's stooped shoulder, and passed the pen and flyer back. The flyer palpitated with excitement as the youngster rushed off excitedly to tell his friends. Robin resumed our conversation as if nothing had happened. 'So, what brings you to The Big E?'

'I was about to ask you exactly the same thing,' I said. If he'd been doing a show you'd know about it. Supersize posters everywhere. I hadn't seen any.

'Little old us?' he said. 'Just soaking up the festival vibe. Oh, and looking for that great movie idea.'

I nodded my head. Weren't we all. Come to think of it, *I* had a movie idea. In fact I had several movie ideas. The male lead usually had a Dublin accent, but in the movie industry, they tell me, it pays to be flexible. I decided to hit him with one.

'Okay,' I said. 'Two actors, twin brothers, one film.'

'Movie,' said Robin. 'It's got to be a movie.'

'Fine. Title? *The Awards Season*. Their movie-within-a-movie[*] wins big at the Baftas, the Globes, the Oscars, The Prix D'Or, others. First twin wins best actor every time, brother nominated for best support, never wins.'

'First twin c'est moi. I'm loving it so far.'

'Thanks. New award every three weeks. They're so busy on the statuette trail they have no time for acting. Following year? New awards springing up all over the place. They're contractually obliged. Same movie, award every

---

[*] *The Siblings of Inishmahone*

week. Year after, same movie, same result. Daily this time. It's the cinematic circle of hell and there's no way out. Climax of the film? Twin One gets Lifetime Achievement Award for services to the film industry. Twin Two overlooked, can't take it any more. Murder. Suicide. Both dead. Credits. Post-credits: 'The film you have just been watching has garnered fourteen nominations at this year's Oscars, including Best Actor and Best Losing Support. Dedicated to the memories of et cetera.'

Robin grimaced and sucked in his breath. 'Ah now, Mr. MacP. Le dénouement. Bit negative. We're looking for something a tad more – édifiant?'

I was about to try again from my vast back catalogue, when I had a better idea. Well, Torquil Pittock's idea to be strictly accurate, and Blaise obviously had her own take on it, but Robin was a draw. *Le Salon Littéraire* would be packed.

'Fancy doing *Book Snuff*?' I said. I knew he'd written a book. *Trajectories*. About his journey from where he was then to where they were, at the time of publication, now.

'We would just *love* to,' he gushed. 'For the cause, *anything*. You know that. We are yours to command.'

Sweet response. I gave him the details. He laughed with apparent delight. Good sign. Mother's teenage diary? *'Yay!!!'* I'd just got to the list of previous winners – He would *die* to be in such company! *Die!* – when he had a sudden thought. 'Ah,' he said. 'Date.' He produced a golden mobile from his breast pocket and flicked.

'Sunday, August 31st?' I said. '6 pm?'

'Let me check that. Just a mo.' Second flick. 'Tsk. I can do the Saturday.'

'Oh.'

'Thing is,' he said, 'Monday, Wednesday, Friday, every second Sunday we're Robin. Tuesday et ceteri et cetera, every *other* second Sunday, Robyn.' Of course. *Trajectories: Me Then to Us Now*. Robin, however, felt the need to explain. 'I realised I was two people, see? Fighting it out. Fighting. It. Out. So I thought, why the conflict? Give them separate days. Problem solved. Today I'm Robin. Robyn says hi.'

'I see,' I said. 'Any chance of Robyn doing it?'

'Ah, well there you see we hit a problem. Robin writes, not as beautifully as you, mayhap, but Robin writes. Robyn, sur l'autre main, doesn't. Robin is a – quote marks – "celebrity standup/author", Robyn is an athlete. Sunday 31st? Robyn not Robin.'

'I see,' I said. Again. 'Any chance of them swapping dates?'

'Love to,' said Robin, 'believe me. Una problemo. The fans wouldn't take it. And without the fans what are we?'

'Nothing,' I said. 'Without the fans we are nothing.'

As I said this he was approached for another autograph. Bald man, huge glasses.

'I am *such* an admirer of your *work*!'

Robin, playfully, signed his glistening pate. The man squeaked ecstatically and was about to rush out to show off Robin's handiwork when he noticed me. Something puzzled him. He gave me the close once over.

'Hold on,' he said, his eyebrows seeming to point accusingly at me, 'didn't you used to be –'

He couldn't finish the sentence. Short concentrated pause. He then clicked his fingers as if his hand would finish it for him. Didn't you used to be pause click click click. Robin giggled girlishly. He couldn't help it. The man's face relaxed. He was ecstatic. 'I made my hero laugh,' he squealed, and raced off to tell the world. And show them his autographed head.

Robin stifled the giggle with a perfectly manicured hand. 'Sorry. Naughty us. Right, where were we?'

'Without the fans.' It may have come out slightly colder than I'd intended. Not that Robin noticed.

'Exactly. Without the fans, mon ami irlandais, nous sommes rien. Tell you what, though. I could do you a charity run.'

'From a sitting position?' I said, hopefully. 'Reading your mother's diary.'

He punched me playfully on the arm. 'Great to see you again. Got to dash.'

Exit Robin. Outside the window I watched as he signed a Fringe brochure on a young woman's back. Quick theatrical bow for the benefit of the gathering crowd, then whoosh! At which point Blaise joined me.

'Don't tell me,' she said as I handed over the basket, 'that was Robin/Robyn.'

'No,' I said. 'Just Robin.'

'Of course,' she said. 'It's Monday. Silly me.'

5

Another sun-kissed Edinburgh morning. I'd just popped out to the corner shop for milk when a literary tour approached the Grassmarket along the Cowgate. It spilled out from the narrow pavement onto the equally narrow street. The tour guide snubbed the traffic with admirable disdain and the odd louche wave. I was intrigued, and moved closer to hear what he had to say. Hands deep in the pockets of his long, black coat, he reminded me of someone, someone I used to know, but I couldn't work out who. He stopped at a building and waved a casual hand in its general direction. His rag-tag band of tourists gathered eagerly around him.

'And this very room,' he drawled, 'first floor, third window on the right, is where Hemingway wrote *The Great Gatsby*.'

The gaggle of tourists started snapping dutifully. All apart from one old couple. The female half *ahem*ed. Her partner sighed audibly.

'Easy now, Lorrie,' he rasped.

By the looks of it he knew what was coming next. The world-weary tour guide turned to Lorrie world-wearily. 'Yes?'

'We beg to differ, young man.' A cultured American accent. One that brooked no dissent.

'Really?' A 'really' of mock interest.

'Sure. Hemingway did not, as you erroneously stated, write *The Great Gatsby* in this very room.'

'No?' The 'young man' paused for effect. 'Come to think of it, you're right. Stop snapping everyone! Point of information. Hemingway did not, as I erroneously stated, write *The Great Gatsby* in this very room. Well spotted. My mistake.' He waved higher up. 'It was *that* very room.'

The old couple's male half, wizened and unkempt, his sun-dried face lined and pock-marked, kept his own counsel. I detected, however, a mocking glint around the eyes. Lorrie, a tall, thin, serious-looking woman with close-cropped white hair and grey trouser suit, bristled with scorn.

'Pray correct me if I'm wrong, young man –'

'Byron, ma'am. At your service.' He bowed deeply.

'– but I was under the no doubt fallacious impression that F. Scott Fitzgerald wrote *The Great Gatsby*. Byron.'

Byron chose to ignore the ironic emphasis on his name. 'So they would have us believe.' And with that he swept off towards the Grassmarket, his ragged band of happy snappers trailing in his wake. I joined, surreptitiously, in. Byron waved a languid hand in no particular direction as he cut a swathe through the crowded pavements. 'Our fascinating tour of Edinburgh's fascinating literary heritage,' he yawned, 'draws to its tragic close on this very spot.' He stopped suddenly in the middle of the narrow pavement and glanced at purse-lipped Lorrie. 'Tell a lie.' He moved a step. 'This very spot.' He turned to his loyal followers. 'Picture the scene. It's high summer. The heat is unbearable.' He plucked a tissue from his pocket and wiped his fevered brow. 'The pavements brimful of life. Black-eyed señoritas. Lustful young bucks. A slow rumble in the distance. To the dump to the dump to the dump. Yes. It's the annual Edinburgh bull run. Dust and sweat everywhere. To-the-Dump To-the-Dump To-the-Dump! But what's this?' He paused, aghast. 'Hemingway, slightly the worse for wear from a hearty breakfast of Jack Daniels and Anaïs Nin, staggers off the pavement –'

Byron, in full flow, staggered off the pavement in front of the charging bulls. A mobile phone rang. Byron froze. 'I distinctly said all mobiles off. There were no mobile phones in 1936.' The ringing grew louder. 'Well answer it then, dammit.' Several tourists took their mobiles out. The ringing continued. All eyes on Byron. Unabashed, he whipped a mobile from the cavernous depths of his coat. Pressed answer. To the mobile: 'Of course I'm wearing the outfit. Tartan trousers. Tartan coat. Tartan vest, socks and underpants.' A slight pause. 'Clan MacBlack.' He gave the mobile a filthy look and plunged it back into the coat. 'Where was I?'

Lorrie was straight in. 'Ernest Hemingway, disputed author of *The Great Gatsby*, having consumed copious amounts of Jack Daniels and had sex with Anaïs Nin, who appears to have been in Edinbro at the time, probably putting the finishing touches to *Huckleberry Finn* –'

'*Moby Dick*, I think you'll find, but let it pass.'

'– staggers off the pavement in front of the annual Edinbro bull run –'

Byron raised a hand, triumphant. 'And is tragically gored –' he grabbed his crotch dramatically '– in the cojones.'

A plaintive female voice from the back. 'Oh my Gosh! How terrible!'

Byron nodded. 'His words precisely.'

'Bulls?' snapped Lorrie. 'Aren't we talking Pamplona here?'

'No,' said Byron. 'We're talking *here* here.'

The female voice from the back spoke up again. Louder this time. 'You have the most beautiful accent. What part of Scotland are you from?'

'Dublin. And you, pretty lady. Where are *you* from?'

'Saskatchewan.'

'Thought I spotted the accent. Wonderful country, Brazil.'

Byron strolled over the traffic island at Cowgatehead and turned right towards Victoria Street.

Lorrie stomped after him. She was having none of it. 'I respectfully put it to you –'

Byron glanced at his watch. 'No you don't, respectfully or otherwise. Because that, I rather fancy, is your lot.'

Lorrie was furious. 'But – what about this?' She pointed pointedly at the *Naked Munch*.

'What about it?'

'*The Naked Munch*? Late fifties? It's why we came on this goddam tour, asshole.' She turned to her aged partner. 'Tell him, Charlton.'

Her aged partner chuckled softly. 'Whoa, Lorrie. Easy now.'

'No, no,' said Byron. 'Lorrie is right. Forgive me. *The Naked Munch*, everyone. Let me check up on it. I'll get back to you.' And he was off up Victoria Street.

'Young man!' shouted Lorrie, pointing at her partner. 'Don't you know who this is?'

Byron turned back. 'Walt Whitman?'

The old man turned to me. 'What the guy say?'

'He said Walt Whitman.'

'Close enough.' He turned to Lorrie. 'Highball time yet?'

But Lorrie hadn't finished. She waved an angry hand at Byron's retreating back. 'Attention must be paid! You hear me, asshole? Attention must be paid!'

As the crowd dispersed I was desperate to ask why attention must be paid, but something held me back. In a funny sort of way, I felt I should already know.

6

When I returned to the flat with the milk, Freya eyed me with approval. I was obviously learning. Blaise was doing whatever it is women do in bathrooms. Whatever it is was time-consuming, but that was fine. I'd spend an hour or so poring over possible contestants for *Book Snuff* while Blaise got ready to visit our first graveyard. To take part you had to have written a book. You also had to be able to prove that, at some point in your life, you'd said something funny. The whole concept was comic, so I needed people prepared to play along. No access to your mother's teenage diary?

'Write it yourself, Een!'

Exactly. I opened my laptop, sipped lovingly at the first coffee of the day and settled down to an author-search with a spring in my mental step. Thousands to choose from. *The Edinburgh International Festival of Literature*. Comedy venues. Celebrities in search of an ego massage or, as in the case of Robin/Robyn, two ego massages and that breakout movie idea. Shame about Robin, by the way. He certainly would have drawn the crowds.

I'd just opened my laptop and got as far as typing *The Edinburgh Int* when the intercom buzzer buzzed. Blaise stuck her head round the door. 'You'll have to go down,' she said, still in her nightdress, 'the clicky thing to open the main door is kaput.'

Oh, well. I closed the laptop and headed down the stone steps. I'd almost reached ground level when the buzzer buzzed again. I opened the door. A tall, imposing woman smiled at me. Weird hat, tinted glasses, large suitcase. I held my ground but stepped back in my head. The hat was like a tiny allotment run to seed. With a hillock-shaped fairy-fort at the centre. You get a lot of that kind of thing in Ireland, but it's the first time I've seen one on a hat. Then it clicked. Could this be Ashley Burnet? Incognito? The hat and glasses said maybe, the oversize suitcase splattered with labels said yes.

'Don't tell me,' I said. 'You want to know if I've accepted the Lord Jesus Christ into my life. It's a long story.'

The woman burst out laughing, grabbed the suitcase and pointed a gloved finger straight at me. 'Sorry,' she said. 'You'll be –'

'I will indeed,' I said helpfully. 'But do come in.'

At which point her mobile rang. I relieved her of the suitcase and hoicked it up the stairs while she took the call. 'Whoa. Stop it right there. The title stays.' Pause. 'Okay. Okay. Remember my first memoir?' Her voice echoed angrily up the stairwell behind me. '*Stroppy Cunt*. That's the one. You didn't have any trouble with that title, so what's wrong with this one?' Short Pause. 'The word is contentious? Are you fucking nuts?' Pause. 'Well you can suck my Antipodean dick.' Pause. 'How do you *know*? Are you denying me the right to have a dick?' By this stage I'd reached the top step, so I pushed the flat door open and ushered her in. 'Okay,' she said, 'so it's a metaphorical dick, but the title fucking stays.'

She pocketed the mobile and whipped her hat off. The effect was startling. A shock of black hair sprang out in every direction. Her trademark. It wouldn't have suited everyone, but it went perfectly with the personality. Full moon. Broomstick. She removed the dark glasses. High cheekbones, piercing green eyes. I'm tempted to say they sprang out too. The full effect was beyond startling. Like a tall, imposing Freya with an electrified human head. She cut across my thoughts and broke the spell.

'It's so good of you to put me up,' she said. 'And don't worry. I'll be as quiet as a wee, sleekit, cowerin', tim'rous fucking moose.'

I somehow doubted that, but said nothing. I parked her suitcase beside Freya's cat bed. 'Blaise is abluting,' I said. 'Tea? Coffee? Oh, and by the way, this is Freya.'

'Hi, Freya,' said Ashley. 'You his familiar?'

I was keen to kill this one at source. 'I have no time for that fantasy stuff,' I said. 'Freya is a cat. That right, Freya?'

Freya mngiaowed. The whatever mngiaow.

'I would love a coffee,' said Ashley. 'If that's not too much trouble.'

'No trouble at all,' I said. 'I'll just grind a few beans in this little beauty here' – I pointed at the grinder – 'and we'll be on our way.' I scooped the coffee in. 'Your book title, by the way. The one they want you to change. What is it?'

Interesting life lesson here. Never ask a question directly before using a faux 19th century electrified coffee grinder. Particularly if you're interested in the answer. She may have responded, I don't honestly know. I took my finger off the grinder button.

'That reminds me,' said Ashley. 'Couple of loose fillings.' She pressed her fingers to her forehead. 'What am I saying? Loose fucking *skull*. Anyway, here I – Blaise, you beauty! It is so, so *good* to *see* you.'

Blaise was framed in the hall doorway, like – best, perhaps, to leave it there, but I'm always stunned by her loveliness after a brief separation. About forty minutes in this case.

'It's so, so good to see you too,' said Blaise. I went back to the coffee-making thing and left them to it. The long hug. The repetition of the so-so-good line with variations. The show-you-to-your-room bit.

The coffee pot had just finished its final perculatory burp when they arrived back and sat down at the table, locked in intense conversation. I tried to get Ashley's attention. 'Black?' I said. 'White?' No response. I moved closer. 'Black?' I repeated. 'White?'

'Oh fuck,' she said. 'Sorry, it's just we haven't seen each other in years. As it comes, thanks.' After which, it was back to the verbal lock-in.

While Blaise and Ashley chatted, I re-opened my laptop, happy to let their word tennis play in the background. They both spoke *sotto voce*, as if someone might be listening in. The odd word or phrase filtered through. "Here for a reason." "Bit hush hush." Which allowed me to get back to my *Book Snuff* search. Hundreds of writers, hundreds of books. I'd just reached full immersion when Blaise tapped me on the arm.

'Okay if we leave the graveyard till tomorrow? It's just –'

Ashley lit up. 'What's this about a graveyard?' she exclaimed. 'I *love* graveyards.'

'We're looking for one in particular,' said Blaise. 'My great-great-grandmother Isabella. Proto-feminist. You know, a feminist before feminism. But now that you're here –'

'Well, I say do it!' interrupted Ashley. 'Today! Now! That coffee has whipped this dilapidated old fuck of a Second Waver up. What did you put in it? Hey! My hat!'

Freya shifted slightly on the flattened fairy-fort. 'Mngiaow.'

'Okay,' said Ashley, 'We'll share. Me outside, you inside. Deal?' Freya gave her an enigmatic cat stare and slid, gracefully, onto the floor. Ashley grabbed the hat, shook it back into its original shape, scooped her hair up and plonked it on her head. 'It is so, so good to be here.' She opened the door with a flourish and waved us through. 'All *right*,' she whooped. 'Izzy, here we come!'

Blaise and Ash strolled on ahead while I dawdled and daydreamed. The sun shone like a celestial thumbs up. The city had given itself over to the festival. Book Tour Byron was back with another group of tourists, wending his way in the opposite direction as we headed up the narrow road that leads from the Grassmarket to Greyfriars Kirkyard. Bigger audience this time, same Byron, still dressed all in black. He waved a lethargic hand in the general direction of nowhere in particular. I vaguely heard 'Gabrielle Garcia Marquez', 'Maria Vargas Llhosa' and 'Sapphic taboos in late 20th century Latin America', but none of the words in between. I was busy trying to fill in the gaps when Blaise and Ash stopped and waited for me to catch up. Blaise looked – troubled is not the word, but same word family. 'You know that clip of you at the *Almeida* theatre from way back?' she asked. 'That comedy festival?' Of course I did. I was in it. 'Well, see that young guy back there? The one with the rakish look.'

'Byron,' I said.

'No,' said Blaise. 'Absence of club foot. Big giveaway. Besides, Byron is dead. No. The young guy in the black coat. Don't you think he's the dead spit of you. Circa, oh –'

Of course! Me! That's who he'd reminded me of! He'd reminded me of me!

This had a weird sort of effect. It's not often you see yourself as you were – in the flesh. I turned and stared at him as he regaled his audience. The hair. He certainly had the hair. And the coat. And the – well, pretty well everything. Rakish? I quite liked rakish. I also endorsed his subversion of the so-called canon. Exactly the sort of thing *I'd* have done at that age. Is there such a thing as a cross-generational doppelgänger? I'd look it up later.

Blaise still looked puzzled. 'Byron,' she said. 'Is that his actual name?'

'I believe so,' I said.

Blaise said nothing as she turned back towards Greyfriars. Trailing behind the two women on the narrow pavement I couldn't help but wonder if she was wishing she'd met me earlier, before the – well, before the ageing process took hold. Despite the August sunshine smiling on this most beautiful of cities, a wave of melancholy washed over me.

> *'The impermulence of all tings, Een, as previously mentioned. The passage of time.'*
> *'The fugiting, if you will, of tempus. Nutting to be done about it.'*
> *'But back to the narrative before you drown in self-pity. How about this. "I sighed a sorrowful sigh and walked melancholily on."'*

I walked on.

'A bit prosaic to our way of tinking.'
'On the plus side, however, it moves the plot along. So on you go.'

Blaise and Ash had just reached the kitsch dog statue near the entrance to Greyfriars Kirkyard when I caught up with them again. People were queueing up to kiss its nose. Why? The heart has its reasons.

'Jesus. Fucking tacky or what.' That was Ashley. Ungodly language for consecrated ground – I merely pass it on.

If you can get past Bobby the dog, the kirkyard has real historic substance. Old but working church, ancient mausoleums built into the high boundary walls. As Blaise and Ashley moved along the gravestones, ticking them off one by one, I was struck by a chilling thought. I'd lived in Edinburgh for some time oh, years ago now, when I looked more like Byron, less like me, and I knew this graveyard well. We were slowly approaching the celebrated grave of a 19th Century worthy, Farquharson Hogg, and I have to admit to a certain trepidation as the women wound their way ever closer. Farquharson's gravestone referenced himself for several self-aggrandizing lines, before memorialising '*His Unblemished offspring Duty*', '*His Unswerving mastiff Repent*' and, as an afterthought, and almost covered over by weeds, '*his wyf*'.

I hardly thought it would pass without comment and expected, at the very least, a verbal eruption from Ashley. And here it came.

'And his fucking wyf!' she exploded. 'I didn't know stonemasons used tiny fonts in those days! And his fucking *wyf*!'

Blaise pointed a warning finger at me. 'Don't say Isabella.'

So I didn't. Besides, my phone had started up. Ashley hooted. 'That will be Farquharson. Or his fucking mastiff.'

I ignored her and pressed answer. 'Farq –,' I said. 'I mean Torquil. Sorry. Bit of interference here. I'll take it outside.'

Out of earshot it was back to business. 'That's better,' I said, although

Torquil hadn't said anything yet.

'Quick catch-up,' he said. 'How are we getting on?'

'I'm on the case,' I said. 'You know Robin/Robyn?'

'Is that an actual question? Of *course* I know Robin/Robyn. It was me who suggested –' I could almost feel his excitement as he interrupted himself. 'Don't tell me! They're up for it! This is sensational! We –'

'Whoa!' I cut across him. 'Robin can't do it. He's Robin Mondays, Wednesdays, Fridays, every second Sunday. Wrong Sunday.'

'Drat. Too late to switch dates. What about Robyn?'

'Ah well, you see. Robyn's an athlete. No book.'

'Double drat. I mean, imagine if we'd managed to get both of them.'

'Not possible,' I said. 'Think about it.'

'I suppose there is that,' said Torquil. 'Anyway, keep on it. Drink soon? You know, compare notes? Maybe –' He seemed to hesitate at that point. 'Sorry. Got to dash.'

End call. I thought about going back in to Greyfriars cemetery, but a man simply can't compete with two close female friends who haven't seen each other for several years –

'You speak the troot, Een, and in so doing show the wisdom of your great age.'

– and besides, Torquil was right. The pressure was on. I had to round up some acts for *Book Snuff*, so I texted Blaise and headed back to the flat.

The Grassmarket was in full swing, the pavement cafes crowded with festival-goers, some in couples, others in raucous groups warming up to take in as many pubs and comedy shows as possible. I spotted a group of young people carrying stage props down the alley beside the *Naked Munch*. The legendary *Traverse* theatre had apparently reopened on its original site. It closed, as I recall, in 1989, relocating to its magnificent state-of-the-art premises at the Tolbooth. The new *Traverse* was still called the *Traverse*, so the old *Traverse* had to look elsewhere for a name. The *Old Traverse*.

Perfect. I'd check it out at some point. Maybe take in a show. Now, though, there was work to be done. I walked on.

As I approached Fraser's flat a police car screeched to a halt outside, lights flashing. I watched, bemused, as DCI Strang, *aka* Liquid Lunch Man, the sure-to-end-in-murder cop from the *Naked Munch*, emerged from the flats next door to ours, waved to the driver and got in. The police car sped off with yet another ear-shattering burst of its siren. I rooted for my key. Odd. Something was pinned to the door, right at eye level. An A4 sheet with a black-ink line-drawing of a woman. Pretty basic – I could have drawn it myself – with one pretty chilling detail. A line-drawn face with circles for eyes and a down-turned, sorrowful mouth, was crossed out with a large, blood-red **X**. That was it.

Basic drawing.
Eyes.
Face.

X

I didn't know what to make of it. Who? When? Why? It's the sort of thing that unnerves you. Then you remember it's festival time. Gothic Edinburgh. I tore it off and wound my way up the turret stairs. The noise of the street faded as the door swung slowly shut behind me. In the kitchen, I was about to crumple and bin the drawing, but something about it niggled. Was it really just a bit of harmless festival fun? Possibly, but why was it pinned to our door? And who had pinned it? Just then, Freya appeared through her 'cat-flap', essentially a sash window left partially open that she could access via a flat extension roof below. She gave me a meaningful look. The feed-me look. I placed the sheet of paper on the sideboard and filled her cat bowl.

*

The imagination has its uses, but it's also, sometimes, a curse. I'd left the sheet of paper on the sideboard, but what about its place in my head? It was in danger of taking over and besides, I needed to get a move on with *Book Snuff*. I consigned it to the out-tray of the mind and opened my laptop. Karima, Blaise's writer friend from Pakistan, was still just a suggestion, and as neither Robin or Robyn could do it, now was as good a time as any to settle the line-up. I had the place to myself. No distractions.

Well, except that I managed to distract myself. Byron. What Blaise said. "Don't you think he's the dead spit of you. Circa, oh –" She never finished the sentence, so let me finish it for her. Circa *last millennium*. This seemed to be hitting me at a pretty deep level now that I thought about it in the solitude of Fraser's flat. Not my idea, but *Book Snuff*, it seemed, had now consigned itself to the out-tray. I sat for some minutes in silent contemplation of the heartbreaking transience of life then, steeling myself, snapped out of it and put my own name into the search engine. *Live at the Almeida*. A short clip, but that's all I needed. It even had a title, *One Short Clip for Mankind*. I braced myself, pressed play and there was my younger self on screen. It may be that, to people of a different genetic makeup, all Irishmen look the same. Not to me, though. I'm Irish. I can spot the difference. I leaned in and stared intently at the screen. The likeness to Byron was uncanny. We could have been – I was going to say brothers, but it was closer than that, more uncanny and unsettling. We could have been each other.

Suddenly, I got up and dashed into the bathroom. An internal, windowless affair. I clicked the lamp above the bathroom mirror on just as the door swung slowly shut, closing out what little natural light filtered in from the hall. I stared at my reflection, now garishly bright. The shock of dark hair was gone, grey and thinning now. Pockets of chin stubble from the morning's cursory shave only made things worse.

I dimmed the light slightly. My face in the full glare had been flattened out to an eerie white, with the added furrows of age. I dimmed the light again. Less shadow, not unlike the sun disappearing behind a Wicklow bog. I dimmed it yet again. All that remained were dark eye sockets and the vague outline of a nose. Almost skull-like.

Bit more.

Bit more still.

The light clicked off.

I was plunged into total darkness.

> *'Is there such a thing as the dark afternoon of the soul, Een? We merely ask.'*

Back to *Book Snuff* and the life-affirming brightness of the kitchen. I'd almost finished typing *Edinburgh International Festival of Literature Programme* in full into the search engine – I'd got as far as *Program* – when the door opened, and in burst Blaise and Ash, locked, as always, in lively conversation. Bearing, as it turned out, lunch. Simultaneously, Freya left her empty bowl, slid over to the table and hopped on the best seat. Ashley gave her a look, possibly admiring, and plonked her hat on the seat next to it. The not-best seat. Freya weighed up her options. Do cats shrug? I don't know. I'm not a cat man. But she weighed up her options, may or may not have shrugged, and hopped onto the hat seat*.

'So,' said Blaise, unpacking an array of cheeses, olives, posh juice and hand-woven bread, 'what have you been up to?'

'Looking up authors for *Book Snuff*,' I lied as I closed the laptop and went in search of plates.

'Found any?'

'A few persons of interest,' I lied again.

Blaise, who was busily chopping cubes of feta to put in the salad, stopped suddenly, her face lighting up as though a brilliant thought had just

---

* *The Cat Sat on the Hat*. Possible kids' story. It's on me, kiddy authors, because I'm not going to write it.

struck her. She waved the knife at Ash.

'How about our very own Ashley Burnet? I think she'd be fabulous!'

What?! Ashley on stage at *Book Snuff*? Apart from *Stroppy Cunt* and the title that dare not speak its name, her essay collection, *Biologically Me*, had graced bonfires the world over, leading to her equally incendiary follow-up, *Bonfire Ash*. Challenging didn't even begin to cover it. Ashley Burnet was getting nowhere near *Book Snuff*. I was trying to work out how to word this tactfully when Ashley saved me the trouble.

'No fucking way!' she said. 'I have zero intention of dying to further your career.'

Well that was a relief. 'Ah! So you know about *Book Snuff* then?'

'Blaise filled me in. Hold on! How about that Scottish comedian guy? You know the one.'

I moved round the table distributing plates and glasses. 'You'll have to narrow it down a bit. I can think of two offhand. Both dead.'

'Red beard. Glasses. Rory Stagg.'

I looked across at Blaise. 'She's joking, right?'

Blaise laughed and grimaced at the same time. 'I expect she probably is.'

Rory Stagg was the total antithesis of Ashley Burnet. The clue is in the name.

'Misogyny with a cheeky boy grin, Een. You heard it here first.'

'Oh, by the way,' I said, 'speaking of controversial.' I went over to the bookshelf and held up the sheet with its crude drawing of a woman.

Blaise wiped her fingers on a table napkin and held her hand out. I passed it over. Blaise's face darkened. 'What's this?' she said.

'No idea,' I said. 'It was pinned to the front door when I got back.'

'Can I see it?' asked Ash. Blaise held it up, Ash grabbed it and blanched. 'Shit.'

'What?' I said. No answer. Blaise stared at the image.

'It certainly looks like someone trying to make a point,' she said.

Ashley whipped out her mobile, snapped a photo of the sheet, speed-tapped something, paused, then stared intently at the screen as the mobile made a faint *whoosh!*

'You okay?' Blaise asked.

'Just checking something,' she said. 'With you in a sec.'

Blaise turned back to me. 'Sounds like you have a few people in mind for the big night,' she said over-brightly. 'Care to share?'

Blaise, I realised, was trying to change the subject. The drawing had obviously touched a nerve with Ashley. Unfortunately, I didn't have anyone in mind. I thrashed about in my brain for a name. Any name. Ashley put her mobile down.

'All quiet,' she said, 'so it's probably nothing.' She turned to me. 'Big night,' she said, also over-brightly. 'Discuss.'

Ah. I had a name. I had no intention of asking him, but at least it would move the conversation on. 'Here's a thought,' I said. 'How about Toby Smyrke?'

Blaise smiled at Ash. 'Didn't you, you know?'

Ashley's eyes flashed. 'I was a bit wild in those days,' she said. 'So yes, we may have had a bit of a – you know.'

My laptop sat on the sideboard. I opened it and quickly typed in Toby's name. 'Hold on,' I said. 'Ah. Here we are. "Toby Smyrke,"' I read from his self-aggrandising website. '"The follow-up to his confirmation-of-genius novel, *Arachnophilia*, with its wilful incomprehensibility and revolutionary spider's web structure, and *Desk* – in which the author's desk narrates its own tortured tale, is his much-lauded twelve-hundred-page one word novel, *word*."' I paused for a quick chortle. 'Hah. I think if you'd had a bit of a you-know with him you'd know. You know?'

'I will say this,' said Ashley. 'Foreplay was a fucking nightmare. He outlined the plot of his first novel.'

43

'*Foreplay*,' said Blaise.

Ash nodded. 'That's the one. The sex itself was more flash fiction.' She did something with her face. 'Jesus.'

'And now there's *word*,' I said. 'Twelve hundred pages? One word? Jesus indeed! I wonder if anyone has actually read it.'

'I have,' said Ash. She topped the juice glasses up. 'After the first 900 pages it gets surprisingly easy to live with. Bit like shell shock. *word*?' She barked a laugh. 'One word yes, but a word containing multitudes. Allegedly. And all those internal fucking adverbs.'

I had wondered. Toby Smyrke loved a good adverb. And, indeed, a bad one. If it's an adverb you'll find it littered through the complete works of.

'So, no to Toby,' I said.

Blaise patted Ashley's arm. 'You wouldn't like to reconsider it yourself?' she said.

Ashley was straight in. 'Definitively, unarguably, not in any circumstances whatsofuckingeverly,' she said. 'I'm travelling incognito, remember?'

Of course she was. I had to set this one in stone. Over my festering corpse would Ash Burnett be taking part in *Book Snuff*.

'Ah, *Book Snuff*'s loss,' I said. 'So what's your name?'

'Sorry?'

'Well you can't go round Edinburgh being introduced as Ashley Burnet, now can you? People would say "Anyone ever told you, you've got the same name as Ashley Burnet."'

'Fair point,' said Ashley. 'Hadn't thought of that.'

'We'd better sort you out with a new one then,' said Blaise. She mulled it over for a moment. 'How about Cindy?'

Ash clapped her hands with delight. 'Cindy!'

'Cindy Ash?' Blaise again.

Ash was ecstatic. 'Cindy fucking Ash! Perfect.'

'So that's settled, then,' said Blaise. 'Cindy Ash it is.'

I re-filled Freya's bowl, simply for something to do. Freya stayed where she was, but she may have winked at me. Excellent. I felt we were starting to bond. Blaise set about clearing the table. I popped the cat-food tin in the pedal bin and glanced over at Ashley, but her upbeat mood had subsided.

She was now deep in thought.

And staring at the X-ed out face.

7

Midnight. Blaise may have been trying to get to sleep. My brain, however, was all a-whirr.

> *'The mind, mind has mountings, Een. Frightful, sheer, no-man faddomed.'*
> *'No, nor lady-faddomed neider. We added that bit, by the way. A very consideratious lover, Gerard 'Manly', but unless a lady was a nun he had no particular interest in her interiority, so to speak.'*

Silence!

> *'Oh, very masterful, Een. Our lips are permulently clamped shut. Honest.'*

I somehow doubted it. Besides, not only did I have three tiny but infuriatingly insistent voices in my head. I also had Ashley Burnet's disturbing response to the X-note in the mix – was someone out to get her? As if that wasn't enough, I appeared to be staring at myself with more than a hint of lunacy, in an imaginary bathroom mirror. I couldn't see Blaise in the darkness, but I glanced over anyway and heaved an involuntary sigh.

'*Book Snuff.*' I said. 'You don't think I'm too old?' No answer. 'Me then, me now. You know?'

Blaise yawned under the duvet. 'Shave your stubble, pat your hair down, you'll be fine,' she mumbled. 'Night night.'

Not much point pursuing that particular subject. I put the imaginary mirror down and clamped my eyes shut. My brain, however, was still a-whirr. Different subject matter. 'Cast your mind back,' I said into the silence. 'Ashley's book, right? The publishers were happy with *Stroppy*

C-asterisk-n-t-s.'

Blaise put her bedside lamp on and rolled towards me. 'Sorry,' she sighed, 'but where exactly are we going with this?'

'Well, they're not happy with another title. I find myself wondering how bad can it be?'

'So ask her,' said Blaise. 'But maybe wait till morning.'

'I already did,' I said. "At exactly the wrong moment. I'd just suggested coffee. Offer accepted. I loaded the grinder. I popped the question.'

Blaise impersonated two seconds of a very loud coffee grinder. Right in my ear. 'You mean that book?' she laughed.

'The very same,' I said. 'So what's it called in English?'

She sat up. 'Are you ready for this?' she said. 'It's going to shock you.'

'I know,' I said. 'If they're happy with *Stroppy* et cetera it must be pretty out there.'

'It is.'

'You surprise me. I thought *C-asterisk* –'

'Cunt,' said Blaise. 'You can say cunt. Cunt is permissible. No problem with cunt.'

'Point taken. So what could possibly be more problematic than –'

'Cunt? Brace yourself.' She paused for maximum effect. '*Woman.*'

I paused. Different pause. '*Woman*?!'

'I know,' Blaise sighed. 'Ashley's modern classic. Great title when it came out six years ago. Now? Problematic word, apparently. They want to change the title for the latest edition. Too exclusive.'

'Okay,' I said. 'Cunt, woman. Woman, cunt. It's been a long day. My head hurts.' I paused. A plaintive sigh pause. 'So why is she here? In Edinburgh. Incognito. Has she told you yet?'

Blaise lay back down, pulled the duvet up, and neatly changed the subject. 'I've been thinking,' she said. 'Why don't you leave finding Isabella's grave to Ash and me. You'll need to concentrate on *Book Snuff*. You know what you're like.'

'What am I like?'

'You know. I don't want you getting stressed. You know what you're like when you're stressed.'

'What am I like?'

'Stressed.'

She had a point. Having said that, this was supposed to be our break.

'I'm pretty sure I can manage both,' I said. 'Besides, I like graveyards.'

But Blaise was adamant. 'Maybe when you've got everything sorted. If we haven't found her by then.'

She was probably right. Besides, the graveyards of Edinburgh were sure to be full of Farquharson Hoggs. Best, perhaps, to leave them to it. Exploding with righteous feminist fury every time they found another 'and his wyf'.

Blaise flicked her lamp off, snuggled under the duvet and stifled a yawn. 'Night night.'

'So why *is* Ash here?' I didn't say that either, but that's what I was thinking as I lay down beside her.

Why was Ashley here?

8

2.32 a.m. We both sat up. The boom boom boom of heavy rock vibrated through the wall.

Blaise groaned and put her bedside lamp on.

'Remember that three-hander play?' I said. 'How's this for a plot-line. Loving couple cat-sitting at the Edinburgh festival. Deranged interloper. Loving couple descend into –'

'We'll work on it later,' Blaise cut in. 'Will you go and have a word – or will I?'

'She's your friend,' I said. 'I'll go.'

'Okay. But be gentle with her. And put something over your penis. Second thoughts. Put the hall light on. Air guitar. Dramatic entry. That should do it.'

I grabbed the nearest thing to hand. Blaise's kimono, silk with a butterfly pattern. I left the hall light off, checked the kimono was securely fastened, and knocked on Ashley's door. Nothing. Curious. The sound had receded since I left the bedroom. I knocked again. Still nothing. An almost imperceptible tap on the shoulder. I nearly leapt out of Blaise's nightwear.

'I don't think it's coming from Ashley's room,' Blaise whispered. 'Or our flat.'

Oh well. As I say, festival time. It made you long for the peace and tranquillity of, say, a lighthouse. We'd just settled back in, lights out, Blaise tucked under the duvet, the boom boom boom now subsided next door, when my mobile rang. What?! 2.47 a.m.?! I squinted at the screen. A sleepy-eyed blur. I couldn't make out who it was. Must be important, though. The late night call. Like the wail of the banshee echoing through

49

the glen, it always brings a slight sense of dread. Bad news about a loved one? Why else would anyone phone this late? I pressed answer.

'I was just thinking. How about –' A distant, excited voice.

'Torquil,' I yawned. 'It's 2.48 a.m.'

'So it is. How about –'

'Could we talk about this tomorrow?'

'Sure,' said Torquil. 'Val Muldoonican?'

'Great idea,' I said. 'I'll check her out.'

Torquil's voice froze. 'Her?'

Twelve seconds later, I put the mobile back on the bedside table. Beside me, the duvet stirred.

'Festival time,' it murmured. 'We'll just have to live with it.'

9

According to my therapist, I'm delusional: I don't have a therapist.

That line came to me as I opened the shutters the following morning. The flat was quiet now. The music had long since subsided. Freya had eaten well. Prawn Surprise – good choice. I felt I was getting the hang of the cat thing. Happy with a job well done, I gazed on the world below. Bars preparing their outside seating, people strolling past in blue-sky festival sunshine. A man standing next to the Covenanters' Memorial, handing out leaflets for a show. He looked remarkably like – hold on! Dan? Handing out leaflets? I'd known Dan since we were children growing up in Dublin, but Dan wasn't a performer. Last I'd heard he was a caretaker at the local convent school in Clontarf. It couldn't possibly be him. I looked again, screwing up my eyes against the bright sunshine. It could. How could I be sure? Too far away to get full facial recognition, but he does this thing with his feet. The six-year-old-boy-who-needs-a-wee-wee shuffle. Sure enough, there he was, doing it right now.

I've fictionalised Dan in some of my other work. *The Book of Blaise*, for instance. Blaise, a beautiful poet, is a fictionalised version of Blaise. I often wonder if she knows. The narrator, 'I', is a ditto me. Dan is in there too, relocated for fictional purposes to Glasgow. Lovely character. Sweet but vague. Lugubrious moustache. Doesn't know how many children he has. And, because I was convinced he'd never read it, or if he did that he'd never recognise himself, I called him Dan in the book. And yes, it was definitely him outside. I'd planned to drop in to the Book Festival later that morning, check it out for possible authors – maybe even take in an event or two. I could say hello to Dan on the way.

Freya had finished her Prawn Surprise and slipped out the back. No doubt looking for love. Or killing things. Whatever cats do. Ash appeared to be out too. Looking for love? Killing things? I'd be inclined to go for the latter. I popped into the bedroom for my shoes. Blaise was sitting up in bed tapping away at her laptop. I avoided looking at the screen. A love poem, perhaps? We live in hope. I held my shoes up. 'Back soon,' I said.

'That's what they all say,' she said. 'Then you never see them again.' Little joke of ours.

'Well, never mind about that,' I said. 'You just get on with your love poem.'

Blaise closed her laptop. 'It's called Canongate Kirkyard Website. I was checking opening hours.'

'I'm sure Ashley will be delighted,' I said. 'The place will be littered with Farquharson Hoggs –'

'– and his tiny-font wyfs,' said Blaise.

'Exactly. A few more graves like that might teach you both the error of your ways.' I raised the Calvinist finger of righteousness. 'Repent!' I bellowed. 'Jezebels!'

Blaise wagged the finger of disapproval, which suggested she hadn't taken me seriously. I raised myself to my full height, glowered at her for comic effect, and closed the bedroom door.

Descending the stone steps to perdition – I was still in character – I reflected on the fact that my DNA might include a soupçon of hellfire and brimstone. As I opened the front door an older couple was passing by outside. Grey-haired and stooped. Holding hands in a public place! I was sorely tempted to bellow "Fornicators!", but held back. Probably just as well, as DCI Strang was standing on the pavement, waving at the driver of an oncoming cop car. He spotted me and nodded a cordial greeting.

'Our friendly local *Book Snuffer*,' he said. 'I'm on the case.'

'Good to know,' I said. 'Always happy to hear from a pro.'

'How many contestants?' he asked.

'Tough one,' I said. 'Three?'

'Any one of whom, correct me if I'm wrong, might snuff it.'

'Metaphorically, yes,' I agreed.

He nodded again. The thinking man's nod. 'From a psychological perspective, now, I'd say your little game show might be seen as a subconscious attempt to get rid of the competition in your chosen field.'

Before I could respond the car drew to a halt beside us, he got in, and off it shot. Very playful – at least I assumed he was being playful – but as I stared after the disappearing car I thought back to his *Book Snuff* prediction. "With a title like that it's sure to end in murder."

I hopped across the road between the slow-moving traffic, spotted Ashley approaching in the distance, and headed towards the still-leafleting Dan. His lugubrious moustache was working wonders. Everyone who passed took a flier. I think they felt sorry for it. He spotted me with his equally lugubrious eyes.

'Is it yourself?' he said.

I've always assumed the question to be rhetorical, but with Dan you just wouldn't know. 'It is,' I said. 'None other.'

'I read your book,' he said. I was thrown and, I have to admit, flattered. He'd bought one of my books. No. Hold on. I'd sent him a copy of *The Book of Blaise*. Ah well.

Dan again. 'Know who my favourite character was?'

'Let me think,' I said. 'Dan?'

'Exactly. You really caught something there. I knew guys like that –' I braced myself. It was inevitable, this oncoming cliché, and there was nothing I could do to stop it. '– back in the day.'

'Glad you liked Dan, Dan,' I said, at which point Ashley strode up.

'Hi,' she said, punching me playfully on the arm. 'You've got a friend. That is such a relief.'

'We went to school together,' said Dan. 'You know –'

'Don't say back in the fucking day,' barked Ashley. And maybe it was something in Dan's expression, but her voice softened. 'Please?'

'Ash – sorry, Cindy – is a writer too, Dan,' I said. 'She wrote –'

'Flier?' said Ashley, stretching out her hand. 'I do love a good show.'

Dan gave her a leaflet and turned his attention to a passing group of excited pre-pubertals who seemed to bond with his hand-out almost immediately.

We bade him farewell – not that Dan noticed – and left him to his leafleting. Ash glanced at the flyer and muttered an irritated 'fuck'. She scrunched it up and tossed it into a handily placed litter bin.

'Not one for you then?' I asked.

She did something with her face. 'You could say that.'

I would have asked her to elaborate, but I was keen to head to the Book Festival while it was still early.

'I take it you're going back to the flat,' I said. 'I'll go over and let you in.'

'Sorted,' said Ashley, rooting in her bag and holding up a key. 'Why? Are you off somewhere?'

'*Book Snuff* biz. I really need to settle the line-up.'

'Got anyone in mind?'

'I certainly have,' I said, lowering my voice to a conspiratorial whisper. 'Anyone who's not Ashley Burnet.'

'Perfect. In that case I have a suggestion. How about Lizzie Borden? Kids' writer. Fucking genius.'

'I take it that's a front cover quote,' I said.

'Close,' said Ashley. 'Look.' She whipped her mobile out. Typed something in. Thrust the phone at me.

Shrinking Violet

Shrinking Violet has magical powers.
She can change size to suit how tall her current boyfriend is.
But wait! Is that any way for a feisty girl to live?
Violet realizes she has to be the right height for herself.
She settles on 12 foot 6.
Is worshipped as a goddess on several Polynesian islands.
And lives happily ever after.

'Lizzie Borden is going to be ****ing huge' – Ashley Burnet

'Sounds great,' I said. 'Where's she on?'

'Ah. Forgot that bit. She's in Denver.'

'It helps if they can walk to the venue,' I said.

'Makes sense I suppose,' said Ashley. 'Any message for Blaise?'

'Tell her I love her madly and to expect my immulent return.'

'Gotcha,' said Ashley.

And, taking advantage of a lull in the traffic, she headed across to the flat.

10

I strolled up Victoria Street, past the *Beau Belle Bar* and on towards the Royal Mile. I was thinking about 'immulence'. It's in my podcast. The three nonagenarian aunts. Some of their loopier flights of fancy have entered our private language. Mine. Blaise's. It's what spending a lot of time together does to you. Ashley may have raised a quizzical eyebrow at the word. Perfectly understandable. No doubt she'd have changed it to imminent by the time she reached Blaise. Not half as interesting as words go, but that's the English language for you. If enough people agree on a particular word that's it. Rubber stamped till the three aunts achieve cult status, at which point, who knows?

> *'Cult status?'*
> *'Pretty immulent if we have anyting to do wit it, Een.'*
> *'And speaking of cult status, isn't that Dublin triple act the Vulvas, soon to achieve immortality as the inspirayshing for bawdy treesome The Merrie Spinsters, as featured in your recently completed novel Hewbris?'*

As I passed the *Church of the Holy Rude*, a loud, commanding 'Macker!' stopped me in my tracks. I executed a half-swivel and came face to face with the owner or, should I say, owners of the voice. *The Vulvas*. All three of them. They'd started their careers dressed in the uniform of their old school, a subversive act in itself. The convent sued and lost. They were now slightly older, no uniforms, one nose ring, one purple Mohican. Weirdly enough, though, the *Vulva* who stood out looked like a head girl from a posh 1950's prep school. 'How's tricks?' she asked. 'What are you up to?'

'I'm –' I was about to follow up with '– doing *Book Snuff* at *Le Salon Littéraire*, actually', but stopped myself just in time. 'Any of you written a book recently?' I asked instead. 'Individually or collectively?'

'Too busy being us,' laughed Nose Ring *Vulva*. 'Why?'

That was a relief. I could imagine them forcing their way onto *Book Snuff* and totally destroying its subtle comic rhythms.

'Pity,' I said. 'I'm doing *Book Snuff* at the festival. You'd have been perfect. Yourselves?'

Purple Mohican *Vulva*'s turn. '*onemanshow* at *The Holy Rude*. We thought you were here to give us your support.'

They now had me pretty well circled. Difficult to know who was going to speak next.

'So why *are* you here?' Nose Ring *Vulva* spoke for all three. 'Ah, it'll be the religion. They say you always go back to it in the end.'

'Not the religion,' I said. 'Care to try again?'

Head Girl *Vulva* tried again. 'It'll be the graveyard, right? Makes sense. You know. At your great age.'

'Now now,' I remonstrated. 'I'm not dead yet.'

'Stick around, Macker. Stick around.'

'So, this *Book Snuff* yoke. What's it about?'

They seemed to be moving in closer, but maybe that was just me.

'Well,' I replied, pausing to collate my thoughts.

'Okay. Give us the short version. We're zoning out already.'

So I did. 'It's about writers dying for their art.' That was as far as I got. They'd spotted someone over my right shoulder and started waving frantically.

'Isn't Edinburgh gas? You can't go outside without bumping into a legend.' That came out as an excited babble. 'Attracta! Do you want to be in your man's show? Star attraction kind of thing. *Book Snuff*?'

Oh me miserum!

Attracta Boyle: multi-award-winning south Dublin novelist[*].

'She eviscerates we Irish for her own pleasure and our own good'
Irish Times

Attracta gave me a withering look and got straight to the point. 'I've read your wannabe novel *Sloot*,' she said. 'It was –'

'– "prolix but underwritten",' I interrupted, '"and would have been better if I'd written it myself. But, given the mundanity of its subject matter" –'

Last word to Attracta. '– I wouldn't have bothered my arse.'

'I'm surprised you lowered yourself,' I said. 'If word got out –'

Attracta smiled, but given the layout of her face it came across as a sneer.

'Oh, listen here to me,' she said. 'Bad publicity is good publicity. I'll do it.'

'Excuse me?'

'Your so-called show,' she said, thrusting a card at me. 'What's it called.'

'*Book Snuff*,' I spluttered. 'That's… that's… great.'

What else could I say? I didn't really have any choice in the matter. You didn't say no to Attracta. Besides, Torquil would be delighted. True, Attracta was a woman, but apart from that, she was a household name in houses around the world. She had *reach*.

'Right,' I said, 'I'll email you the details.' I shuddered at the thought of her mother's teenage diary. Her best sex scene? Shudder didn't even begin to cover it. Ah. I had it. 'Amongst other things,' I said, 'we'd like you to entertain us with your most humiliating rejection slips.'

Attracta puckered her nose. 'I don't do rejection.'

'Fine,' I said. 'You can tell the audience that.'

---

[*] Copyright laws, fortunately, prevent me from including a sample.

'Oh, I will. I will. Tell you what. I'll share yours. The ones you should have got.'

'Very droll,' I said.

'I can think of several words to describe it,' said Attracta, sneer-smiling again, 'but droll isn't one of them. Anyway, got to go. I'm running late as it is.'

Of course she was. Attracta always ran late. It fed her sense of self-importance. Make 'em wait.

A short, and possibly relieved, pause as she sauntered self-lovingly off.

'Right,' said Purple Mohican *Vulva*. 'That went well. Anyway, back to business. *onemanshow*. Are you gracing us with your presence or what?'

'Hold on there,' I said. '*onemanshow*? First, there's three of you. Second, you're all clearly –'

Nose Ring *Vulva* giggled impishly. 'You're making assumptions there, Macker, based on outmoded biological doodahs. We, however, are old school. The clue is in our name. But don't, for Jayzus' sake, grass us up. We'd never work again.'

> *'They're absolutely right, Een. We well remember the heyday of the Katlick church in Ireland.'*
>
> *'A naughty trio of spinster ladies wit lovers spanning the known globe? It didn't augur well.'*
>
> *'Fortunously, we managed to purloin tree mudder superior outfits from a teatrical costumiers in Fumbally Lane, so we were never unemployed.'*
>
> *'The Katlick Church is now in disarray, but wait'n we tell you.'*
>
> *'If it's not one religion it's anudder.'*

'To answer your question though,' said Purple Mohican *Vulva*, 'a different male joins us onstage at the end of every show –'

'– a non-speaking, penis-friendly part –'

'– to justify the title.'

I may have grimaced. 'Not me, I hope.'

'No way. Has to be a name.'

'It's the free fringe, Macker, so it's on us. Bring –'

'– ah, hold on. He doesn't have to.'

'I have a friend,' I said.

'Come on now. Social workers don't count.'

'Only joshing. Let us know when you're coming and we'll fumigate the Royal Box.'

11

After bumping into the *Vulvas* and Attracta I almost got caught up in the middle of a large group of megaphone-wielding unicyclists advertising *The Ladyboys of Banknock* down the Royal Mile. Another student theatre company blasted out a medley from Samuel Beckett's *Breath – The Musical* which, along with the crazy hedonistic atmosphere of the entire city in mid-afternoon sun-baked festival mode, made me yearn for the relative peace and harmony of Fraser's flat. To rest and recover some vestige of normality, some semblance of sanity, because I had a weird sense of the world becoming unmoored. Or maybe it was just the inside of my head about to explode.

Mayhem of the festival, peace and tranquillity of the flat. If I seem to be labouring the point here, I have my reasons. As I climbed the stairs, cool and quiet after the street outside, there was a burst of raucous laughter from the living room. Crazy, hedonistic, peace-and-tranquillity-shattering laughter. I opened the door. Blaise and Ash, hooting. That was it. No-one else there. But hold on. My podcast was playing in the background. Did they find it *that* funny? I felt, I can't deny it, quite emotional. Any negative thoughts I might have had about Ashley Burnet staying were put on hold. But only for the length of that sentence.

'A fucking *lighthouse!*' she shrieked. 'That is fucking *priceless!*' She calmed down slightly when she saw me. 'Blaise has just been telling me about your aborted holiday. Fucking –'

I was totally confused. 'I don't follow,' I said. 'We were double booked.'

'What's this about a double booking?' said Ashley. 'There's no poetry in a double fucking booking. The lighthouse was blown up by a feminist collective dedicated to the removal of phallocentric erections on our otherwise female coastline. Now *that* is fucking poetry!'

Blaise made slightly bashful eye contact. 'I'm a poet,' she said. 'I opt for poetic truth. A double booking doesn't have quite the same cachet. Oh, and by the way, is this what you call immulent?'

Neat change of subject. I pressed pause on the podcast.

'We were listening to that,' said Ash. With what looked like a put-upon pout.

'No, you weren't,' I said. 'You were hooting over it. The podcast – *my* podcast – was playing in the background, alone and unloved.'

'Beautifully articulated bollocks,' said Ash. 'We were rapt. *Rapt*.'

'She was too,' said Blaise. 'I put them all on a loop.'

'Listen to this,' said Ashley. She stood up, smiled enigmatically, and planted herself stage centre on Fraser's rug.

> *'You're blushing, Een.'*
> 'I am not blushing.'
> *'Well den, you've got that global virus ting. Stand well back, we're high risk.'*
> *'Unless you are blushing. In which case, fess up.'*
> 'Okay, okay. I'm blushing. Happy now?'
> *'Indeed we are, Een. Ecstatically so. Ting is, we've just come up wit a title for our forthcoming memoir. Too Old to Die. It would hardly work if you killed us off and the book came out postumous.'*
> *'If you can't believe the title you're hardly likely to buy the contents.'*

I was astounded. That was Ash in full flow, but it could have been me and the aunts. It was beyond spot on. Ashley bowed from the waist. 'More? How about this?'

> *'We'll be popping in when you least expect it, Een. Not, we hasten to add, when you're fairing l'amour wit your beautiful beloved. Well done, by the way. You're not the worst.'*

'Are you seriously suggesting –'

'Quick exit, girls. I tink we may have strayed into uncharted waters.'

Ash folded her arms in mock outrage. 'They certainly fucking had.'

Me? I was lost between admiration for the uncanny accuracy of Ash's delivery – her version of me could have been, well, *me* – and shock at her seemingly total recall. In spite of the fact that she patently hadn't been listening when I came in. She was pretty obviously enjoying herself.

'Know what my favourite episode is?'

'I shudder to think,' I said.

'*Three Aunts on a Pond*,' she said.

'Sorry?'

'The one about the Barbarous Ducks.'

'You're delusional,' I said. 'There's no such episode. And as for your Barbarous Ducks –'

'Hold on,' said Blaise. She leaned over to the laptop, tapped a few keys and pressed play.

'Sorry we're late, Een.'

'I wasn't expecting you, ladies, so technically speaking you're not late.'

'That's very consideracious of you, Een. Isn't it, girls?'

'Not so. You shouldn't be here in the first place.'

I said nothing, but I honestly didn't remember recording this.

'Well be that as it may, we were held up. We were passing that lovely lily pond on the way here.'

'It's not on the way here, Florrie, unless you're coming from Scuntorpe, which we weren't.'

'It's Dorrie, Florrie. Get a grip. You're Florrie.'

'I knew one of us was. Anyway, there they were, Een. Tree ducks. A lady duck and two gentlemen ducks.'

> '*Except they weren't gentlemen. If you follow. Their willies – close your ears for this one, Een.*'
>
> '*Too late, Dottie.*'
>
> '*You're probably right. He heard willies. Oh, and you're right about Dottie too. For once! Anyway, where was I?*'
>
> '*Their tings. They're like corkscrews, apparently. So there we were, tinking the lady duck might lean more towards the Sapphic, if you follow. And who could blame her? Would YOU fancy a corkscrew up your –*'
>
> '*He doesn't have one. Behave yourself!*'
>
> '*So in we went. The tree aunts to the rescue.*'
>
> '*Operayshing Rescue Lady Duck.*'
>
> '*Hence the title, Een. Tree Aunts on a Pond.*'
>
> 'Surely, ladies, that should be Three Aunts *in* a Pond.'
>
> '*Well observed, Een, but erroneous. We walked on water. Little trick we learned from the maestro. Baby Jesus. All those years ago.*'

Blaise pressed stop and overrode my stunned silence. 'Hold on,' she said. 'Next episode.' She pressed play.

> '*Delicate subject, ladies, but I don't remember writing that last episode.*'
>
> '*Could be an age ting, Een. Tought of that?*'
>
> '*Don't be daft, Dottie. He's a veritable spring chicken.*'
>
> '*Or, should we say, duck. Is there such a ting, Een? Spring duck?*'
>
> '*Sounds a bit dodgy.*'
>
> '*Could be one of those Cockney rhyming slangers.*'

'Happy now?' said Ash.

Happy? Confused, more like. Discombobulated. Stupefied. Take your pick.

'I simply don't remember writing any of that,' I said.

Ashley narrowed her eyes and did something with her lips. *'Maybe it was us, Een. Didn't tink a dat, did you?'*

Did I mention my head about to explode in the tropical mayhem outside? This brain-frazzling episode almost made me want to go back out there. Bit late for that now, though, so I opted for the voice of sanity. 'The three aunts,' I sighed, 'are fictional.'

'So they would have us believe,' said Ashley, and wisely changed the subject. The three aunts, however, those ever-present voices in my head, didn't.

'We know what you're tinking, Een. The female characters are so well realised, a woman couldn't possibly have written it.'
'Let alone tree batty oul wans wit a laptop.'

My head was then invaded by the most infuriating high-pitched giggles.

'Before the exhilarating delirium of your podcast we were discussing feminist waves,' Ashley's voice broke through – and mercifully the giggles faded. 'We'd just done Wave Six.' She sighed. 'It's been pretty dispiriting since the Second Wave heyday. So. Seventh Wave. One line descriptor?'

And maybe it was the influence of the podcast, but the three aunts, giggles now abated, continued to bounce around in my brain.

'You'd never tink of it yourself, but try this one, Een.'

A good idea for once, so I did. 'Seventh Wave,' I declaimed. 'One day, all women will be men.'

Good one-liner. Hadn't a clue what it meant. Ashley stared at me in shocked disbelief. I moved closer to the knife block. Just in case.

'Well tickle my scrotum with a floppy dildo. You're a fucking – what's that term?'

'Idiot savant?' said Blaise.

Ashley hooted. 'That's the one. You're an idiot-fucking-savant.'

I moved away from the knife block and sought refuge, instead, in the grinder.

'Happy to help,' I said. 'Coffee?'

12

In response to many calls from Torquil, most of which I'd managed to miss, not to mention the many midnight texts he'd sent, signing off with x, xx, or xxx and once or twice, bizarrely, a blood red heart, I made up my mind that today was the day I'd update him. I'd spent the past few days failing to find anyone to add to Attracta, and possibly Karima, for the big night.

Blaise had chosen Karima, Attracta had chosen herself. In spite of visiting comedy venues and a trip to the official Book Festival, I'd got nowhere. Quick example. Comedy legend Senga Mingin standing outside the *Stand Comedy Club* plugging *See You, See Me, See Ma Fuckin Show*. Not that she needed to plug it. She was, as I say, a legend. She didn't recognise me, fortunately – too busy recognising herself – but a show is not a book, so no need to worry on that front. Until this follow-up bellow: 'And while you're at it, read mah fucken tie-in fucken book!' I headed, metaphorically speaking, for the hills.

I was tempted to contact Rory Stagg, reputation notwithstanding, but I'd probably have to jump through all sorts of management hoops to get a response. I'd also trawled through every venue on the internet in my search to find the perfect *Book Snuff* panel. Several possibles, a couple of probables, no definites. Oh, well. Time, perhaps, to speak to Torquil face to face and see what he suggested. I tried his mobile. Straight to message. Feeling the need to get away from the laptop for a bit I grabbed my jacket and headed out to find him. A police car sat outside, engine on. Young officer in the driving seat, drumming her fingers on the steering wheel and staring straight ahead. DCI Strang stood beside a nearby bin, sucking violently on what looked like the tip of a cigarette.

'Ah. Mr *Book Snuff*,' he said. 'How's the murder tally today?'

'Spe expecto,' I said. 'Speaking of which, we had an A4 sheet pinned to our door. Woman. Head crossed off with a large, blood-red X.' I watched him closely as I spoke. Would he brush it off with a quip? He sucked on his butt and ruminated briefly.

'Old copper's motto,' he said. 'Give us the corpse and we'll do the job.' He chuckled and took another deep puff. 'I wouldn't worry about it. Sounds to me like someone trying to get an audience.'

'What?' I said. 'You mean a marketing strategy?'

He tapped ash onto the pavement. 'It's certainly got *you* talking about it.'

To be fair, his theory made sense. That, after all, had been my initial thought. Fringe show. Hold off on the details. Get them talking. Word spreads like wildfire. Everyone wants to know what the show is. DCI Strang went over to the car and tapped on the window. It purred open.

'Entertain our friend here with stories and songs from his native land, Shin, while I finish this.' He coughed, also violently, and went back to the bin, inhaling deeply.

Shin smiled warmly. 'It's Sinéad,' she said. 'He seems to find two syllables a bit of a stretch. The stories and songs bit? My dad's Irish. Montserrat mother, Irish dad. Hiberno-Caribbean.'

'Same here,' I said. 'Without the Caribbean.'

Butt stubbed, Strang flicked it into the gutter and made his way back to the car.

'Where's the cops when you need them?' said Sinéad, then to Strang, 'Hop in there, Sir. Bit of a domestic in Pilton. One fatality.'

'What's his name?' said Strang, easing his bulk into the passenger seat.

Sinéad gave him a mock long-suffering look. 'Nice try sir, but I suspect the victim is female.' She turned to me. 'Likes his little gender jokes,' she sighed, then, 'Nice meeting you. Dad's from Clontarf. Know it? It's in –'

'Dublin, by any chance?' I said.

She smiled again – a warm, of-course-you-know-it smile – turned on her blue lights and siren and roared off, startled tourists leaping out of the way. Dan, across the road, didn't even look round. Unusually, he wasn't surrounded by young people reading his fliers. I waited for a lull in the traffic and headed over.

'I read your book,' he said.

I was about to say you've already told me, but something stopped me. I'm not sure what. Something. 'So what gives with the flier?' I asked.

He handed me one. 'The kids, like, you know?'

I glanced at the title. *Straight Swap*. Six-year-old twins. Wrong body stuff. Meet a helpful 'therapist' online. Get the doings done. Body lop here, skin graft there. Bingo. Don't tell the parents, though. Family trauma when they find out. It's tearing them apart till Dad figures he's a woman and Mum – well, you can work that one out for yourself.

> *'Don't tell us. Mammy heads for the exit and joins a women-only commune in Letterfrack.'*
> *'We can't say we blame her, Een. Time, perhaps, to bring back that wonderful kiddy programme from the early days of television. What was it called again?'*
> *'On the Psychiatrist's Knee.'*

Thank you, ladies. As I was saying. Dad is now Mum, Mum Dad. Problem solved. Happy ever after. Credits.

I looked up from the flier.

'Hold on,' I said. 'Six? But your kids are – what?'

Dan looked a bit agitated. Tough one.

'Sixteen?' I said. 'Eighteen?' Dan now looked totally lost. I felt bad about bringing it up. Besides, it was a fringe show. They were probably playing the parents. I squeezed his arm. 'Sounds like a hit, Dan. Well, better get on. Catch you later.'

I headed off, still troubled by Dan's slightly absent manner. At the corner, I turned back to wave. But I'd already lost him to his fliers.

13

Le Salon Littéraire at George Square. The obvious place to start my search for Torquil. Besides, I'd been meaning to check the Square out anyway. A beautiful residential area when it was laid out in the late eighteenth century, it has since been defaced by progress. The central area was now buried in tents, makeshift bars, come-all-ye toilets and fake grass. I peered into the *Salon Littéraire* tent. Rows of closely packed chairs, platform stage at the far end, lighting rigs, a sound man checking the electrics for whatever show was on next. He gave me a friendly wave, so I strolled over.

'*Book Snuff*,' I said. 'My gig. Sunday 31st. Mind if I check the stage?'

'All yours,' he said, and got back to work fiddling with wires and switches.

I hopped onstage and turned to face the rows of empty seats. I hadn't been on a stage for some time. The recent pandemic. Writing a couple of novels. No call for my services. It was probably natural, then, that my mind flashed back to the past. Me as I was then. Hand on the microphone stand. Faint suggestion of a smile. Without thinking, I broke into a line from my act.

> '*My wife left me this afternoon.*
> *Four thirty.*
> *(GLANCES AT WATCH)*
> *Still, time is a great healer.*'

The sound man stopped what he was doing. 'Sorry to hear that,' he laughed. 'Midnight show, is it?'

'No,' I said. '6pm.'

The sound man grimaced. 'Ah, Torquil's gig!'

'The very same,' I said. 'You don't happen to know where he is?'

'Should be around here somewhere,' he said. 'Tell you what. When you find him, maybe ask him to ease up on his intro. Sixty minuter last night. Started at 6. He was still gabbing away at 8.30.'

'Bit long-winded, is he?'

'It's all relative, mate. If we're talking dawn of time till now – quick intro. I mean, have a dekko at this.' He indicated his mop of snow-white hair. 'Last month? Jet black. Then I met Tork.'

At the mention of Torquil's name my mobile went. 'Bloody hell,' I said, checking the screen. 'The legendary impresario himself. I'd better take it.'

The sound man grinned. 'Funny that,' he said. 'He's forever rabbiting on about this sexy Irish bloke he's having a thing with.'

'Lucky guy,' I said.

He caught the tone, nodded in mock agreement, and grabbed a speaker lead. 'Back to work,' he said, 'and roll on September.'

I gave him the thumbs up, took the call and headed for the tent flap.

'Torquil,' I said, 'I was just talking about you.'

'*Really?* Who to?'

'Oh, you know. People.'

'Well, as it so happens,' he effused, 'I've been talking about you too.'

'Really? Who to?'

'Friend of yours. Says you're his biggest fan.'

I quickly ducked under the flap and into the daylight. Across the fake grass, outside a rentakabin office, I could see the tall, straight-backed figure of Torquil, mobile phone jammed to his ear. Facing him, in casual shorts and a back-to-front baseball cap, stood none other than standup comedian Dorian Wilde, jabbing his finger animatedly at a flyer.

'Good to know,' I lied. 'So who exactly are we talking about?'

'Dorian. Dorian Wilde?'

'Biggest fan? Well, that's one way of putting it.'

'Great,' said Torquil. 'He's very excited about *Book Snuff*.'

'Aren't we all,' I said. 'Tickets available from the usual outlets.'

'Okay-y-y,' said Torquil. 'So I take it that's a –'

'No, Torquil. It's not a no. Don't say that when he's standing in front of you. It's a *Fantastic!* My people, his people.'

'Right, I'll – where are you, by the way?' His head was swivelling like a demented periscope.

No way did I want to have a face-to-face with Dorian Wilde. I had to get out of there. Fast.

'Locked in my study,' I said. 'Working, working, working.' I made my way towards the exit. Swiftly. Surreptitiously. 'You?'

'I'm – it's just –'

'Just?'

'It's just – there's a guy looks exactly like you –'

'Where, Torquil?'

'At the venue.'

'Weird. Could be related, I suppose. They do say all Irish people look the same. Unless you're Irish.' Reaching the exit I joined a group of Japanese tourists quietly heading away from the square.

'But – but – Dorian. How did you know he was standing in front of me?'

Good point. I had to think fast. 'Call it an educated – Whoops! Forgot to charge this thing. My power's about to –' I was out. I was off. A quick dash to the corner and freedom. I could still hear Torquil hello-ing in my hand. Then, click! He was gone.

As I strolled the city streets on my way back to the flat, I found myself wondering how Dorian Gray might fit into the *Book Snuff* setup. Short answer?

He wouldn't. Readers of *Sloot* will be interested to know that comedy wunderkind Foetus O'Flaherty was based on the same Dorian. Harsh but justified fictional journey given the career of the real-life version. Huge success in Dorian's foetal years, followed by a decade in the doldrums. Foetus was a bit of a nightmare, and so was the real-life Dorian. If he ever found out that Foetus was based on him –

No reason he would, though. He was hardly likely to read the book.

> *'You never know, dough, Een. He might just pick it up in a charity shop for 50p somewhere.'*
> *'Signed by the autor to his tree beloved aunts.'*
> *'Very intertextualitous if he did.'*
> *'Don't you tink?"*

As I was saying! He was hardly likely to read the book. I was feeling pretty relieved at this thought when I almost walked straight into Ashley Burnet, well, Cindy Ash, standing outside, of all places, *Qwe(e)rtyuiop Books*.

'Cindy. What a pleasant surprise.' She seemed startled. 'But I thought you and Blaise were visiting a graveyard?'

'Ah. Yes. Well. We were. We were. Just said our goodbyes.' There was something odd about her response. As if she was hiding something.

'So,' I said. 'Which one today?'

'Today? Hold on. Yesterday was St. Engelbert of Dumbiedykes. Today? Let me see.' She looked away as if thinking deeply. 'St. Enoch of the Barbed Wire Underpants.'

'You're joking, right?'

Cindy pursed her lips. 'I never joke about the dead. It's – why, it's disrespectful.'

Her lips were pursed. Her eyes? Her eyes may have danced with merriment. Tinted glasses. Impossible to tell.

'Anyways,' she said, 'you're just the guy to help me out here.'

'You don't say.'

'I totally fucking do. I mean, take a look at *this*.' She pointed at the *Qwe(e)rtyuiop* window display but, before I could do as requested, she swung the door open and ushered me in. 'Come on, big boy. Let's rock.'

'Settle down,' I said. '"Cindy".'

Ashely dropped her voice. 'Shit,' she whispered. 'Gotcha.'

The same assistant – Kaite *she/they*, according to her multi-coloured name tag – who'd been there when I first visited, was busy rearranging the children's section, a psychedelic blur of rainbows, sequins and glitter, just inside the front door.

'Hi,' she smiled at us. 'Looking for anything in particular?'

'As it so happens,' said Cindy in her best polite voice, 'we are. This lovely man here. His partner is none other than the author of seminal slim volume *The Crone Diaries*. Endorsed, I believe, by none other than Ashley Burnet. You know. The *Woman* woman. That Ashley Burnet. I was hoping you might have a copy to send to the folks back home in Oz.'

Quite a speech, delivered sweetly, but she lost Kaite's smile at *Crone*, and compounded her loss at Ashley.

'I'm afraid we don't stock such a book,' fake-smiled Kaite.

'Thought you mightn't,' said Cindy. 'Radical bookshop. You have to be careful not to dilute the brand, I suppose. You know. Lady stuff. Well, thanks for your help.' She turned to me. 'What say we have a quick browse.'

'Of course,' said Kaite, unsmiling now and with ice in her voice. 'I'll be right here, should you need me.' She left the children's books to sort themselves and took up her position behind the counter, from which vantage point she stared antagonistically at Cindy.

'*Hey*!' An ear-drum-bursting *Hey*! More Ashley Burnet than Cindy Ash. She'd just spotted a whole table devoted to *Qwe(e)rtyuiop* Book of the Month.

Handbag: a Memoir

Torquil Pittock

'Heartbreaking. Indispensable. NECESSARY!' – *Guardian*

Ashley Burnet meets Torquil Pittock? I was seriously tempted to swear.

'Desist, Een. Desist, desist, oh desist.'

The three aunts in my head again. Good advice for once, though.

I desisted. And instead wandered into the children's section, hoping for a safe haven from Cindy. And Torquil's *Handbag*.

I love children's books. I've written a few myself to very little avail. I flicked through a few of the titles on offer, mostly from the same imprint. *Nonbinarybird Books*. Pride of place? *Uncle Frank's MAP.* Six-year-old Harry spends the weekend in Uncle Frank's flat and goes on a journey of self-discovery. On a quick skim, all routes lead to Uncle Frank's bedroom.

'Revelatory'
Guardian

I then flicked through *A Child's Garden of Erotic Verse*

'Seminal'
Guardian

and was immersed in *The Zebra Who Found His Spots*

'You'll want a new family too'
Guardian

when I heard ill-suppressed hooting

> *'Hold on, Een. You left out the one next to it.* Willie & Dino*. *Little Willie befriends a giant dinosaur wit a sneezy cough. But is he really a dinosaur or a gynormous –'*
> *'Don't say ejaculating you-know-what, Florrie. He's blushing enough already. You were saying, Een. Ill-suppressed hooting –'*

from the *Handbag* table. Cindy/Ash, clutching Torquil's memoir, rippling with mirth. I made the mistake of looking over. She flipped the book to the back cover blurb.

'Listen to this,' she snorted across the shop. '"Poor little orphan baby. Found at a railway station. In –"'

'A handbag, by any chance?' I suggested. 'Settle down, Cindy. This is hardly a fit subject for levity.' I was quoting the title of my own podcast, but what the hell. It's hardly advertising. Cindy (!) settled down. Momentarily. Seconds later? Off again, but louder.

I glanced over at Kaite *she/they*. The face said it all. Luckily, the hair was already blue. I turned back to Cindy. 'I'll go further,' I said. 'It's hardly a fit *bookshop* for levity. Tell you what. We'll buy a copy. You can hoot on the pavement outside.' I took one over to the counter and turned back to Cindy. 'Behave yourself,' I ordered as I grabbed my wallet.

Too late. 'You'll never guess –' she'd gone beyond a hoot at this stage. 'The railway station,' she spluttered. 'You'll never guess where.' She was almost weeping now. As was the assistant.

Tears of laughter.

Tears of rage.

Back to Cindy.

'Bracknell.'

Tiny voice, but she managed to get it out before exploding again. She

---

* All four titles by Nonbinarybird Books' wunderkind, Larry Woodcock.

held the book up and waved it in the air. 'This guy has serious fucking mother issues. Pages two, six and twelve.'

I had to do something here before she read the relevant sections out. Change the subject. And help, or so I thought, was at hand. *Eighth Wave.* Obviously a trendy new publisher, they had their own stand near the door. Interesting selection. *From Altar Boy to Handmaiden: My Journey Through Modern Ireland.* I'd actually read that one.

'Oh, look,' I said, intending to shift the subject from mother issues to Ireland.

'Same ting, Een. But do go on.'

Cindy looked, then walked over and pointed at the sign.

'Now that,' she said, 'is interesting. Why Eighth?' She turned and held Kaite in a tinted-spectacle stare. 'Seven waves surely. As with feminism, so with the mighty ocean. Seven waves. Building slowly in height from number one.' She flung her arms out to heighten the drama. Kaite flinched. I ducked. Back to Cindy, her arms rising and falling. 'Number seven? The highest wave. Then back to number one. One to seven, back to one. One to seven, back to one. And so ad infinitum. That, at least, is what you're led to expect.' Cindy snapped *Handbag* shut. 'So what's this with number eight?' She fixed me with her steely but playful gaze. 'You might be ahead of me here,' she said.

I wasn't.

'Wait for it, Een. It's a cracker.'

I waited. Cindy stood on the balls of her feet, drawing herself up to her full height, arms aloft, and roared the final line. 'The eighth wave's a fucking tsunami!'

I glanced over at Kaite, silently throbbing Kaite, and lowered my voice.

'Very droll... *Cindy*,' I said.

Cindy smiled bashfully. 'Oh. Right. Cindy. Sorry.'

I paid for the book, Kaite thrust it into a paper bag and passed it over. I turned to Cindy.

'Right,' I said, handing her the book. 'We're leaving.' I gave Kaite my best empathetic look. 'The problem with day release,' I said. 'You never know what to expect.'

She – they? – glowered at me. Purple hair now, might have been the light.

14

Outside, Senga Mingin* stomped past, thrusting leaflets at innocent passers-by. '*See You, See Me, See Ma Fuckin Show!*' she bellowed.

Ashley, now back to demure Cindy, tutted audibly. 'Language, dear,' she admonished. 'There are gentlemen present.'

---

* Real name Agnes Boake.

15

The festival had reached its zenith. During the day the city was bursting at the seams. Revellers, revellers everywhere. And the heat! Blaise and Ashley were usually off grave-hunting or lunching out, so the flat was a relative oasis of calm, especially if the windows above the Grassmarket were kept firmly shut.

By night? Debauchery and drink. The Grassmarket vomitorium in full festive swing. An occasional burst of boom boom boom through the walls, lasting about 15 minutes, then stopping as suddenly as it started. The sound of an inebriated Ashley hooting in the guest room. The late-night call from Torquil.

This particular night, the last two, at one point, combined. 2.07 a.m. Torquil had phoned for 'a quick catch-up'. Couple of new possibilities for the *Book Snuff* line-up, he suggested excitedly. Any other business I needed to discuss? I was about to suggest that I could pop over for a chat, preferably during daylight hours, when a roar from Ashley's room vibrated through the wall.

'"I don't *have* a mother!"' Pause for a prolonged hoot. 'This is fucking genius!'

'What was that?' asked Torquil, interrupting himself mid-flow.

'Grassmarket,' I said. 'It's the festival, remember? Why?'

'Oh. Nothing. It's just… nothing.'

'"I don't have a fucking mother!"' howled through the wall again.

'Alcohol and mental health, Torquil. Talk soon.'

I pressed end call, put the mobile on the bedside table and sat up, careful not to disturb Blaise.

Thanks to Torquil, I was now wide awake. Serendipitously, though, an idea for *Book Snuff* had just popped into my head. I always keep a notebook and pen handy. I'm also pretty good at jotting down ideas in the dark. You simply never knew –

> *'When the muse might strike, Een. Very foretinking.'*
> *'And so it came to pass.'*

Blaise turned over towards me, still full of sleep. 'What is it now?' she groaned.

'Nice idea for the event,' I said. '*Who Said That?* Bit of an ice-breaker. Can't think of any examples offhand but –'

'Good. Sleep on it. Night night.'

'Hold on a sec. Got one. "St Enoch of the Barbed Wire Underpants." Who said that?'

A pause. No eye contact, so I couldn't see what she was thinking. She turned away from me and yawned theatrically.

'The Dalai Lama,' she sighed. 'Night night.'

16

Blaise, showered, dressed, makeup immaculate, was immersed in a Facetime call at the kitchen table.

'Here he is now, Karima,' she said. 'You can tell him yourself.'

I stepped into shot behind Blaise and waved at the screen. 'So, Karima, you're up for *Book Snuff*.'

Karima woggled her hand. 'Maybe, maybe not,' she said. 'I'm not sure I want to die for my career just yet. I'm still in the prime of life.'

'Fair point,' I said. 'Such a waste.'

'Now, if you were to guarantee I would lose,' said Karima. 'That I could live with.'

'Beautifully put,' I said. 'Done.'

'In writing?'

'Two witnesses,' said Blaise. 'Ashley Burnet. Me.'

'Perfect,' said Karima. 'I hope this gives you some indication that I've already entered into the spirit of the thing. I'd love to do it.'

This all happened first thing. Blaise, who was becoming increasingly concerned about the talk she was giving in a few days at the Scottish Women's Library, was now off at the National Library again, Ashley was still in bed. I was on the hunt for my third writer. It would help if I chose at least one of them myself. Besides, tempus was fugiting fast. 'Might be an idea to include a man.' That was Blaise's contribution before she hurried out. Bit under-represented, apparently. I accused her of being wilfully humorous as I waved her off the premises. Good point, though, so as soon as she'd gone I fed Freya, who purred her thanks graciously, made a fresh pot of coffee and rubbed my hands together.

'Got to find me a man,' I pretty well wailed.

Just then, Ashley stumbled from her room and headed for the bathroom. I glanced over. She seemed totally preoccupied, so no ribald rejoinder, but Freya had certainly heard. 'For the event,' I reassured her. It's the way she was looking at me. The Free Presbyterian cat look. I felt the need to clarify. 'I'm a happily married heterosexual male man,' I said. 'And a radical monogamist to boot.' Outmoded term, to boot, but it seemed to go with Freya's Bible-thumping face.

Back to the laptop. The Book Festival. What an array of talent. Male. Female. Other. And such a wide range of subject matter. I got sucked in. You know the way. Two hours later and you can't remember what you were looking for in the first place. Where was I? Ah yes. Books. I was struck by the titles of some, the authors of others.

My own particular favourite? Benjamin Quirke's memoir *Staring at the Wall: A Writer's Journey*. A special mention, too, to Icelandic noirist Persson Perssondottir's novel *Perpless*. Great tag line: 'If you don't read it, you'll never find out what it was they didn't do.' Quirke was in Edinburgh for the Book Festival, but back in Dublin on the 31st, no doubt staring at his next novel. Perssondottir was featured at the Spiegeltent, speaking through a translator. The translator's mother's teenage diary? Not what I had in mind, so when Ashley went back to her bedroom some time later I still hadn't found me a man.

When I eventually closed the laptop for a break Freya was staring at me. I was about to stare back when the flat door opened. Blaise. Beautiful as always, but visibly upset.

She held up a Frida Kahlo doll – in one hand the body, in the other the head. The neck had been stained with what looked like blood-red ink. Blaise put them on the table. 'Someone must have shoved them through the letterbox,' she said. 'What on earth is going on? First the note on the door with a silenced woman, now this.'

Just then Ashley staggered in, her long black hair springing wildly from her head. 'Fuck me up to Fucksville! What did you people put in that whisky?'

She was about to expand when she took in the pieces of doll on the table. 'What's this?' she said. 'Frida Kahlo double act?' Quick pause. The pause of recognition. 'Ah.' She took her mobile out, clicked and scrolled, looked puzzled, then snapped a photo of the doll. 'So, where did these come from?'

'Pushed through the door,' said Blaise. 'I found them when I came in. But who? And why?'

Good questions, and I thought I might have an interesting lead. While Blaise and Ash, deep in animated conversation, disappeared down a warren of feminist rabbit-holes, I went over to the bookshelves and examined the painting on the wall of the living-room, *The Tussle for the Keg*.

'Third question,' I asked, loud enough to startle them back to ground level. 'Who's Morag?'

'Not now,' said Blaise. 'Please.'

I pointed at the print. Blaise sighed and followed my finger.

'Lovely,' she said. 'Très Kitch. So, what about it?'

'Not the print,' I said. 'The arrows. See? Morag? Me?'

Blaise looked closer. 'Bloody hell,' she said. 'I hadn't seen those.'

I had her full attention now. 'So what exactly is Fraser trying to say?'

A short pause for Blaise to think it through. 'Hold on.' A slightly longer pause to compose herself. We waited expectantly. Then she was off. 'Okay. Morag is Fraser's ex. I knew them both at university. Then, out of the blue –' she waved a hand to indicate the flat '– the invitation to cat-sit.'

'You said ex,' I said.

'Bit of a tempestuous relationship,' she said. 'He liked to call her Mad Morag of the Mountains –'

'Cheeky cunt!' Ash interjected.

'Well, she was a bit wild in those days, and to be fair she grew up in the Highlands.' Blaise laughed, 'But yes. What you just said.' She laughed again. 'Anyway, they split up. As far as I know she went back to Orkney. Which is where they'd met.'

Ashley was riveted. 'Any chance she's here? At the festival?'

'I suppose she could well be,' said Blaise.

My turn. 'Interesting. Would she know about Fraser and –'

'Hilary,' said Blaise helpfully. 'She'd couldn't not know. He plastered the wedding photos all over social media before they left.'

'This Hilary,' said Ashley. 'Good deal younger, maybe?'

Blaise shrugged. 'Isn't it always the way?'

She lifted the framed photo from the sideboard and held it out to Ash, who took it and peered closely at it. 'Don't tell me. Fraser with Frida Kahlo.'

'Hilary,' said Blaise. 'But you're right. She's certainly got the look.'

'Hold on though,' said Ashley, propping the photo back in its place. 'Fraser and Hilary aren't here right now.'

'But maybe Morag of the Mountains doesn't know that?' I said.

Blaise thought about this. 'Maybe,' she said. 'Then again –'

'Maybe not. Okay,' I said. 'But let's keep an eye out for this Morag. Appraise her of the situation. Fraser isn't here, we are, so don't take it out on us. We need to locate her before she shoves something else through the letterbox.'

'Like what?' said Blaise.

'A paraffin rag? Unlit, but psychologically combustible.'

Ashley studied the *Tussle* print closely. 'So we're on the lookout for a red-headed, wild-eyed loon at the Edinburgh festival. Shouldn't be many of those around.'

Blaise laughed and looked again at the print. 'It's not a particularly good likeness,' she said. 'And besides, Morag is not a man.'

The case was seemingly cracked, though. Man takes up with younger woman. Ex-partner not happy. Takes it out on trophy wife. It certainly made sense. Oh, and finding Morag wasn't really an issue. Forget the paraffin rag.

That was me being dramatic. No sense dwelling on it, so I tossed the headless Frida, and her bodyless head, into the pedal bin and thought no more about it.

Or did I? Funny how the mind works away beneath your conscious thought. I lay awake that night. Pitch black in the bedroom. Raucous festival noises from the street below, the usual burst of thumping music from a nearby flat, Blaise breathing gently beside me, Ashley in the next room hooting at that bloody book, when I thought I sensed something. Difficult to describe. Something *untoward*. Which is where the sub-conscious mind kicked in. Back it went, unbidden, to Morag. How had Ashley described her? A red-headed, wild-eyed loon. Put that together with a paraffin rag through the letterbox and here's what you get. Paraffin rag, lit at one end. Flame licks up the stone steps, grabbing hold of anything flammable on its way. Through the flat door. Old flat, dodgy gas pipe, and there's your explosion. RIP Blaise, Ash, and me.

In the darkness, I grabbed my mobile from the bedside table and slipped out of bed. Barefoot, I fumbled for Blaise's silk kimono, then inched my way over to the door, slipped silently out, closed it gently and switched the phone torch on. Quick trip down the cold stone steps to make sure everything was as it should be. Nothing to report. Back upstairs. I was about to click the torch back off when I stepped on something sharp, crunchy, wet. I leapt back in fright and shone the torch on it. A discarded eggshell. But why? How had that got there? I flashed the light beam across the room. The contents of the pedal bin lay strewn across the floor. First thought – an intruder. Or a poltergeist. Which was worse? Hard to say.

I stood there working it through, still in a state of shock.

Second thought – Ah! Pedal bin. Discarded contents. Cat. I put the torch on the table and sat down, trembling. Of course. Bloody pedal bin, bloody cat. No sign of Freya – a sure admission of guilt. The mess, however, remained. I'd made sure to feed her, so why on earth had she done it? Who knows, for who can comprehend the feline mind? It's probably just what they do to pass the time. Which left the real question, why had I suddenly become so jumpy? Were things beginning to get to me? *Book Snuff*. Ashley Burnet. Morag. Rogue mammals. Beheaded Fridas. Eggshells underfoot. Feeling pretty flustered, I scooped the strewn contents back into the bin, gave the floor a quick sweep, clicked the torch off and inched my way back to bed.

17

The following day I went for a head-clearing walk, but it's funny how the mind continues to work away beneath your conscious thought. Even when the matter has been resolved.

To be fair, Ashley had based her description of Morag on a well-known painting of what appeared to be two feral Scotsmen, but she'd been right about the red-heads. The festival streets swarmed with them. Particularly the Royal Mile. Possibly a convention, but whatever the reason, there they were. Everywhere. They didn't look particularly wild-eyed or loonish, but it was still only early afternoon. Give it time.

Which set my mind racing down the paraffin rag route again as I turned into the downward-winding Cockburn Street. Serendipitously, however, I spotted the *onemanshow Vulvas*, some way from the venue, leafletting for their event. I say serendipitous, as their youthful exuberance tossed the paraffin rag into the pedal bin of my brain.

Purple Mohican *Vulva* threw her hands up in possibly mock delight.

'Fancy seeing you on Cock Burn Street, Macker.'

'It's pronounced *Coburn*,' I corrected. 'None of you is called Mad Morag of the Mountains by any chance?'

'Would you go 'way with yourself,' laughed Nose Ring *Vulva*. 'You know we're not. Why do you ask?' She switched to mock serious. 'Not that he needs a reason, girls. He's Macker. He moves in mysterious ways.'

They'd reverted to coven mode and switched to referring to me in the third person. A quick interjection was called for, or I'd be surplus to requirements. Or worse. 'I'm on the lookout for a red-haired, wild-eyed loon called Morag, from Orkney, who may or may not have posted certain items through our letterbox with malicious intent or, to put it another way, malice aforethought.'

Head Girl *Vulva* patted my arm. 'Guess who swallowed a Thesaurus for breakfast.'

They stared at me in silent contemplation for a very short moment. Admiration? Awe? Difficult to say. Then they were off.

'Are you crazy, you big ride? Orkney? *Orkney?!*'

'Unless you hadn't noticed, Irish is part of our usp.'

'Help him out there. Look at the age on him.'

'Okay. usp. Unique –'

'I know what usp is,' I chided playfully. It was the assumption. To be fair, they were right. I didn't. Well, until they said Unique. But I wasn't telling *them* that. Besides, I didn't get the chance. They were off again.

'Further point of information, Macker, referring to our previous incarnation.'

'None of us has red hair.'

'We're not the word that dare not speak its name.'

'And I can't vouch for the others, but I've never been to Ringsend in my life.'

Ah. Of course. The *Vulvas* started out as *The Red-headed Whores from Ringsend*, a literary reference, but had to adapt to social pressure. *The Red-headed Sex Workers from Ringsend*, however, didn't work. Wrong rhythm. So. No red hair. Not whores. Not from Ringsend.

'That's three points,' I said, 'but thanks for clarifying.' I raised my hand for silence. 'And before you tell me it's a quote from a poem, adieu, gentle ladies, adieu.'

A few choice ripostes followed me up Cockburn Street, but it was the final one that stopped me in my tracks.

'btw,' – and yes, I know what it means – 'we purloined your filthy versepome for the show. *Polyamóry in Yatatata*. Bye-ee.'

An office worker with a carton of coffee almost came to grief behind me as I jerked to a halt. 'Sorry,' I said. No point trying to explain. I could hardly explain it to myself. *Polyamóry in Ballydehob*. It's in my latest novel, *Hewbris*. Which hadn't been published yet. So how could they possibly know the verse?

I twirled round to ask them.

They'd gone.

In my experience there's a logical explanation for everything. Even if it's illogical. Take the above scene, for instance. Could it be that my fictional take on the real-life troupe was so accurate that I'd managed to anticipate their actual material? Is it possible I'd written it into my as yet unpublished book and, without them even reading it, it had metamorphosed into fact? This, on top of everything else that was going on, was beginning to make my brain hurt. It was saved, from a migraine or worse, by displacement, when I found myself no longer striding deep in thought over the venerable cobbles of Old Edinburgh, but face to face with a wall completely obliterated with festival posters. Pretty garish, most of them. Gurning comedians. More gurning comedians. I noticed a sad little effort from career-floundering egomaniac Dorian Wilde:

The Far Side of Funny
Just when you thought nothing else could go wrong – it gets worse.
'Yesterday's man' – Chucklers & Chuckling

Old trick this. Turn lousy reviews to your advantage. Pride of place on the wall, though, was

Rory Stagg – Wife Beater*

Bloody hell. Is this what it had come to? An image of Stagg, standing at a microphone looking very pleased with himself. I noted the asterisk.

It suggested footnote. And so, on tiny font inspection, it proved.

*I beat her once at a game of darts. It doesn't get a mention. I just liked the title.

With one leap he was free. He'd just beaten her to the double top. Hilarious.

Next to the obliterated wall was a pavement café with a couple just leaving a table. A free outside table at the Edinburgh festival? I grabbed it. In the early days of my career I would have gone for a pint. Possibly more than a pint. But not any more. A flat white extra hot was exactly what I needed. All I had to do now was figure out a way to go in, order a coffee and come back out without losing the table. Tough one. I didn't have a jacket. My mobile phone would get nicked. I could always leave my notebook and pen, but what if they fell into the wrong hands?

I was swimming my way through this mental soup when I realised that the woman at the next table was smiling at me. I say smiling at advisedly. Something was amusing her. True, I may have been acting a bit strangely to the outside eye. Even for Edinburgh at Festival Time. I was reminded of my comedy guru, Professor Emeritus Larry Stern of CDU. With particular reference to his seminal study, *The Unintentionality of Comic Genius*. Was that me? Here? Now? I grimaced inwardly. Possibly outwardly too.

The woman glanced over again, somewhat furtively this time, her face half-shielded by a magnificent mane of autumn-leaf-coloured hair. None of the wild-eyed loon about her, though.

'Excuse me,' I said. 'You're not Morag from Orkney by any chance, are you?'

She laughed openly, freed of the need to stifle her mirth. 'No,' she said, 'I'm not Morag. Nor am I from Orkney. Great chat up line, though.' She leaned towards me and lowered her voice. 'I've been happily married for seventeen years, he's due back any minute, and I'm not prepared to jeopardise a beautiful relationship for a brief dalliance with a smooth-tongued Celt. Nice try with Morag, though. And here he is now.'

"He" was six foot five in a rugby shirt. Some team or other. England. That's it.

'Is he annoying you, darling?' he said. To her. About me.

She waved it away. 'Not at all,' she said. 'He wanted to know if my name was Morag. From –'

'Orkney,' I said helpfully.

Her husband may not have been the brightest. 'Good line,' he said. 'Must –'

Not-Morag's smile fled. The sun darkened in the clear blue sky. 'Must what, *darling?*'

Her husband looked startled. 'Oh, nothing.' But it wasn't nothing. He knew it and, perhaps more importantly for the unfolding drama, she knew it too.

'Let me finish the line for you, *darling*,' she spat sweetly. 'Must use it myself.'

Fortunately I hadn't ordered, and the writer's desire to take notes was outweighed by the desire to save my own life. 'Darling' scowled at me as I left, which seemed a bit unfair. *He* was the 'good-line' thief, not me.

I was elbowing my way slowly through the crowds and street performers along the Royal Mile, slugging from a much-needed bottle of water, slightly out of breath in the mid-afternoon heat, when a man on a bicycle shot across my path and disappeared down a side street. Shock of white hair. Scarf flowing behind him in the breeze. He was, I can hardly bring myself to write it, Professor Emeritus Larry Stern to the life. Professor Emeritus Larry Stern is a fictional character! From *Sloot*. CDU is a fictional university, also from *Sloot*. Yet here he seemed to be – in the living, cycling, three-dimensional flesh. First the *Vulvas* purloining a song I'd never made public, and now a character from my fictional story set in Dublin, materialising on the Royal Mile in Edinburgh!

Having said that, the world is full of crazy, shock-haired cyclists, many of them wearing scarfs. Hold on though. This was Edinburgh in August. You don't wear a scarf in high summer. Another thing. Flowing behind him in the breeze?

There *was* no breeze.

I've noticed I do a lot of walking in my books. *Sloot*. *Hewbris*. This. Walk, walk, walk. It allows the mind to wander where it will. I don't drive, but as far as I know you can't let the mind roam quite as freely behind the wheel. As I passed St. Giles' grave-free cathedral I thought of Blaise and Ash. St Englebert of Dumbiedykes? St. Enoch of the Barbed Wire Underpants? I'm not of the Protestant persuasion, but I know of no such establishments. So what exactly were Blaise and Ash up to when they disappeared for hours at a time? I bookmarked the question for later.

I turned left onto George IV Bridge, past Central Library and the National Library, then right, down the picturesque curve of Victoria Street with its elevated walkway, towards the *Beau Belle Bar* and the Grassmarket. People crowding every pavement. Spilling onto the cobbled road. Posters covering anything that didn't move.

You know that rabbits-in-a-tree game you play with small children? You can't see the rabbits, but once seen you spot them all over the place. Same with Rory Stagg. His 'wife-beater' posters once seen couldn't be unseen. Walls. Lamp-posts. Centre stage on the window of the *Beau Belle Bar*.

As if drawn in by the relentless publicity machine, a rowdy gaggle of women trooped into the *Beau Belle* as I passed. All wearing the same bright red t-shirt. On the back? An image of a gigantic set of forked antlers and

Stagg Night
A F***ing Hoot – Kuntz

Curiosity aroused, I followed them in. Lovely bar. Small and traditional. One long narrow room with seating on either side, in the style of oak pews. Central aisle leading to the bar. Bit like a drinker's church, come to think of it. I used to worship there – ah, one for the memoirs perhaps. Inside, the women trooped up to the altar to order drinks. The punters parted. These women weren't the sort you messed with. Standing beside the door to the gender-neutral Ladies with his heavily ironical face on, Liquid Lunch Man himself, DCI Strang. With pint. His colleague, Sinéad, in civvies. Soft drink.

Strang grinned at me. 'Anything to report, squire?'

'A decapitated doll was shoved through the letterbox,' I said. 'Frida Kahlo. In two parts. Body. Head.'

'Now that is interesting,' said Strang. 'Make a note, Shin.'

'Will do, Fult – sorry, *Sir*.'

'I didn't hear that,' said Strang. 'Drink anyone?'

'Not for me thanks,' I said. 'I'm driving.' I turned to Sinéad. 'That's a lie. I'm working.' I nodded at the rowdy gaggle of Stagg Nighters. 'Research.'

Right on cue, one of them raised her voice above the general babble. Dagenham, I think. I'm pretty good on accents.

'Fing is,' she said, 'my Gav's nor a wife beahah. Never 'as been.' She spotted me looking at her. 'We're noh married, see?' Her pals' failure to laugh was perfectly understandable. Heard it. Used it themselves. My failure could have been problematic. Luckily for me, she was too busy laughing herself to notice. She leaned over. Conspiratorially. 'They say all Scotch people are cunts, love. Know what I say? Whar abah' Rory Stagg? Eh? Eh?'

Strang shrugged philosophically. 'I'm off out for a fag,' he said.

'Ooh er, missus.'

Not me. The woman.

Sinéad finished her drink. 'Research?' she said.

'I'm a writer,' I said. 'Everything is research.'

'What about me?' she said. 'Am I research?'

'Of course,' I said. 'Ambitious cop. Waiting for Strang to retire so you can apply for his job. Happily married, no kids as yet, and you live in a two-bedroom flat in Marchmont. Close?'

'Spot on,' she said. 'Apart from most of it. Come on, I'll escort you out.' She nodded towards the Staggers, who were now reassuring the barman that he wasn't a cunt either. 'Safe passage.'

I was relieved to notice as I passed that The *Naked Munch* window was spared the indignity of a Rory Stagg poster. There was, however, a fresh one advertising an event the following day.

Sewer Special
Chuck Weill
August 21st. 1pm

A genuine Wow! Moment. Chuck Weill! The Very Special Guest for the Sewer magazine relaunch. That, I hadn't expected. Though it made perfect sense. If he was still alive, at any rate. The event info was superimposed over an image of his seminal masterpiece, *Ridin' in the Mayflower*. The original cover featuring Chuck Weill himself, in a pair of boxer shorts, fag in hand, three-day growth. Bottle of Jim Beam. Ancient Olivetti. Tapping away. Great image. Iconic. I read it aged 17. Believe me, it was the cool thing to do. Oh, *yeah*! I didn't say that. It was the mind again, off on one of its little journeys. It pencilled in the time, smoked an imaginary *Lucky Strike* and strutted, Chuck Weillily, on. I, naturally, went with it. Regular walk, mental strut.

'A superannuated teen, Een. Very alluring.'

Dan was in his usual place at the Covenanters' Memorial, shuffling from foot to foot. I returned with a shock from Chuck Weill-land to reality.

Robyn, of Robin/Robyn fame, stood facing him, relaxed-looking in a purple mini-skirt with low-cut fuchsia blouse over a generous bust, offset by knee-high stiletto-heeled black leather boots. She was talking at speed in a highly animated way and whacking a *Straight Swap* flyer against her naked and athlete-muscled upper thigh to illustrate her point. 'I'll fire this on to Robin,' she gushed as I passed. 'He will be so, so *thrilled*.' Nice to see her engaging with Dan. I positively warmed towards her and, by association, her other half. I thought about stopping for a chat, but no. Whatever they'd found to bond over, this was serious engagement. I'd never get a word in. Besides, time to get back.

I left them to it. Robin still rhapsodising, Dan still shuffling on the spot.

Freya mngiaowed pitifully when I went in. As well she might. Guilty as charged. I'd disposed of the bin bag on my way out, so there I let the matter rest. Second thoughts, though. The guilt was mine – I'd forgotten to feed her again. I'd just finished opening a tin of Cockle Delight, and Freya was hungrily tucking in, when Blaise arrived home. No Ashley. As good a time as any to bring up the subject of their little trips out together.

'À la recherche du plot imaginaire, Een. We'll hold your coat.'

'Any luck?' I asked.
'Sorry?'
'You know,' I said. 'The graveyard. Saint – where was it today?' Blaise looked – difficult to know how to put it – shifty?

'Oh, that?' she said. 'No, no. We – we never made it. Ash was meeting some – let's call them contacts, so I went along.' A slight pause. I held my nerve, because Blaise hates lying. Something to do with Strong Moral Centre Syndrome. I checked my watch. Twelve seconds in: 'Okay okay okay! We haven't been visiting graveyards per se,' she said. 'But seriously, best you don't delve.'

'*Per se?*' I said. '*Delve?*'

Blaise ushered me over to the sofa at the far end of the room, sat down and patted the seat beside her. I sat. She leaned towards me and whispered, as if her co-conspirator, wherever she was, might be listening in. 'Ashley is planning something. Not to put too fine a point on it, this isn't a chance visit.'

'Not a chance visit from Australia?' I said. 'You surprise me. Of course it's not a chance visit. So what exactly is she planning?'

'Okay,' sighed Blaise. 'She's been treated pretty shabbily by certain parties and, well, her plan is to set certain things in motion to – how best to put this? – redress the balance.'

'Certain things,' I said. 'Bit vague.'

'You could say that.'

'I just did.'

Blaise patted my hand. She sometimes does this. It's meant to mollify. 'Look, it's all a bit – you know – at the moment.'

'No,' I said. 'I don't know. So tell me.'

'Ah well, you see. Bit of a conflict of interest there. She said if I told you I'd have to –'

I knew what was coming next. A total cliché. I expected better of Blaise, and she a poet of no small standing. Besides, we have a cliché jar. 20p for a cliché. 40 for a tired cliché. Fifty quid for Thunk.

But I was wrong. What she actually said was far, far more chilling than "kill you". 'She said if I told you, I'd have to answer to a hard-line feminist collective.'

Blaise had the good grace to look abashed, so there I left it. Probably a midnight get-together of the coven on Blackford Hill. I was more than happy to be excluded.

'Given that I don't know what it is,' I said, 'your secret is safe with me.'

'Exactly. Oh, and don't forget Glasgow.'

'Of course not. We live there. That bit?'

'No. We're going there tomorrow. That bit.'

Are we?' I said. 'Why?'

'My talk, remember? 2pm? At WLS.'

Women's Library of Scotland.

I almost expleted. She'd been working on this talk for months. It had been booked ages ago. I'd promised to go along. A quick break from the lighthouse was what we'd intended, but I'd totally forgotten about it in the mayhem of the festival.

'Oh, and I have the perfect title,' Blaise beamed at me. '*Scolds Unbridled*. What do you think?'

'Women's Library? *Scolds Unbridled*? A marriage made in feminist heaven.'

Blaise seemed happy with this. I, on the other hand, nursed a secret sorrow. My heart sank as I realised that was Chuck Weill out. A chance to relive my youth. On the assumption that Blaise would be off doing whatever she did with Ashley, I'd gone and booked a ticket.

As I ground the beans to make us a pot of coffee, I thought of using the pressure building around *Book Snuff* as an excuse. I even thought of fabricating a meeting with Torquil Pittock to finalise details. His texts and missed calls were becoming ever more frequent, so a meeting made perfect sense. But no, I'd promised Blaise I'd go. I simply couldn't bear to let her down. Her sad face is a thing to behold. It contains within it the sadness of the ages. Complex people, women. Giving birth may have something to do with it. I know men do it these days, but it's traditionally been the woman's role.

I kept my own male sadness in check – with my face it's difficult to tell anyway – but it persisted into the evening. I'd been genuinely excited about seeing the icon that was Chuck Weill. Weird sensation. I couldn't dissociate Chuck *now* from me *then*. On the cusp of manhood. Reading his riveting prose. Teenage hormones on fire.

'Is there something the matter?' said Blaise, as she stood at the sink washing and trimming a colander of string beans for dinner.

'Nothing whatsoever,' I said. 'I was simply lost in a reverie.' No sooner had I finished the sentence than I had second thoughts. Teenage hormone thoughts. 'Well, there is something,' I said. 'My loins –'

'Loins Schmoins,' she said, waving a string bean playfully. 'Big speech tomorrow. Work to do on my notes.' She popped the bean in the steamer and dropped her voice to a seductive whisper. 'Just remember, my love. We'll always have Scrabster.'

Scrabster. Early days of our relationship. Cancelled ferry. Single bed at the *Fisherman's Arms*. We told them we'd take turns. We didn't. But that was then. This, at the time, was now. I was about to press the point when her mobile rang. I put my loins on hold. Simple method. Rather than dwell on those happy youthful hours reading *Ridin' in the Mayflower*, I brought to mind my schooldays and, more particularly, the venerable Brother Machree. Not, I would have to say, that he was particularly venerable at the time.

Blaise was now in full flow, the mobile tucked against her shoulder as she finished preparing the last few string beans. 'No, no, Ash. It's great that you're meeting people. We'll see you when you get back. Good timing, actually. I was just making dinner. I'll go easy on the beans. Early night tonight too. It's my big day tomorrow. (PAUSE) Women's Library of Scotland. (PAUSE) Really? That would be – (PAUSE) No, no, that would be perfect. Of course you can. I'd love that. See you later then.'

Blaise put her mobile down. 'With one leap he was free,' she said. 'Ash wants to come to the Women's Library with me tomorrow. Makes sense. You can stay here and –'

'But I was all set to go,' I said.

'No you weren't.'

Blaise was right. I gave in without a fight.

18

Almost midnight, still no sign of Ash.

'She's probably just letting her hair down,' said Blaise, plonking her finished speech notes on the bedside table. 'Oh well,' she sighed. 'Long as she keeps her hat on.' And she squeezed my hand and disappeared under the duvet.

Short pause. Loud music through the wall. And this, along with the vomitorium, three texts from Torquil, and a waking nightmare about Brother Machree in his underpants, kept me busy till 4.32. Which is precisely when Blaise squeezed my hand again.

'Are you awake?' she whispered.

I was now. Blaise sat up.

'Still no sign of Ash,' she said. She looked worried. 'It's just not like her. She knows we're heading off first thing. What if she –'

She didn't finish the sentence. In a way, she didn't have to. My imagination finished it for her. A teeming bar in central Edinburgh in the early hours. An inebriated Cindy tosses her hat to the four corners of the room and reverts to Ash. Fiery Ash. Drunk, bellicose, gloves-off Ash. Spoiling for a –

I didn't finish the mental sentence. 'Phone her,' I said.

'What?' said Blaise. 'We're her parents now? I can't do that.' She sighed a frustrated sigh.

Then – 'Just do it,' I said. So she did. 'Phone's dead,' she said, dejectedly. 'So what do I do now? Ash has enemies everywhere. What if she's –' We were both thinking the same thing.

'Phone the police,' I said.

No response, so I thought about it again.

'Better still, relax. She's probably in some late-night dive sweet-talking Senga Mingin. She'll arrive back at dawn bleary-eyed, crash out for rest of the day. I'll do the Glasgow trip. Okay?'

Blaise smiled weakly and lay back down. 'Okay,' she said. "You're probably right. Night night.'

Bloody Ash. On the plus side, she wasn't doing *Book Snuff*. With that uplifting thought in mind I fell into a deep, much-needed sleep.

19

I groaned myself awake. Blaise was sitting in bed poring over her notes. She took her reading glasses off. I yawned and stretched.

'Ash came in at six,' she said. 'There's no way she'll be up on time.'

'Cast your mind back,' I said. '4.32am. "I'll do Glasgow." Okay?'

I was making light of it. Bloody Ash again, though. Secret meetings? Out till dawn? On the plus side, she still wasn't doing *Book Snuff*. I glanced at my watch. 08.40.

'Right,' I said. 'Quick coffee while you get ready.' I crawled out of bed, grabbed Blaise's kimono and pulled it on, fortunately, before I opened the door. Because there, standing in the kitchen, fully dressed, arranging a pile of freshly baked croissants on a plate, was Ash. Her mobile phone sat charging on the worktop.

'Ready to *rock*,' she whooped. 'Fuck me. Love the flowery outfit. And there I was thinking you were last of the trouser men.'

'Sleep well?' I asked, my voice dripping with irony.

'Like a baby,' she replied chirpily. 'And hey! Look what *I* got. Takeaway coffee. And these scrumptious little beauties.'

'Triff,' I said. 'I'll take a coffee in to Blaise. Whose dressing gown, by the way, this is.'

'Relax,' said Ash. 'It kinda suits you. The gay sumo wrestler look.' I was about to change the subject before she said featherweight, when she changed it herself. She whipped *Handbag* from her handbag. 'Just finished this.' She tossed it on the table. 'Not one motherfucking woman in the whole book. No mother. No sisters. No female friends. In the whole book! His. Anyone else's. I mean, weird or fucking what?'

At which point Blaise emerged fully dressed and smiled at Ash. 'You must be pretty exhausted,' she said. Sweet on the surface, slight acidity underneath.

Ash flinched. She knew Blaise well enough to see behind the sweet. 'I met Toby.' She gave Blaise a pleading look. 'You know. Twelve hours on his masterpiece, quick haiku.' She feigned blasé. 'But *hey*! That's me back!'

Two heys? I could see she was putting the cheery, upbeat tone on for effect. Probably desperate to crash out. Might as well sort it now.

'I told Blaise I'd do the Glasgow trip,' I said.

Ashley looked genuinely shocked. 'No no no! Me me me!'

So that was settled. Her her her.

I watched from the window as they headed off, across the Grassmarket, past Dan, who looked confused at Blaise's friendliness. He'd met her several times before. With me, granted, but still. He thrust a couple of leaflets at them and they continued on their way, striding up Victoria Street, until they rounded the corner and disappeared out of sight. I turned my gaze away from the window and fed Freya, who'd started mngiaowing meaningfully. I'd really got the hang of cats by this stage. Feed them regularly, like humans. Otherwise, leave them to it.

Freya happily eating, I pulled a chair out from the table and opened my laptop. I started to type in *Sewer* magazine, intending to get a bit of background info for the Chuck Weill gig later today. After all, I hadn't heard of him for years, if not decades. Then I thought - no, surprise me, and deleted the search. He'd be older. That much I knew. *Ridin' in the Mayflower* had been such a massive part of the zeitgeist in my adolescent years. Everybody read it. I say everybody. Males. I say males. Young males.

Boys becoming men. As you can tell from the prose style here, I was probably a bit trippy. I tried to calm down with three more coffees and a bit of heavy lifting on *Book Snuff*. After all, I was still one author short, and the big day was drawing close.

Speaking of short, my investigations revealed that Jan Slipowitz was in town. She'd had a short book of comic vignettes published in the late sixties and seemed to have spent the past half century drawing people's attention to it. I wasn't sure I wanted to add to the brand.

Other than that? Nothing. In frustration, I shut the laptop lid. I still had a couple of hours to play with before the Chuck event, so I took a short trip to Bruntsfield. For nostalgic reasons. I lived there, oh, years ago now. There's a graveyard nearby, an actual graveyard, so I thought I'd surprise Blaise and who knows, maybe even locate Isabella myself. I imagined myself staring accusingly at Ashley Burnet, who'd been leading Blaise astray, with a dramatic reveal of Isabella's final resting place.

Big graveyard, however, no Isabella.

I was crossing the historic Brunstfield Links, a gently sloping grassy area with natural rises and dips, where the game of golf is said to have originated with one of the King Jameses in the fifteenth century, when I spotted iconic wordsmith Abe Altman. Abe's dry Jewish wit is perhaps best experienced through his act. Is? Was? He must have been getting on for ninety at this stage.

> *'Ninety, dough, Een. That's nearly as old as us.'*
> *'You never know. He might have played a quick round wit King James.'*

Probably well retired by now. Which might explain why he was playing a round of miniature golf with himself on the Links.

'Abe!' That was me.

'A moment if you will. Slight problem with my niblick.'

Probably an age thing.

'I'm sorry to hear it,' I said.

I felt a bit of a pang here. Abe would have been perfect as the third guest writer for *Book Snuff*. He's written some wonderful off-kilter books. And the aforementioned act? Surreal humour with musical accompaniment on the handheld Glockenspiel. But late eighties? Problems with his niblick? He'd be upset if he had to refuse. I hadn't brought the subject up, but decided to change it anyway. 'Just had a quick look round Morningside Cemetery for Blaise,' I said.

He stroked his ball with what may have been a putter, then stood up straight and patted my arm with his free hand. 'I'm terribly sorry to hear it,' he said. 'Such a vibrant lady. So young.'

'No, no,' I said. 'Not her. She's trying to locate her ancestor's grave. Isabella. Late 19th Century. Bit of a radical by all accounts. No luck so far, I'm afraid, but the search continues.'

Abe mulled this over as he holed the ball in eight, removed it, and sheathed his putter. All remarkably sprightlily* for a man of his advancing years. 'Excellent round,' he said.

'I'm delighted to hear it,' I said. 'Five under par? Twelve?'

Abe shook his head and sighed. 'I knew I'd forgotten something.' He examined his ball as if it might help him out, pocketed it, and returned to the matter in hand.

'A thought,' he said. 'Mere postulation on my part. Is it possible, by any chance, that your lovely lady is Jewish? Whole or part thereof?'

'Not that I'm aware of,' I said. 'To be honest, I've never actually asked her.'

'Rabbi in the family? That's usually a clue.'

'Not, again, that I know of. But why do you ask?'

'Bit before my time, but it's a well-known fact. All 19th Century radicals were Jewish.'

'Try telling that to Karl Marx,' I said.

'Next time he's in town,' said Abe. 'Oh, and would you mind?' He

---

* Not, technically, an adverb. Possibly © Toby Smyrke.

pointed at his golf bag. 'Bit of an issue with the lower thoracic vertebrae.' I grabbed the bag and followed in his wake as he headed slowly down the links. 'Bear with me,' he said. 'A short ten-minute walk should do it.'

'You have a theory,' I conjectured.

'You conjecture correctly. To elucidate. I had the great pleasure of dining at your official residence some years back. Main course?'

'Kneidlach,' I said. 'I remember it well.'

Abe had three helpings. I knew, now, where this was going.

'Wonderful cook,' said Abe. 'And an equally wonderful poet. The two don't often go together.' They didn't in this case either. I'd done the cooking. Let me qualify that. The kneidlach I reheated from the local Jewish deli. But I could see what he had in mind. Blaise female, Jewish cuisine. Put the two together, Blaise Jewish. Possible, I supposed. I'd simply never asked.

We were now three minutes into our ten-minute walk. Understandable, this being the Edinburgh Festival, that we'd eventually cross paths with a fellow performer. And so it came to pass that Rory Stagg, of wife-beater fame, hoved into view with top comedy agent Amelia More. Rory put his arm around the small of Amelia's back and pointed at us with his free hand as they approached.

An icy smile from Amelia that didn't meet her eyes. Or her mouth.

'This is Mimi, by the way,' said Rory. 'Just married. Oh, and speaking of just, Abe, just read your latest. Right up there.' He moved across to Abe, who seemed happy with the direction the conversation had taken.

> *'A quick interjection here, Een, if we may.'*
> *'Now's your big chance. Ask your one there –'*
> *'The power behind the trone so to speak.'*
> *'– if your man is free to do your illustrious event on the tirty first.'*

I'd actually got there before them. I moved closer to Mimi. 'Quiet word?' I said. 'I'm hosting *Book Snuff* at *Le Salon Littéraire*. Last night of the festival. Any chance –'

'And you are?' said Amelia More. She knew who I was. Rory had just told her. What she meant was *you're nobody*. I stared into the frozen ponds of her eyes and mentally withdrew the offer. At which point Robyn, of Robin/Robyn fame, raced past. Different sparkly tracksuit. Turquoise. Same cheery wave.

'To the crags, amigos! To the crags!'

Amelia waved excitedly, eyes aflame with networking zeal. 'Robin-n-n!' she squealed.

'Wrong Robyn,' I corrected her. 'I think you'll find this is Tuesday.'

No response. Pretty glacial with it.

'*Guardian* interview, Rory,' she said sharply as if tugging on an invisible leash. 'Chop chop.' And they were off.

So, at an infinitely slower pace, were we. I assumed Abe would return to the subject of Blaise's Jewish heritage and her alleged culinary skills, but after he'd finished complimenting Rory's good taste, with particular reference to Abe's book, and recounted his glowing testimonial word for hyperbolic word, we arrived at our destination. *Sciennes Jewish Burial Ground*.

'Two points, Abe,' I said. 'The gate is locked.'

'Lest we remember,' said Abe sadly.

'Second point. The graves we can see there. The ones at the front? They're all in Hebrew. Do you happen to speak Hebrew?'

'Not fluently,' he replied. 'A word here, a recipe there.' Short pause for thought. 'Blaise, however, might.' At the mention of Blaise's name his eyes took on a faraway look. 'You know, even at this distance – what? 2 years, 3 months, 17 days – I can almost taste the melted schmaltz of her matzo balls.'

20

Back to the flat. Time to get ready for Chuck.

Linen suit.

Mobile, notebook, pen.

Glasses.

I checked myself in the bedroom mirror. Hair under control. No traces of silvery stubble lurking in chin crevices. Classy outfit. Not bad for a man approaching the foothills of late middle age. Temperature-wise, the suit was cool. Okay, the word cool has two meanings. I like to think it suited both.

Close to the time, but not too close to look needy, I skipped down the stone staircase and out into the buzzy festival sun. I may have stood on the pavement as if advertising the latest Italian chic. Man of a certain age in linen suit. Little comic interlude over –

> *'Or was it, Een? Comic, that is.'*
> *'Or were you, perhaps, exulting in your testosteroneous masculinity?'*

I'd just returned to the real world when a text pinged in from Torquil.

keep missing you must meet up asap x

No time for that now. Busy busy busy. Dan, as always – or so it seemed – was doing his leafletting thing across the road. I waved over as he stood holding out a flyer for the next sympathetic passer-by. He looked, I would have to say, inexpressibly sad. Funny the way the mind works, though. I found myself thinking, could it be the droopy moustache? Would he look happy if he stood on his head? Or moved to Australia? I then felt bad about thinking this. There seemed to be something not quite right about Dan these days. I'd pop over for a chat later, but not now. Now was time for Chuck.

As I approached the *Naked Munch* DCI Strang flicked a cigarette butt into the gutter and preceded me in. He flashed his police badge at the startled loon-pants kid, who now wore a *Fuck the Pigs* t-shirt.

Fuck the Cops? Fuck the Pigs? You'd think he'd have learned, but no. They never do. Meekly, the kid waved Strang through. I flashed my ticket and followed Strang inside. I picked up a complimentary copy of the fiftieth anniversary edition of *Ridin' in the Mayflower* from a nearby table and flicked it open. Introduction by Toby Smyrke. Who else? It fitted snugly into the linen jacket pocket.

At the next table people were queueing to pick up their free drink before finding a seat. As I waited in line I took in the transformation of the *Naked Munch*. Its usual set up of tables and chairs had been replaced by theatre-style rows with a small raised stage at the far end. On it sat a brown leather armchair, a small table and a mic stand.

My turn to choose a drink, and I should have guessed. Chuck Weill event. No water or juice, no alcohol-free. Just beer, beer, beer.

> *'You foreswore it, Een. And you've held a steady course ever since.'*
> *'The inspirayshingal lecture circuit beckons.'*

I took a bottle just in case. Dry throat syndrome. It was pretty hot in there.

> *'We spoke too soon.'*
> *'You know how it is, Een. One bottle leads to anudder.'*
> *'Scrap the lecture tour.'*
> *'A night in the cells more like.'*

The way I figured it, a quick mouthful would hardly set me off. Besides, it went with the general ambience. And the suit. And the book. And, it has to be said, the clientele. It was predominantly male. Strang slurping his beer, probably plotting an end to the smoking ban. Toby Smyrke, deep in conversation with a fawning acolyte. Oh, and Lorrie, the abrasive American woman from the Byron walk. She was there too, standing over at the side looking a bit lost. No sign of her elderly partner on the premises which, you would have thought, might cheer the poor woman up. Curmudgeonly old sod. If I'd been her his absence would have cheered *me* up. But I didn't have him in my life, I had Blaise, the very thought of which cheered me up.

Glad she wasn't here, though. Blaise and Chuck Weill? Possible song: *When Two Views Collide*. I chose a seat on the end of a row near – but not too near – the front, took the *Mayflower* book out and studied the cover. Chuck with his fag, his three-day growth, his bottle of booze. And the Olivetti! Retro cool before retro was a thing. Chuck Weill, sixties icon. Totally immersed in his writing and simultaneously aware of the camera's hero-worshipping gaze. And that mesmeric, ancient face! It looked as if several people had already lived in it. He'd have been – what? – thirty-one? Weird to imagine what the passing years had done to that craggy face, with the fags and the booze and the flop houses and the fights and – I'm getting carried away here. I'll tone it down for the final draft, but… what a life! He'd probably roll onstage in an urn.

I flicked through the book while I waited for the big moment. Hard to know what I'd make of his writing now. Changed times. I was also that bit older. More, I like to think, mature. Back to the book. Title: *Ridin' in the Mayflower*. Plot: Chuck has been commissioned to cover the Miss America pageant for a hip monthly. He ingests every illegal substance known to man with his midget (*sic*) sidekick, Geronimo, while – I think the title gives the rest of the plot away. Every contestant, if he's to be believed, falls for his grizzled charms. Except Miss Nebraska, a martial arts expert from Wahoo. Toby

Smyrke's one paragraph intro ran to 48 pages. How did they get him to stop?

I was about to skip to the last line to see if he finished the sentence, when a series of taps on the crotch-level microphone suggested we were about to start. I closed the book. *Fuck The Pigs* kid stood centre stage in a borrowed jacket, three sizes too big, closed over the t-shirt message. He stole a sideways look at Strang. Is it possible to look sheepish and cool at the same time? No, it isn't. Especially in your dad's borrowed jacket.

He crouched to microphone level.

'Few words about *Sewer*,' he mumbled, at which point I zoned out. I know what a few words can turn into in the hands of a mumbler. Beer in one hand, book in the other, I re-examined the Chuck Weill cover image. A moment in time. Cometh the hour cometh the – Snap! I was brought back to the real world by the sound of applause, the whistling, the whooping.

Chuck Weill walked slowly towards the makeshift stage and sat laboriously down in the battered leather armchair. The stage was pallet-height, the author slightly hunched. I had to sit up straight to see the top of his head. I was about to try peering between the people seated in front of me when 'This is a great man! This is a great, great man!' I turned to see Lorrie, the Byron-walk American. Standing at the back. Finger jabbing at Chuck. I did a double take. Was it possible? Of *course* it was. Chuck was none other than her grumpy old partner, Charlton. Wispy-haired and wizened now, like young Chuck reimagined as a sun-dried prune.

From the stage he focused on Lorrie with his rheumy eyes, seemed about to say something, but thought better of it and opened his book instead. Also slowly. Also laboriously. An affectation? Difficult to say. I discreetly shuffled my seat over into the makeshift aisle. Perfect. I now had a direct line to his face, his hands, his – his essential Chuckness.

He began to read. Slow and low at first. He then continued slow and low. That was the Chuck Weill style. Part way through – hold on. I'm going to switch to present tense to suggest immediacy, because this is quite a moment.

Chuck is reading. He stops. Mid-sentence. What is he doing here? Where is he going with this? He puts the book down. Slowly. Laboriously. Affectation? Jury still out. He fumbles in his jacket. Wait for it. Removes a pack of *Lucky Strike*. I'm not advertising here. It has to be *Lucky Strike*. Flicks one into his mouth from the open pack and, with the practised ease of millennia – he straddles at least two, remember? – he sparks a match on his stubble – okay, okay, his shoe – match raised to cigarette, puff, puff, puff. I glance over at the fuck-the-cops kid. He's palpitating. He's an anarchist, but this is against the law. I glance over at Strang. He *is* the law. Strang is gazing with adoration at his hero. His hero, meanwhile, picks his book back up and, after a protracted wheezing fit, continues reading. I won't transcribe what he read – this is *my* book – but if you're into bedrooms, barroom brawls and braggadocio, Chuck is your go-to guy. He'd just gone in search of the American Dream in room sixty-nine – "I clocked the sign on the door. Miss Alabammy. DO NOT DISTURB." – when my mobile rang.

I was sitting on my own in the aisle.

Directly in his line of fire.

I whipped the phone out and desperately tried to mute it. I'm not good with mobiles. But you'd think on this occasion, with an icon of American letters glowering at me from, what, about 12 feet, I'd finally crack it out of fear. Nope. I pressed everything. It seemed to be ringing for days.

'Hellfire, fella!' Chuck barked. 'Answer the goddam thing.'

I knew how to do that, so I did.

'Shoot,' I said. Not my usual opener, but it seemed appropriate for the time and place.

'Blaise asked me to call. Just to say we might be late, okay? Interesting times here. We –'

Ashley. Great timing.

'Look,' I interrupted. 'I can't talk to you now.' Chuck was staring at me. 'I'm at a – a thing.' Note the reluctance to specify.

'A thing?' That was Ashley. 'What thing?'

Chuck was giving me a sour look. I felt trapped in a pincer movement. No way out.

'A Chuck Weill reading.'

'Chuck fucking *Weill*? I *know* Chuck. Put him on. Tell him I'm in Sydney.'

Christ! Of course she knew Chuck. This was the last thing I needed, but Chuck was still staring. Imaginary Stetson. Low-slung holster. So I caved in. 'It's Ashley Burnet,' I said. 'She's in Sydney.'

'Best place for her,' said Chuck. 'Reminds me of my first wife.'

'I heard that,' said Ash. 'Ask him was that *before* he shot her.'

'I'm not asking him that! She says was that before you shot her?'

Chuck shrugged. 'Ruthie? She was ten years older'n' me. She'd be dead now anyways.' A ripple of possible delight from the audience: did he really say that? I say the audience. Most of the audience. A couple of women in the aisle seats in front of me sat stony-bodied. Possibly matching faces. Chuck motioned towards the mobile. 'Lemme talk to the lady.'

Chuck wanted to talk to Ashley, Ashley wanted to talk to Chuck. A golden opportunity to relive my youth and Ashely Burnet invades it. But what was I supposed to do? 'Chuck wants a word,' I said. 'I'm passing you over.'

I felt like reverting to even younger me and sulking, but managed to snap out of it. I walked up to the stage, passed the mobile over, stood there feigning cool in my cool linen suit.

'We know what you're tinking, Een. Where's the paparazzi when you need it?'

'Well, missy,' drawled Chuck, 'it's been a long, long time.' (PAUSE) 'Whoa, lady.' Less of the drawl now. 'Ruthie was a good old gal, no question, but hell it was an accident. Cuba. Melon on the head.' (PAUSE) 'Settle down, lady. The tequila missed. The hallucinogenics missed. Chuck Weill did not, repeat not, miss. Same with Delia, same with Sal.' (PAUSE) 'Correction, Miss Burnet. I tried clean. Lord how I tried. Late eighties to two thousand six. Didn't write a goddam thing.' He sucked on his *Lucky Strike* and stared out at the audience. 'You hear that, young writer guys out there? Learn from an old man's mistakes.' Back to the mobile. 'Gotta go, babe. There's a whole mess of people here want a piece of Chuck.' He waited for the sounds of approval to die down. 'Any message for phone guy?' (PAUSE) 'Chuck Weill is God.'

The audience burst into spontaneous applause. He pressed *end call* and tossed the mobile back. 'Maybe not her exact words.' Hoots of appreciative laughter.

Chuck lit a cigarette from a cigarette. Cool if you find that sort of thing cool. *Fuck the Pigs* kid did. Strang did. I glanced at the two women as I made my way back to my seat. Front view this time. Let me put it this way: they may have strayed into the wrong event. Chuck Weill took a long, deep pull on his *Lucky Strike*. He held it in, exhaled, appeared momentarily to forget where he was.

'Darling.' His lady-love, Lorrie, implored from the side of the room. 'Why don't you –'

Chuck Weill flicked his ash at the transfixed front row and peered out at her. 'Say, I thought I left you cuffed to the bedpost.'

You weren't supposed to laugh at that sort of thing, but the audience spread its legs and did just that. So did Lorrie. 'Shoot, Charlton,' she hooted. 'You are *so funny*!'

He dropped the dry tone for a snarl. 'Chuck, lady! Chuck!'

Lucky for him Blaise wasn't here, I thought.

Lorrie was more emollient. 'A great, great man,' she repeated, but more tentative, less of a jab this time. 'You could maybe take some questions now, hun?'

Chuck ignored her. 'Anybody got a question out there?' Between *question* and *out* a hand shot up. 'Tall guy with the mortician's face,' said Chuck.

Toby had written the introduction, but Chuck didn't appear to know who he was. Toby, unfazed, unfolded himself to his full height and came at his question like the class swot. 'Your work, Mr. Weill, is sublimely, ingeniously, resonantly, nay *exuberantly* of its time, yet it exists, if I may make so bold as to project backwards to the Big Bang and forward to the end of days, for all time.' He glanced proprietorially at the young man beside him, then turned with reverence to Chuck. 'Any advice for the aspirant author?'

Chuck Weill tapped a fresh cigarette on his knee, 'Never use one small word where twelve big ones will do,' he croaked, smiling at his own playfulness. 'Oh, and fuck adverbs.'

I could see Toby mentally editing his twelve hundred page masterpiece down to three paragraphs. I'm tempted to say he left shortly afterwards, deflated, his Winchester education no earthly use to him now. Not a bit of it, though. He deferred to the great man. Sorry. The Great Man. Toby Smyrke. The Great Man. A room erupting with testosterone. Not to mention the gentle waft of fumes from my hand-warmed bottle. Alcohol content? Probably very little, but this may have added to the effect. My hand shot up. 'Fancy doing *Book Snuff*?' I couldn't believe it. How had this happened? I had no way of knowing, but I did know one thing. It had.

'*Book Snuff*,' said Chuck Weill. 'Sounds kinda quirky. What the hell's *Book Snuff*?'

Book Snuff
Kinda quirky – Chuck Weill

That's me with my marketing hat on. I was on a roll here. 'Well,' I may have drawled, 'three writers onstage. One of them gets to die for her art.'

Chuck winced at the *her*. I ignored him*. 'Great Career Move. Except she doesn't really. Die, that is. It's all explained on the night. Climax of the Book Festival.' My cliché-detector kicked in. Don't say Yours Truly. Too late. 'Yours Truly to compère. All you need – let's see. Most humiliating rejection slip – taken. Best sex scene – taken. Ah. An extract from your mother's teenage diary.'

Chuck Weill – I'm tempted to say lit up.

'Well now,' he definitely drawled, 'will you take a look at this.' He tossed his cigarette butt at *Fuck the Pigs* kid – 'Help me out here, sonny' – started rooting in the inside pocket of his jacket and took out his wallet. Opened it, withdrew a yellowing and folded sheet of paper, held it up. 'Got it right here, folks.' He motioned over to poor, put-upon Lorrie. 'Get this guy's details, hon,' he said. 'Chuck Weill is back, folks. And this time? He stays back.'

Perfect scene-end line there. Pity, because it wasn't the end of the scene. He did the one last question routine. The two women. Both hands shot up.

'Can't do both,' said Chuck. 'Come on, guys. Anyone else?' No-one else. He flicked another cigarette from the pack. 'Slug it out there, ladies, get back to Uncle Chuck.'

'That's no problem, Charlton,' the older of the two tall slim blondes said in a relaxed American accent. He may have bridled at the name but said nothing. 'The Misses America in the book. With the honourable exception of Miss Nebraska and her reverse neck choke, did you actually sleep with *all* of them?'

Chuck chuckled. A low, conspiratorial chuckle. 'A gentleman never reveals his secrets.'

'But you did in the book,' she said.

---

* I also ignored the tiny giggles in my head. *'Us again, Een.'*

Chuck chuckled again.

'When I wrote the book, lady, I was no gentleman.'

The woman paused for effect.

'Okay. Got that.'

Shorter pause.

'My mother was Miss Ohio.' Full stop pause. 'Dad.'

A collective intake of breath from the audience.

'Only joking. She thought your book was mis-titled.'

'Oh yeah? And *her* title?'

'Horseshit.'

End of scene.

I stood outside the *Naked Munch* as the audience dispersed.

Two deliriously trippy women. Heading back to Ohio, no doubt, mission complete.

A morose-looking Toby with his young acolyte. Off to prune his adverbs?

Strang. He seemed quietly pleased with the way things had gone. He lit up and came over to where I stood. 'Nice move on *Book Snuff*,' he said. 'Hot ticket when this gets around.'

'I take it you'll be there,' I said.

'Work night, sadly,' he said. 'But you know what they say.'

'Give you the corpse?'

He shrugged and headed off. I was about to head off myself, but where? I'd just booked the legendary Chuck Weill for *Book Snuff* and Blaise and Ashley were still in Glasgow. I had the rest of the day to myself. Dan, I noticed, was standing where I'd last seen him, holding out a leaflet. Not that he particularly needed to. The queue for tickets for his kids' show snaked out of the close leading to the venue. A noticeboard outside was plastered with five-star quotes.

STRAIGHT SWAP*

'The perfect show for your six-year-old daughter – especially if she's a boy'
Guardian

'And vice versa'
Guardian

'We are so, so jealous! Grrrrrrrr!!!'
Robin/Robyn

* Sponsored by Pharmaceuticals-R-Us

I was about to take a closer look at the reviews under the quotes when who should round the corner but Byron in his trademark black, followed by a group of rapt tourists. He was probably about to shake them off and escape up Victoria Street like he'd done before, but at the precise moment he reached the *Naked Munch*, out came Chuck and Lorrie. The Miss Ohio episode hadn't swayed his core fan base and Chuck, after a lengthy book signing, was back in the saddle. As the happy couple emerged, Byron jerked to a halt. Comedy jerk. Exactly what I would have done at his age. Touch of silent film legend Finlay Jameson's classic two-reeler, *The Jerk*. Then he let rip.

'Attention must be be paid!'

The line, as delivered, was dripping with irony.

'It's from a play, Een, by celebrated American playwright Arthur Mullard.'

I remembered it from the first time I came across Byron's Edinburgh Old Town walk. An apoplectic Lorrie to Byron. 'Attention must be paid! You hear me, asshole? Attention must be paid!' And now this. Byron's playful revenge. I got it. Chuck got it. Lorrie, on the other hand, was deeply moved. 'You,' she said, 'are a *good person*.'

Byron, however, still embraced the irony. I caught the mischievous glint. 'And this,' he declaimed, pointing at the *Naked Munch*, 'is where legendary authoress Enid Blyton composed her late-flowering masterpiece, *Five Go Mad on Mescaline*.' He bowed from the waist to his followers. 'There endeth the lesson.' And off he strode up Victoria Street, leaving them trailing forlornly in his wake.

Lorrie was apoplectic. 'And just who in tarnation,' she fumed, 'is Enid Blyton?'

'Old girlfriend probably,' muttered Chuck. 'Difficult, at this stage, to tell.'

21

Something about Byron fascinated me beyond my powers of understanding. Have I used the word visceral yet? I certainly hope not*, and I'm not going to use it here. Having said that, Byron's very existence affected me in an almost animal way, so I set off in hot pursuit. Up Victoria Street – his followers, who were now openly muttering their displeasure, breaking up into their constituent parts and replanning their afternoons. Along the Royal Mile. On the left-hand side there's a narrow wynd leading to the lower end of Cockburn Street. Byron swung into it and hurried down the steep stone steps. I quickened my pace. Half-way down, as if freed from the accursed mob, he slowed to a dawdle. I slowed too. Interesting wynd. Historic it goes without saying. Everything about Edinburgh is historic. Except for the new stuff. The wynd – back to the wynd – was out of the sun. Narrow steps descending between towering centuries-old tenements. Darkness. A sense of foreboding. Was that the haar in from the sea, the bitter sea beneath the lowering sky? Was Byron, black-clad, brooding, doppelgänger Byron –

I was about to build on this filmic image when I passed a wynd-dark wall defiled by publicity posters. Four Rory Stagg posters in a square. Superimposed over each of the four, a slightly smaller poster, but you knew it was Rory underneath. His Staggness stuck out at the edges. Inference? This was a deliberate act, an act of provocation. The superimposed posters were meant to block out the posters underneath. And what were they advertising? Nothing.

---

*Editor's Note: You have. In spite of my earnest entreaties.

Every single one was purest white. At the bottom right-hand corner, however, in tiny-for-a-poster letters, #usp. It didn't make a great deal of sense. #usp? Incomprehensible and yet, somehow, intriguing.

Further on, a single poster. Same thing. Rory at the edges, otherwise whited out. I went closer this time. The #usp poster looked like it had been printed on, the print then whitewashed out. Like a palimpsest. You could almost see the shape of letters, as if they were struggling to make their presence felt beneath the whiteness. Or then again, maybe it was a trick of the lack of light on the steep narrow stairs descending between tall ancient buildings.

Byron was now approaching the foot of the steps, and I was about to set off again in pursuit, when a deranged-looking man with electrified hair came barging past me from above. He screeched to a halt by an ancient oak door and grabbed it by the knob.

'Excellent news,' he roared, swivelling towards me. 'I've just invented and cured schizophrenia in collaboration with myself!!!'

'Delighted to hear it,' I said as I tried to push past. 'Just give me a bloody flyer.' Bit testy, but this was a narrow wynd. A brief respite, you would have thought, from the relentless self-publicity of the Royal Mile.

He paused for a demented second and fixed me with both mad, swirling eyes. 'You're delusional, laddie. The word flyer does not presently exist in any lexicon of note.' He grabbed the knob with renewed intensity. 'Hector McGregor, Doctor of Lunacy. Struck off in the year of Our Lord 1873 for reasons of insanity, but we won't go into that. You'll have read my weightless tome, *Snap Out Of It, Man!* Every mental illness cured in a sentence!!!' He smirked with uncontrollable glee. 'Available, I need hardly add, in all the best bookshops. Well, bookshop singular.' An ear-splitting roar. '*The Divided Shelf.*' He let go of the knob, whipped a blood-stained meat cleaver from the folds of his morning coat, and leaned closer on the strangely deserted wynd. 'Meet Eugene!' he leered, glancing around as if to check no-one else could hear. 'The world is a madhouse, laddie. Why? Philosophers through the ages have waxed lyrical on the subject, but here's my theory.' He moved closer still and dropped his voice to a bellow. 'Ladies,' he confided, 'control the means of reproduction. Some mistake there by a non-existent deity *I* would have thought. A dropped 'd' on the instruction kit is my best bet. For Ladies read Laddies.' He raised the cleaver higher, and grabbed me with his free hand. 'Eugene's job? To rectify matters.'

Backed against the wall I felt its icy cold seep through my jacket. Edinburgh at festival time was always crazy, but this was something else. McGregor smirked triumphantly. 'What, I conjecture, if ladies were laddies and laddies were laddies too? Revolutionary, I grant you, but thanks to Eugene, a great wrong will be redressed!'

Eugene? What? As in Eugenics? He seemed to read my thoughts, and emitted a deranged cackle. 'The word hasn't been invented yet, but Yes, laddie! Yes!!!'

Best, I thought, to humour the man. 'I see,' I said. I was reminded of my witty riposte on the subject at Fraser's flat.

'Our witty riposte, technically, as autors of same, but go for it, Een.'

'So you'll be one of those Seventh Wave Feminists?'

He quailed visibly, as if I'd brandished a crucifix. 'The F-word, laddie, doesn't enter the Queen's Gibberish for aeons. Its sole purpose? To dismantle what we lovingly call The Patriarchy.' He raised Eugene to eye level. 'Our job? To remantle it. Next stop? The Master Race!'

From somewhere deep behind the thick oak door – was that the plaintive cry of a small child?

'Hel-l-l-p!'

'Methinks the lassie doth protest too much!' roared the good doctor. 'A few slight rearrangements on the torso front and he'll be back on his stumps in no time. Come, Eugene! There's work to be done!'

He sheathed the cleaver, pushed the door violently open, and with a final 'Only the mad are truly insane!' he slammed the door behind him. Moments later a muffled roar from within. 'Put me down this instant, nurse! I'm affianced!'

Then? Silence and, on closer inspection, no door. A stunned pause while I processed the above. Real life? Hallucination? Was he a vision or a waking nightmare? This was Edinburgh. Difficult to tell.

I waited for the briefest of brief moments for my heart rate to return to normal, shrugged philosophically, and continued my descent. Did I make McGregor up? Had this little episode been caused by sitting with my nose too close to that beer bottle? I hadn't sniffed alcohol for years. Had it, perhaps, returned to haunt me? Plausible, I supposed. I picked my brain up off the cold stone steps and tried to recall how I'd got here. Byron! But Byron was now long gone. I turned, retraced my steps up the darksome wynd, and headed back towards the Royal Mile.

In glorious festival sunlight.

22

As I advanced, brows probably knotted, up the Royal Mile, with its fire eaters, buskers, leafleters, moving statues, general mayhem, I began to wonder if I was, perhaps, losing it. The lunacy that is Edinburgh at festival time. The unsolved X sheet pinned to the door. The beheaded Frida. Byron, the cross-generational doppelgänger, Mad Morag of the Mountains, the phantom late-night boom boom boom, the Ashley Burnet/Cindy Ash double act conspiring to drive me nuts, Torquil's constant texts and calls, Robin/Robyn's irrepressible joie-de-vivre.

And now, to cap it all, Hector MacGregor and his blood-stained meat clever Eugene.

'Voices in your head, Een. Don't forget voices in your head.'

Don't interrupt! Voices, as I was about to say, in my head. All this, and the psychological pressures of my impending performance beginning to assert themselves. It reminded me of a conversation I'd had with Blaise just after I completed *Hewbris*. I'd made the point that I seemed to feature psychologists a lot in my work. Her response? 'Now why do you think that is?'

I turned left onto the relative sanity of North Bridge. Then down the relative madness of Victoria Street. As I approached the *Beau Belle Bar*, the same group of women I'd bumped into before were standing outside, staring up at the Rory Stagg poster on the window. Except this time it was blanked out, like the others I'd seen, by #usp. The Staggers looked confused and, strangely, hurt.

'Censorin our boy? Nah. We'll take our shekels elsewhere, thank you *very* much.' As they turned to go one of them caught me looking at the blank where Rory used to be. 'Can't say a blinkin fing these days.' Yes. It had to be Dagenham. I was pretty sure of it, and what moved me was the hurt in her voice. Not to mention the blinkin. She may have seen me as a man of breeding, unused to the cut and thrust of Dagenham phraseology, but whatever the reason it brought out my empathetic side. It also, and this is never a bad thing, took my mind off myself.

'Could it possibly be,' I said in my best man-of-breeding voice, 'that you're looking at it the wrong way, ladies? Might it, perhaps, be instructive' – I'm writing this from memory, it probably wasn't quite as flowery – 'to approach it from a different angle. Brilliant marketing strategy from Team Rory. Proof? *You're* certainly talking about it.'

The response was immediate and touching. 'Sodding buggery, Rube. The gentleman is right.'

'And you, kind Sir. Is that an Oirish accent we detect?'

'It is indeed,' I said. 'I was born in Birmingham, but got elocution lessons from a Mrs. O'Reilly.'

'Wise move, eh, girls?' They waited till their laughter died down. 'So what brings you to Edinbra don't mind us awksin?'

I was going to deflect the question with "cat-sitting", but there was something about them. A warmth. A shared humanity. I softened. 'I'm hosting an event on the last night of the festival,' I said, trying not to sound boastful. '*Book Snuff*.'

'Blimey. An Irishman who performs. Whatever next?' They waited till their laughter died down. Again. 'So where's this *Book Snuff* on, then? Can't go if we don't have the details. Stands to reason.'

'Leave it out, Trace. Ever 'eard of bookin' online? We'll be there. That right, ladies?' General agreement. Much laughter. 'Right, follow me, everyone. The drinks,' she shouted at me over her retreating shoulder, 'are on us.'

I slipped quietly off. I'd got caught up in a similar situation with an Irish nurses' night out in Tooting some years back. On the plus side, you can only lose your virginity once.

'Before you met your lovely lady, Een, we sincerely hope.'
'You being certifiably monogulous.'

Before Blaise. Of course. Long, long before. I reached the Grassmarket, to return to the present, with my manhood intact. As I approached the Covenanters' Memorial, Dan was still there. I was about to go over for a quick word when my eye was caught by Fraser's living room window. The one with the shutters. An animal instinct, perhaps, but I could have sworn I saw something – someone – move. I screwed my eyes against the brightness. Was that a face staring out? But how could it be? Blaise and Ash were in Glasgow. Fraser was in Crete. I was out. Probably my imagination. Paranoia? The mind slipping its moorings? I shaded my eyes with my hand. Something – no, someone – definitely moved.

Skirting round a doleful, abstracted Dan I ducked across the road. Over to the flat's main entrance. The door – I halted abruptly – was ajar. The face at the window: might it have been an *actual* face? Had someone broken in? I was deeply unsettled. *Snap out of it, man!*

I made my way slowly, tentatively, up the winding stairs.

'Hello?' I called.

A timid hello. No response.

'Hell-*o*?' I tried again. Better, but still no response.

I was now at the top. I don't want to sound melodramatic, but I didn't want to die. What to do? Call the cops? I'd probably get DCI Give-us-the-corpse Strang. "*I'm* the corpse." "You don't sound very dead." "I will be when you get here. Happy now?" I was torn between not wanting to die and not wanting to look foolish either. I braced myself for violence and flung the flat door open.

'Torquil?!

In the middle of the living room, even taller and more erect than usual, stood Torquil Pittock. Huge glasses, huge matching eyes. Gulping the gulp of fear. No violence, then, but I was still pretty wound up.

'How did you get in?' I asked. Asked? Possibly demanded.

His Adam's apple – what is it about Adam's apples and fear? – was like a terrified mouse in a sock. 'The – the door was open. I tried ringing up. No answer. Thought, you know, you'd popped out for, you know, milk or – or something?'

But – hold on. How did he know my address? He answered before I asked.

'I've – I've seen you go in. It's the – the Grassmarket. You know? I just wanted to check up on, on, you know – the line-up?'

He was gabbling now, obviously startled by my sudden appearance. I have to admit the door open thing was a possibility. It made sense. We'd gone away for the weekend once – a Blaise poetry event in Kinlochbervie, as I recall. Came back, I'd left the bloody door not just ajar, but wide open. Fortunately, we live in Glasgow so nothing was touched, but even so. And now I'd done it again. This would be the last time I'd do an imaginary linen suit fashion shoot leaving the flat. I took a deep breath. I was still on edge, but it wasn't Torquil's fault. Just me and bloody doors.

'Okay,' I said. 'Glad that's sorted. No harm done.' I pulled out a chair from the table and gestured to him to sit. Torquil didn't. Still gulping the gulp. 'Anyway, you wanted to talk about *Book Snuff*. Quick question. Me as compère. Three acts. How do you fit in?'

'I, sort of, introduce the evening,' he said, regaining his composure.

I was reminded, oddly enough, of the sound man's hair. Time to assert myself. But subtly. 'Great. Then what? You disappear?'

He was about to answer when his eyes lit on the table. *Handbag.* Upside down, but identifiably his memoir.

'Ah,' I lied. 'My copy.'

'Yours?' he said, beaming with pleasure. 'I'm – I'm –'

Speechless? I thought he might be.

'Have you – read it yet?' He was still jumpy, but the gulps were dying down.

'Not in toto,' I said. 'It's one to savour, don't you think?'

'Oh! God! That is so – *humbling*.' He pressed his hands together as if in prayer and half-bowed towards me.

I paused to let him savour the humbling, then – 'The section on your mother,' I said. I was fishing here. I knew of no such section.

'There isn't one,' he said.

'Correct me if I'm wrong, Torquil.' I said. 'Could be an Irish thing, but this is a memoir, and I've yet to meet a man without a mother.'

'I meant section,' he said. 'There's no such section.'

'My point exactly,' I said. 'Interesting omission.'

'It was an editorial decision,' he said. His tone? Defensive aggressive. Best, perhaps, to leave it there for now.

Moving swiftly on. 'The line-up,' I said. I counted them off on my fingers. 'Karima Lucknawi. We've chatted online. All set to arrive on the Friday. She's going to be great.' Torquil may have grimaced. 'Attracta Boyle.' He nodded, relieved. Big name. No need to expand. 'Then there's me, of course. What can I say? Great career move.'

A short pause for dramatic effect. Torquil looked puzzled. 'But that's – that's just you and two authors.'

I'd been holding off on this one. 'Wait for it,' I said. 'This one will kill you.'

But before I could kill him, he glanced at his phone. A text had just pinged in. I ceased to exist. He trembled, sat down at the table, and clicked play on a moving image. I looked over his shoulder. Was that – no, it couldn't be. A shocked Torquil turned towards me and handed me the phone.

A short video on repeat. *Qwe(e)rtyuiop Books*. Exterior. Night.

Covering the window, a large poster. Blank. White.

A tall, hooded figure walks into view. Stops in front of the window. Points at the poster. Turns towards the camera. Slowly pushes the hood back, long black hair springing out. Smiles mischievously. Pulls the hood back up, then walks away.

I may have looked shocked myself. I passed the mobile back.

Torquil's voice rose a couple of decibels. 'Oh my *gosh*!' he squeaked. 'That total *witch*! She must be in Edinburgh!'

'Oh,' I said. 'Right.' Not a fan, then. I didn't say that bit. Best to change the subject. 'As I was saying,' I said. 'This one will kill you.'

He glanced back at the mobile. Super squeak plus. 'Not –'

'No,' I said. 'Not Ashley Burnet.'

He settled back down. The relief. The re*lief*. 'Three women? I just didn't think, you know –'

He was lying, but I left it. 'Chuck Weill.'

'Chuck Weill? Wasn't he on at the *Sewer* relaunch earlier? Gutted I couldn't make it. Didn't he –'

'Kill his wife? That's the one.'

That may not have been what Torquil meant. But he nodded. Then he nodded again. 'Excellent.'

That was it. Third author. I was about to point this out when Freya slithered through the open kitchen window.

'Makeshift cat flap,' I said. 'Bit of a security risk, but what can you do? Anyway, meet Freya.'

Freya ignored Torquil. Torquil ignored Freya. Then, clearing his throat self-consciously he said, 'Look, there was one other thing.' He sounded hesitant. No eye contact. I had to make do with the back of his head.

'Hit me.'

He spun round to face me. 'No! I could never –'

'Figure of speech,' I said. 'You were saying.'

He was gulping again. 'Was I?' he said. 'Sorry, I've – I've just remembered something.' He unfolded himself from the kitchen chair and pretty well dashed towards the door.

'Busy busy busy?' I asked, bemused.

'That's – that's it. I'll – I'll see myself out.'

'Well,' I said, 'at least you know the way. Unless, of course, you want to follow Freya. Quick hop onto the low roof, down to that wall, slither off and there you are.' An attempt at humour, but he didn't see it that way.

'Sorry,' he said. 'I should have –'

'Relax,' I said, following him to the door. 'There are no dead bodies.' He seemed to shrivel up as he descended the winding steps.

'– phoned,' he squeaked, and disappeared from view.

I closed the flat door, went back inside, stopped, went back down the turret steps to the front door, double checked it was locked, went back up to the flat. Peace at last? No. The Ashley Burnet video Torquil had just shown me had taken up residence in my head. Difficult to know what to make of it. The video itself. Torquil's response. My main feeling, however, was one of relief. She wasn't doing *Book Snuff*. Lucky escape. He didn't know she was here. Or that she was an old friend of Blaise's. Nor did he need to. I'd had enough mental turmoil for one day, so I tried to leave it there.

Back in the kitchen, I fed Freya, and found it strangely soothing watching her eat. I toyed with the idea of popping out for a quick word with Dan, maybe even take him a cup of coffee, but I'd also had enough of stairs for one day and besides, I still had a lot of boring admin stuff to do for *Book Snuff*, so I settled down to that. I checked the time. Blaise's event would be well finished by now, but I hardly expected her to come straight back. Ash had said they'd be late. They were probably socialising. Old female friends, female acolytes, newfound female fans.* More than likely locked in intellectual discourse in a female-friendly Glasgow pub. I didn't expect them back any time soon.

---

* I'm not labouring a point here. Her event was at the WLS. The clue is in the W.

A couple of hours passed quietly, after which it was back to the event itself. I now had all three acts. Could be quite an evening. Karima, Attracta, Chuck. I tend with these things to rely on natural chemistry and spontaneous wit, but it's as well to have something in reserve. Attracta, for instance. "Please welcome the late Attracta Boyle." Perfect intro, given her unwillingness to ever arrive on time, but it sounds better if it just pops out. Pre-planned it loses its edge. Better to wrong-foot the recipient, leading them – Attracta in this case – to an equally spontaneous snide retort. Or ritual humiliation.

Works both ways. I was off. "There's no such thing as good publicity, Attracta. Who said that?" Before she could respond – "Hitler, Attracta. Hitler." Attracta. Hitler. Get the subliminal link in early. The audience would be rooting for her to win.

Off? I was more than off. I was now rocking the joint. I jotted down a few Who Said That's. Examples:

'When in Rome criticise what the Romans do.' The Pope.

'I may disagree with everything you say, but I'll defend to the death your right to be wrong.' Stalin.

> 'Brilliant game, Een. Okay if we play?'
> 'We'll take your failure to staunch our fortcoming incessant flow as a yes. So how about diss one for starters.'
> '"You're only as old as you are." Who said that?'
> 'Metusaleh. Speaking of which, did we ever tell you about our romantic dalliance wit the same gent?'
> 'A somewhat disappointing lover, Een, the way he could never get it u –'
> 'Dottie! Spare the poor boy's blushes.'
> 'It's Florrie, actuously, but point taken. To be fair dough, Een, it was only two hundred and forty-six years before he died. Of course they didn't have Viagra in those days. It was eider find the tree of us irrisistible or do a Mahatma Gandhi. "Enough wit the stocking tops and the come hidder looks, ladies. I'm celibacious."'

'But back to Who Said That.'
'"My mother is a woman and so, on Tuesdays, Thursdays, Saturdays and every second Sunday, are we."'
'Okay, Robin/Robyn didn't say that, but he would have if he'd tought of it.'
'Whoops! Burn us at the naughty stake, Een. They! They!'

"You're only as old as you are?" I liked it. I took some time out for a sandwich and a mug of black coffee – no milk! – and let rip till my teeming, three-aunt-infested brain could take no more. Relax time, then. Quick bath.

'Discreet veil if you don't mind, Een. You'll be on full show in all your naughty, naked nudity.'
'It's not that sort of book.'

Relax time.
Quick bath.
Cut.

I'd just emerged, refreshed, revivified, and applying a towel to my hair, when the flat door swung open. Blaise. Ash. Well that was a relief.

'You look startled,' said Blaise. 'A bit flushed, in fact. Expecting someone else?'

Blaise came over and patted my hair down. 'On the plus side,' she said, 'you remembered to wear the kimono.'

'Oh, I don't know,' laughed Ashley. 'Master of the house, dingle-dongle-dangling, dripping from the shower?' She whipped her mobile out. 'Whaddya say?'

'Hold the penis,' I commanded. 'Better idea. *Qwe(e)rtyuiop Books*. Exterior. Night.' I was looking straight at Ashley as I said it. 'A hooded figure –'

Ashley cut across me. 'Fame at fucking last, eh?' She tugged off her hat and let her long black hair spring crazily out.

I could have mentioned Torquil, but best, perhaps, to leave it there.

'So how did it go at the Women's Library?' I asked. Blaise and Ash exchanged an inscrutable glance.

'Will you tell him, or will I?' Blaise said.

Ashley scooped her hat off the floor, removed her glasses and sat down. Mock deflated. Her gleeful laugh gave the lie to that. 'This lady, gal, woman, call her what you will, this stroppy cunt got us royally fucking barred.' Then, under her breath, 'Hopefully for life.'

'Don't tell me,' I said. I knew Blaise. 'Not a restaurant, not a bar stroke bistro, not, the Lord save us, a strip club in Govan.'

'Women's Library of Scotland,' said Blaise. 'Pending an apology –'

'– for emotional damage and hurt caused,' Ash finished the line. 'Blaise had just finished her *Scolds Unbridled* talk. Brilliant, by the way. Fiery. Passionate. Divisive. Q&A session afterwards. First question. Man in the front row.' Ashley grimaced. Stood and drew herself up to her full man height. Dropped a couple of octaves.

'My question –' she boomed, '– comes in four distinct and separate parts. Blaise, cool as fuck: Would you mind if I died of old age at some point, let's say part three? Nanosecond pause. Seemed like years. Then? Temper tantrum. Cindy – that's me, by the way, hi – tried to calm him down. He was getting hysterical. Sorry. Wrong word. Suggests female. Pontifical. The pontifical cunt was getting pontifical.'

Poor sod. Up against Ashley. Little did he know.

'You tried to calm him down,' I said. 'How?'

'I tickled him under the chin and said *diddums*. Well, *fucking diddums*. It seemed to set him off. Minutes later, we were thrown out. Barred for life.'

'Oh! And there's an interesting twist,' said Blaise, hardly able to suppress her glee. 'Go on.'

'Women's Library of Scotland, right? He's the new director.'

Ashley let rip with a series of snorts.

Long pause while she struggled to catch her breath. She sank back onto her chair, eyes full of tears, and took a very deep breath.

'Second interesting twist,' she gasped. 'The cunt's a fucking dyke.'

23

Lying in bed some time later, I try to grill Blaise about the twenty-second *Qwe(e)rtyuiop* bookshop video. Does she know about it? Has she seen it? Was she in any way whatsoever involved? She stonewalls. I try again. She stonewalls again.

'All will be revealed,' she says, 'in the madness of time. Whoops. Fullness.'

As it turns out, she was right first time.

24

The following morning, I showered. I shaved. I headed for the kitchen. For once, Blaise and Ash had got up before me and were now sitting at the table, huddled round Blaise's laptop, engrossed. I say Blaise and Ash. Blaise, Ash and Freya. Front paws on the table, back paws on a chair or, more accurately, on Cindy's hat. As soon as I entered she slid down and over to the open window. She made eye contact and licked her lips before she hopped out. Obviously fed, then. Nice of her to let me know. I thought about removing the hat and sitting down, but settled for peering between their shoulders instead. Old footage. A book event by the look of it.

'Sydney Festival of Chuck,' said Ash. '25th anniversary of his so-called fucking masterpiece.'

Ah. That explained it. The book was now fifty, so twenty-five years ago. Chuck had more hair, Ash was exactly like Ash, only more so. She turned the volume up.

> 'You may not be aware of this, Chuck, but I wrote the intro for the Australian edition.'
> 'Did you, missy? Well I never saw that.'
> 'Neither did anyone else. Wasn't printed. It mentioned pre-pubescent boys and wanking in the same sentence — Whoa, Chucky, you wouldn't hit a woman on camera, now would you?'
> 'Never stopped me before.'
> 'Hold on. I've got a better idea.' She picked her water glass up and positioned it on top of her head. 'They tell me you're an excellent shot. One request, though. Not the fucking face.'

Ashley pressed stop. 'It gets a bit hairy after that.' She smiled up at me. 'Maybe when you're a bit older.'

I wasn't listening. An advert had appeared at the side of the screen. *Time to chuck that old linen suit?* Bloody cheek, but the chuck word brought me, more importantly, back to Chuck. Touchy subject. I placed a hand on both their shoulders. 'There's something I need to share,' I said.

'Group therapy!' whooped Ashley. 'Tell you what. You first, nobody next.'

Blaise was more circumspect. 'Oh dear,' she said. 'Is this going where I think it's going?'

'Probably.'

She gave me the full effect of her beautiful, brown eyes. Mesmeric with a dash of troubled. 'Did you have a drink yesterday?'

Oh. Right. I hadn't been expecting that. 'Let me put it to you this way,' I said. 'I had a drink but I didn't have it. If that makes sense.'

'Makes sense to me,' said Ashley. 'You held it in your firm, manly hands, maybe even rested it on your firm, manly crotch, but you didn't imbibe. Unlit *Lucky Strike* dangling from your steely hunk lips.' She patted Blaise playfully on the knee. 'It was a Chuck Weill event. Guy's got to fit in.'

I may have bridled at this. 'It was all they had,' I said. Not a great response, but it was the best I could do with the material on offer. 'Dry throat syndrome? I thought, what harm in a quick sip?'

Blaise smiled the empathy smile. 'I wasn't being judgemental,' she said. 'So where does the need to share come in?'

I steeled myself. 'He's doing *Book Snuff*.'

Ash hooted. 'What? Chuck Weill? Well fuck me rigid with a wet welly. You are fucking priceless.'

That, I supposed, was one way of putting it. 'Blaise?'

'Agreed,' she said. 'Without the welly.'

I'd have to say they'd taken it pretty well. As a bonus, I was reminded yet again that Blaise had originally asked Ash to be on the panel. What if she'd said yes? Chuck Weill/Ashley Burnet – the nightmare scenario. The relief. *The relief.* But I kept that bit to myself.

'Okay,' said Ashley, getting up from the table and grabbing her mobile. 'Quick call to my esteemed fucking publisher. Back soon.'

She went into her bedroom and closed the door.

'Glad that's all settled,' I said. 'Coffee?'

'Good idea,' said Blaise. 'We were going to head out in a while. A la recherche de l'Isabella perdue. Fancy coming?'

'What?' I said. 'You mean you're going to an actual graveyard for once?'

Blaise dropped her voice. 'Ash is all organised now,' she said. 'She's a bit more relaxed. So, yes. An actual graveyard.'

'Anywhere in particular?' I said.

'St. Cuthbert's Kirkyard. But maybe you've too much to do?'

'No, no. Good idea,' I said. 'I have all three authors booked for the event. Time, perhaps, for a well-earned morning off. Coffee first?' I opened the fridge. 'Ah, milk! I'll just pop out.'

Just then Blaise's mobile lit up on the table. She checked the message.

'Text from Fraser,' she said. 'He wants to know how we're getting on.'

'Like a flat on fire,' I said as I headed for the door.

'Very reassuring,' Blaise called after me.

'Maybe check whether he's had any contact with Morag,' I called back. 'Speaking of a flat on fire.'

Outside was overcast but warm. Bustling with people as always, many of them redheads. I was closing the main door – making sure it was locked this time – when a passing woman stopped.

'You're Blaise's partner, right?' she said and, before I could answer, 'I just love her poetry. It's so –' She searched for the apposite word.

'Poetic?' I said helpfully.

She laughed. A warm, friendly laugh. 'I'd heard you were funny. Doing anything this year?'

'I am, actually,' I said. I couldn't help myself. 'I wasn't going to, but Torquil Pittock – don't know if you've heard of him –'

'Of course. *Le Salon Littéraire*.'

'Anyway, he asked me to do the last night of the festival. *Book Snuff*.'

'Do tell me it's crime,' said the woman. 'I'm here for the crime. I love a good murder.'

'Well,' I said, 'it would be helpful if no-one *actually* got murdered. But yes. Let me put it this way. Snuff is not a reference to nose tobacco.'

'I'll book straight away. What date was it again?' She pulled a mobile from her shoulder bag.

'31st.'

'Ah. I'll be back on Orkney by then. Work beckons. Anyway, give my best to Blaise. We must have her up for a reading.' I may have looked confused. 'Stromness Library. I'm the head librarian.'

'Oh, right. Orkney. I'm sure she'd love that,' I said. 'Sorry. Who shall I say?'

The woman laughed again. 'Silly me. I just assumed – Morag. I used to be married to Fraser. Lived right here in fact.' She nodded at the door I'd just exited. 'He's on his second honeymoon, I believe.'

'I know,' I said. 'We're cat-sitting.'

'Well, if you see him, tell him I said congrats.'

'Really?'

Morag must have sensed my surprise. 'Whyever not?' she smiled. 'We said our goodbyes a long time ago. Usual disagreement over who owned what, but no kids. That's the main thing. Anyway, must dash. Got a show to go to. Say hi to Blaise.'

I watched as she walked away. Her hair. In a certain light, I suppose you could call it red.

As soon as Morag was out of sight I leaped back upstairs, two stone steps at a time. In the flat door.

'Don't press send!' Blaise's finger was on her mobile. She looked up, startled. 'It's not Morag,' I gasped. 'I've just met her.' I pointed at Blaise. 'She's not a killer, she's a librarian. Totally different thing.'

'I've already sent it,' said Blaise. 'Relax. Bit daft mentioning the ex-wife on his honeymoon.' She put her mobile down. 'Don't you think?'

Rhetorical question. I ignored it, clicked the kettle on and opened the fridge with a flourish.

No milk.

We opted for the scenic route to St. Cuthbert's Graveyard. Blaise and Ashley forged ahead. Women on a mission. Across the Grassmarket and up Castle Wynd South. Flight upon flight of steep stone steps, but excellent exercise and not without its pleasing vistas. I stopped every so often to take in the vistas and allowed my mind to flit where it would. This, you might recall, was the original plan for the Edinburgh break. Meditative walks with a smattering of ancient graveyards. Bliss.

As I reached the half-way point, I looked up to see where Blaise and Ash had got to. They were flagging slightly on the seemingly everlasting steps, but chatting on regardless. When, to my horror, a pale blue Lambretta appeared, and with a deafening roar came bumping crazily down the steps. It rocketed straight towards Blaise and Ashley. Ashley dived out of the way just in time. Blaise screamed as it narrowly missed her. The bike screeched past me, skidded at the bottom onto the road narrowly missing a truck, and disappeared. I raced up to the two women. Blaise was shaken. Ashley was shaken. We were all shaken.

'Did you see him?' said Blaise.

'Fraid not,' I said. 'Slim figure, strangely straight-backed, black leathers. Couldn't see the face with that reflective visor down. Are you sure he was a him?'

'You can tell by the knuckles,' she said. 'And the calves.'

The Knuckles and the Calves. Good title. I don't know why that floated into my mind, but it did. Strangely straight-backed, though. Ridiculous thought, but if Torquil had a motorbike it would be a Lambretta, and he'd definitely sit on it like that. He also seemed to hate Ash with a vengeance, but it surely didn't run to attempted murder? Besides, I gave myself a shake, Ash was Cindy, not Ash. She sank down onto a step, breathing rapidly.

'Are you okay?' I said.

Ash winced. 'I'll live,' she replied. 'For now.'

'Tell you what,' said Blaise. 'Why don't we all go back to the flat? You look pretty shaken up, Ashley. I know I am. Besides, I'm sure Isabella won't mind.'

Ashley turned away from the wall and smiled wanly.

'Another day dead,' she sighed. 'Just a thought.'

We retraced our steps in sombre mood. On the wide Grassmarket pavement, tourists and festival goers sat drinking at outdoor tables, the bustle and chatter a welcome reminder of why we were here in the first place. Dan, at his usual place, was lost in his leafleting. I dawdled for a while, watching him. The long, sad face. The small boy shuffle. Mesmeric.

Blaise and Ash, arms linked as if for mutual support, were now at the flat's front door. I tore myself away from the contemplation of Dan and followed them over. The door was open, and Blaise was holding an envelope in one hand, a sheet of paper in the other. She handed me the envelope. No name or address. She then handed me the sheet of paper. Blank. I turned it over. Also blank. Ashley grabbed the sheet. She, too, turned it over, her face drained of blood.

'Fuck it all to fuck,' she said. 'The note on the door. The decapitated Frida. The Lambretta. And now this. Saying nothing, saying everything.'

'What? You mean it's all connected?' I asked, confused.

'Looks like it,' she said. 'Seriously, you two don't need this. I should go and stay in a hotel. Give you guys some peace.'

Possibly a reflection of my mental state, but I was toying with recommending a guest house in Sydney when Blaise got in before me. She put an arm round Ashley, who seemed to crumple slightly.

'Relax,' she said. 'We're all in this together.'

'Tell you what,' I said as we climbed the shadowy turret steps to the flat, 'I've been promised tickets for a free fringe show. Maybe we should just skip the graveyard, take it easy for a few hours and go along tonight.'

Ashley breathed out in a loud whoosh. The anguished look on her face gave way to a brave smile for the imaginary cameras.

'Tickets for a free show?' she said. 'We wouldn't want to waste *them*.'

'You sure?' asked Blaise.

'Sure I'm sure,' said Ashley, suddenly straightening up as we entered the flat. 'Sure I'm fucking sure.'

'Fighting talk,' I said. 'Let's do it.'

Ashley bunched her hands into pretty impressive fists.

'I'll go further,' she snarled. 'Let's *fucking* do it.'

25

Several coffees later, at least one of which had a dash of whiskey in it –

> *'Tree dashes, Een. Tree. We're sticklers for accuracy.'*
> *'Oh, and as we're in Scotland, whisky.'*
> *'It reads like a doggy name, but that's the way they mis-spell it. Isle of Ulay single malt.'*
> *'We shared a bottle once wit legendary Scottish autor Hugh MacDiarmid'.*
> *'A lover of prodigious appetite, Een. For the whisky anyway. A Scotch autor if you will.'*
> *'But back to the set text.'*
> *'Several whiskies later, at least one of which had a splash of coffee in it.'*
> *'Stop that, Florrie. The colour, Een –'*

– had returned to Ash's face, so we approached the *Church of the Holy Rude* that evening in good spirits. Blaise casual chic, me in my linen suit, Ash with her hair well-tucked up in a dramatic new wide-brimmed Cindy hat, and a pair of brand-new tinted specs. Things felt a bit more relaxed. Nice night out, no pressure.

On our way to the show I even accepted a leaflet from a young student type, a sure sign I was feeling pretty mellow. No Hector McGregor 'Give us a bloody leaflet' moment this time. I was about to pocket it for later when Ashley whipped it out of my hand.

'What the fuck,' she said. 'What the fucking fuck.' She stopped and held it up.

X

Marks the Spot

A crime caper with an unusual twist!

The victim is a...

WOMAN!!!

DCI Strang had been right after all. The note pinned to our door had been nothing more than a clever piece of fringe marketing. Here was the exact image – line-drawing of woman with X-ed out face – but this time with added text and venue details. Infuriating, yes, but it had certainly got us talking. And here we were again. Last word to Ashley. 'What the fucking, fucking, fucking fuck.'

That about summed it up as, laughing with relief, we strode with renewed vigour towards the venue.

First people we saw among the small group standing outside the *Church of the Holy Rude*, *aka* Venue 198: cop-car Sinéad, looking more relaxed out of uniform, chatting happily to a cheroot-smoking female friend.

'DCI Strang,' I exclaimed to her friend. 'You certainly look different off-duty.'

Sinéad laughed. 'I know,' she said. 'I seem to be drawn to smokers. This is Cyd.'

'My sincere apologies, Cyd,' I said. 'You're a step up from Sinéad's boss.'

'Oh, Fulton's not so bad,' said Sinéad.

'Isn't he retiring at the end of the month?' asked Cyd, exhaling a small cloud of smoke.

'Allegedly,' said Sinéad. 'Sorry. Introductions.' She turned to Blaise and Ash. 'I'm Sinéad. This is Cyd.'

I put my hand up. 'No, no. *I'm* sorry. That was my job. This is Blaise. And this –'

'– is Cindy,' said Ashley. About as demurely as she could manage. Just as well she butted in. I'd almost inadvertently grassed her up.

'So,' I said. 'Going in?'

'Soon as I've put this out,' said Cyd, expertly flicking the lighted tip into the gutter. 'Best get in before this lot.' She motioned behind me. I turned to look. The *Vulvas* were spilling noisily onto the pavement from a brightly coloured cycle rickshaw.

'No need,' I said. 'I think you'll find –'

Before I could finish the sentence, Purple Mohican *Vulva* was off.

'Howaya, Macker! Janey, we didn't have you down as a ladies' man.' She flashed a smile at 'Cindy' and Blaise, Sinéad and Cyd. 'Howayiz, girls.'

Nose Ring *Vulva* linked arms with me playfully. 'Come on and we'll bunk you in.'

'I think you'll find it's a free event,' I said. 'But a quick word first. About my bawdy verse, *Polyamóry* –'

'*The Merrie Spinsters*. You based them on us, Macker. Fair's fair. We're only taking back what's already ours.'

This didn't make sense. I did indeed, as already mentioned, base *The Merrie Spinsters* on them. But *Hewbris*, the book that featured the ribald triple act, as I've said before, wasn't published yet. *Polyamóry in Ballydehob* was a bawdy verse secret known only to me and my sympathy reader Blaise.

> *'And us, Een. But we know what you're tinking. How did they know?'*
> *'Best way to find out? Ask them.'*

'But how did you know?' I asked, still confused.

Nose Ring *Vulva* squeezed my arm and disengaged. 'A woman always knows. Three women? Always plus. Show to do. Bye-ee.'

We followed them in with the rest of the sizeable crowd and took our seats. Or, more accurately, pews. What is it with these churches? I'm not religious, but whenever I go somewhere like the *Church of the Holy Rude* for a performance, I fully expect to be damned to the flames of hellfire for all eternity. I'd settle for nothing less. Yet here I was, about to watch a sizeable group of women on the main stage – an abomination unto the Lord in itself!

The Church of the Holy Rude?!

Women?!!!

Where was I? Pews. I was sitting between Blaise and Cindy on one side, Sinéad and Cyd on the other. Blaise and Cindy, I'm pleased to say, were not holding hands. Sinéad and Cyd were. Cyd may have noticed me noticing.

'I think Dad wanted a boy,' she explained. 'Interesting response when I took my first girlfriend home. "But I thought you'd be pleased." Let's just say he wasn't.'

Sinéad leaned across. 'Wasn't me,' she said, 'or I'd have nicked him.'

The lights dimmed slowly to off. Showtime. I'll draw a discreet veil over the next 47 minutes of full-on *Vulvas*. They conjured up a vision of post-post-Catholic Ireland that made me glad I'd settled for abroad. But why, you may ask, 47 minutes? It was at this point that the one-man show element kicked in. Career-floundering egomaniac Dorian Wilde, Foetus-O'Flaherty-from-*Sloot*-inspiring Dorian Wilde, strutted out from behind the backdrop. One fist raised in triumph, eyes glued to his mobile.

'Get this,' he whooped as he reached his beloved other half – the microphone. 'Breaking news.'

All three *Vulvas* were straight in. 'Excusez-nous, you self-centred, non-speaking-part fuck.'

I could feel Ashley Burnet rippling with merriment under her disguise, the brim of her enormous new hat flapping in perfect time.

'Settle down,' I whispered, '*Cindy.*'

Dorian Wilde ignored the French request. He wasn't listening to the *Vulvas*. He was, however, listening to himself. '"Dorian Wilde's stunning anti-comedy, *The Far Side of Funny*,"' he read, '"wins Samuel Beckett award for –"'

'– self-regarding shite!' exclaimed Nose Ring *Vulva*.

But Dorian still wasn't listening.

'Succeed again!' he cried, strutting towards the back exit. 'Succeed better!' And he was gone. The award had unleashed a monster. The crowd loved it.

Head Girl *Vulva* grabbed the mic. 'Bit of a problemo, people. *onemanshow*. That's the title, but we've lost our non-speaking man. Anyone out there volunteer?' Cindy leapt to her feet and held a finger over my head.

'That you, Macker?' Purple Mohican *Vulva* this time. 'Sorry. Must be a Name.'

'Pity,' I called out. 'I could have advertised *Book Snuff*. August 31st. George Square at eighteen hundred hours. Book in advance to ensure –'

'–disappointment. For pity's sake, Een.'

Een? Head Girl *Vulva* had called me Een. Exactly like the three aunts. How very – *chilling*.

'It's supposed to be a non-speaking part,' Head Girl *Vulva* admonished. 'You're fired! Anyone else?' A spotlight swept the space.

'Hand over there!' Nose Ring *Vulva* exclaimed. 'The lady behind the lady in the enormous hat!'

The lady in the enormous hat was Cindy.

Hand lady's response? 'Correction. Man.'

'Sorry about that. You have very artistic fingers,' Purple Mohican *Vulva* replied. The audience laughed. 'We can't see the rest of you,' she continued. 'Question. Can *you* see *us*?'

'You mean there's visuals?' a deep voice responded. 'I thought it was a radio play.'

Non-lady man was witty, I'll give him that. Clever quip. Someone in the audience ran with it. 'Off with her hat!'

Nice rhythm. Catchy. It bore repetition. Someone near the back took it up. 'Off with her hat.'

A man in row two. 'Off with her hat.'

All three *Vulvas* in unison. The whole – with a few free-thinking exceptions – audience. All turning and twisting in their seats to stare at Cindy and chanting.

'Off with her hat!'

'Off with her hat!'

'Off with her hat!'

Cindy stood slowly up. Tall. Commanding presence. Tinted spectacles. Voluminous hat. There was something about her. The height. The presence. The hat.

The chant died slowly down. Silence. Then, dramatically, Cindy whipped her hat and specs off to reveal iconoclastic legend Ashley Burnet. Tall. Commanding presence. Flashing green eyes. Wild witch-black hair, as featured on so many of her books, springing free.

'Happy now?' She stood, defiant and fearless, like Pirate Queen Gráinne O'Malley on the prow of her ship as she sailed up the Thames to confront the English queen.

The response was instant and stunning.

Silence.

More silence.

'Thanks, missus,' said Nose Ring *Vulva*. 'You can sit down now.'

Ashley sat down, a bit stunned herself, I'd have to say. Not one person had gasped in recognition – that this was Ashley Burnet, feminist firebrand. It was – why, it was *outrageous*!

The *Vulvas* pointed behind her.

'We can now see the man behind the hat. None other than the legendary… Jake Fedora!'

'Question: can we be in your next film?' The *Vulvas* spoke with one excited voice.

'We call it a movie,' said movie legend Jake. 'But yes. That's why I'm here.'

Ashley had her hat back on, her hair scooped back up inside it, as we queued to file out of the church. 'Just off to powder my nose,' she said quietly. 'Won't be a minute.'

Blaise linked arms with me. 'Younger audience,' she said, her voice low and confidential. 'She's been writing her new book for seven years. A lot of them were still in nappies.'

'Shame,' I said. 'She looked pretty –'

'I know what you're going to say,' said Blaise. 'Pretty deflated. Ego as big as the Ritz.'

'My exact words,' I said. They weren't. Ego yes, Ritz no. Beautifully put, though.

'But,' she continued, 'just because Ash has a huge ego doesn't mean she's not important. Or, whisper it softly, vulnerable.'

I nodded in diplomatic agreement. We walked outside and, moments later, Ashley emerged. No crack about cocaine being the powder of choice. She hadn't been gone long enough, probably just wanted a moment to herself. We were about to set silently off when Cyd and Sinéad came out. Straight over.

'Got to dash,' said Sinéad. 'Late shift, but great meeting you all.' She looked directly at Ash. 'You're Ashley Burnet, right? We are such big fans.'

'First time Sinéad and I met,' said Cyd. 'Bookshop. Both in to buy *Woman*. One copy left. The rest is romance.'

'Oh my *gawd*,' whooped Ashley, suddenly recovered. 'I am totally fucking *speechless*.'

26

Dusk was slipping into darkness as we made our way home. The clouds from earlier in the day had cleared, and a full moon bathed the bustling old town streets in a silvery glow. Ash was back on full-moon, lunatic form as she strode expletively on. Fuck this, fuck that. Fuck the guy on the Lambretta. She was veering towards the positive, upbeat, just-some-nut-on-a-scooter take when, halfway down Victoria Street –

KERRASSSH!!!

'Holy fucking fuck!'

That was Ashley, as Blaise grabbed her arm and pulled her into a doorway. I automatically leapt for the relative safety of the wall. In front of us on the pavement lay what at first glance looked like it had been a huge chunk of glass, shattered now into a thousand glistening pieces. It had narrowly missed Blaise and Ashley as it plummeted from somewhere above. I knelt and carefully picked up a dagger-shaped shard. It wasn't glass, it was ice, the smaller fragments already starting to melt.

I stared at the ice, then slowly ventured out from the wall and looked up. Above us was the elevated Victoria Terrace with its walkway that served a row of shops and eateries.

A manic scuffle of feet from the terrace, then silence. Ashley let out a further stream of abuse, directed now at the disappearing feet, but there was nothing we could do. The culprit would be long gone by the time we'd made our way via the connecting steps up to the terrace. What remained of the icy boulder lay a foot from where Ashley had been walking, melting fragments glistening in the full-moon light. Whoever it was – it seemed pretty obvious now – was out to get her.

No, not get. Murder!

As if summoned by the thought of that very word, DCI Fulton Strang meandered out of the *Beau Belle Bar* opposite, smoke already lit. He saw me, waved his cigarette tipsily, and swayed over. Blaise and Ash stayed huddled in the safety of a shop doorway, locked in half-whispered conversation. I met Strang half way.

'My friend,' I said, pointing to Ashley. 'Guy on a pale blue Lambretta tried to run her over this morning –'

'Fled the scene no doubt,' said Strang, his voice amiable and slurred. He'd been in a pub. It was that time of night.

'Yes,' I said. 'On the Lambretta.' It was intended to sting. It didn't. I pressed on. 'Now this. A block of ice. Pushed over the wall of the terrace up there. Missed her by that.' I extended a forefinger and thumb.

Strang thought about this for a long moment. 'So,' he slurred, 'missed by the thickness of this fag. Possible malicious intent. Tell you what. I'm off duty at the precise moment –'

'You surprise me,' I said.

'– but I'll get the lads from forensics round in the morning. Check the ice for fingerprints.'

A mock salute and he was off, still swaying slightly, down towards the Grassmarket. I thought about looking for a sober cop, but what was the point? We couldn't prove anything. Check the ice for fingerprints? 'Christ,' I snapped. 'Why does everyone have to be a comedian these days?'

Strang turned slowly back. 'It's part of the Hippocratic Oath, Sir,' he called boozily. 'Speaking of comedy, how's the event shaping up?' Before I could answer, 'Bad feeling in the gut. A sense, shall we say, of unease in the bowels and the lumbar region.' And, giggling like a schoolboy at his own wit, off he swayed woozily. Again. I turned back to Blaise and Ash, who were both peering intently at Ashley's mobile phone.

'Got to go,' Blaise called to me. Ashley marched on ahead, still transfixed by her mobile, tap-tap-tapping the keys like a deranged one-armed pianist. Blaise waited and linked arms with me. We walked slowly to put some space between us and Ash.

'She's got a date for her book launch.' Blaise said quietly.

'What? Oh. Right. Hold on. Book launch?' First I'd heard of it. 'Exciting news. Where? When?' Even as I said these words my heart sank. Sydney? Next year? I hardly thought so.

Blaise slowed to a halt and turned to face me.

'Okay,' she said. 'You're bound to find out sooner or later. Dawn tomorrow. Outside *Qwe(e)rtyuiop Books*.'

This was beyond crazy. And yet. And yet. 'Makes sense,' I said. 'If you're certifiable. Which –' I pointed at Ashley careering on ahead, stooped over her mobile '– she clearly is.'

Blaise sighed but said nothing. There was nothing to say.

Because Ashley clearly was.

Our lovemaking was wild and passionate that night.

Tell a lie. Hot chocolate. Teeth. Sleep. Before that, Blaise had sworn me to secrecy, then given me a brief synopsis of the following morning's plan. A 5.30 start. Up and out. That was all I needed to know.

'I'll try not to wake you,' she said as she set the alarm on her mobile and switched off the bedside lamp.

'In which case,' I said into the darkness, 'I'll have to wake myself.'

'What? You're not thinking of coming.'

This wasn't a question, and Blaise sounded more than a little defensive as she said it.

'An Ashley Burnet book launch?' I said. 'It's not women only, is it?'

'Not – exactly.'

'Well then,' I said. 'Try to stop me.'
I paused to let the three aunts in.

'Very masterful, Een. You won't be gainsaid.'
'And tanks for the headspace. You're a very good boy.'

'But tell me this,' I continued. 'Why dawn?'

Blaise sat up and clicked the lamp back on. I could almost hear her brain whirring as she tried to frame her response. 'Okay. You deserve an explanation. Remember I said Ash had been treated badly? She was invited by Edinburgh Uni to deliver the keynote speech at the annual summer symposium. End of August. Very prestigious. She said she'd be honoured. Then it was cancelled after she'd booked her flight. Administrative error, apparently.'

'Except, of course, it wasn't,' I said.

'Exactly. Some-poor-palpitating-student-might-get-upset error more like. So Ashley thought –'

'Language,' I said.

'Okay. In laywoman's terms she thought, I'll come over anyway and do something. Get my own back on the –'

'Administrative staff,' I said.

'Thank you,' said Blaise. 'Although *pusillanimous cunts* is possibly snappier.'

'Fair enough. But I fail to see the link between a book launch at dawn tomorrow and a cancelled speech somewhere else on a totally different date.'

'Honest answer?' said Blaise. 'She wouldn't tell me. Said if she told me she'd have to –'

'I know, I know. Answer to a hard-line feminist collective.'

Blaise smiled her mischief smile.

'No,' she said. 'Kill me.'

27

That night.
Grassmarket as Bacchanalian Vomitorium.
Thumping music.
Ashley not hooting at *Handbag*.
Three increasingly bizarre Torquil texts.
The final one consisting of a love heart and two kisses.
Blaise's mobile alarm.
Up.

28

An early morning mist was hovering over the sleeping city as we headed out at 5.30 as planned. Me, Blaise, Cindy? No. Me, Blaise, Ash. Sans hat. Sans glasses. Fiery green eyes. Regal bearing. Black hair wilder than ever.

Grassmarket to Cowgatehead, up Candlemaker Row, bit of a zigzag route then around the University area with its incongruous mix of brutal concrete erections and centuries old granite architecture, to Potterrow, left into West Nicholson Street and there you are.

Qwe(e)rtyuiop Books.

Blaise and Ashley forged on ahead, locked in conversation. I followed on behind and tried to reclaim my head for whatever it used to think about left to its own devices. Nothing. Complete blank. Not even a whisper from the three aunts. Ashley Burnet-induced shellshock?

I was about to walk faster in an effort to catch up when an odd-looking couple passed Ashley and Blaise and did a double take.

I say odd. One was shiny-pate bald, the other sported a wild mop of candyfloss pink hair. Nothing especially odd about that you might think, except that in this case, the bald one was the woman. Nothing odd about that either, come to think of it. Forget odd. This was Edinburgh. Festival time. Perfectly normal. Except for the double take. Fans of Ashley, fans of Blaise? Difficult to say.

'Book launch,' I said as they hurried past. '*Qwe(e)rtyuiop* at dawn.' You never knew. It might bump the launch numbers up.

By the time I arrived at the bookshop, the mist was burning off as the sun rose higher. A small group of women were there already, silently arranging piles of books onto a trestle table set up in front of the bookshop.

Two women with stepladders were preparing to attach something to the window just below the *Qwe(e)rtyuiop* sign. The whole scene was being filmed by – you may be ahead of me here –

'We are indeed, Een. Yet anudder woman.'

I stood back at a discreet distance as Blaise was welcomed, in total silence, with warm hugs and broad smiles. Some of the women I recognised as friends of Blaise, 'friends of Blaise' being a term to denote people of a certain persuasion – wave-wise, that is. I was simply there as an observer. I stood back. I observed. Ashley, I noted, was now nowhere to be seen.

Moments later the poster unfurled across the shop window.

Aha! An even bigger version of the blank, #usp ones I'd seen before. With, in bold black print, the following:

WHITE INK

a memoir
hand-written in breast milk
by
Ashley Burnet

'An incendiary firebomb' - Joy Scarralotes
#usp*

*#untamedshrewpublications

In front of the giant poster, the trestle table, with blood-red tablecloth, now sporting a display of books, with pristine white covers.

Just then the not-odd-looking couple I'd passed earlier appeared at the end of the road. With a small group of like-minded friends.

Idiosyncratic dress sense, idiosyncratic hair. Up early? Up all night? The incomers formed a small group, huddled beside a skip filled with builders' rubble. Whispering among themselves.

The women carried on regardless, setting up piles of the white-covered books, but you could tell the mood had shifted. Difficult to describe exactly how. Not a cloud-over-the-early-morning-sun change, but a sense of expectancy. An electricity. A tension. More people, many of them women, arrived silently and approached the table.

More people also approached the huddle, which became, as numbers grew, more vocal, less huddled.

Suddenly, a tall hooded figure in a full-length, coal-black cape swept dramatically up the street. The camera turned and followed its every move. Finally, it stood, centre-stage, in front of the bookshop window and held the pose, totally immobile, for a beautifully-timed dramatic moment. Then, in an equally dramatic movement, it whipped the hood off. Ashley Burnet. Powerful. Imposing. Cascade of beyond black hair tumbling wildly around her shoulders. Across her mouth broad black duct-tape in the shape of a cross. Collective gasp. Ashley raised a black-nailed hand slowly to her silenced mouth, yanked the tape off with a theatrical flourish and dropped it, eyes averted, into a strategically placed bin. She then moved to the table's solitary chair behind a row of books, swept the cape aside, sat down and, cinematically framed by the bookshop window, smiled for the camera, her regal bearing, even seated, suggesting a woman you wouldn't mess with. The assembled women burst into spontaneous applause as she began the serious business of signing copies – pen, not breast! – and handing them out gratis to a growing line of Ashophiles, the camera filming hungrily on.

Suddenly, without warning, a large, bearded, muscle-bound figure in bulging, military-fatigue shorts and a paisley pattern smoking jacket several sizes too small, turned the far corner and stormed towards the huddle by the skip.

Not a cloud in sight, but it was as if the dawn sky suddenly darkened, the temperature suddenly dropped as he got closer, acting like he expected to be recognised. Bit like Jake Fedora without the charisma. Or the charm. Too many steroids would be my guess. Even his jacket-straining, muscle-bound arms looked apoplectic. Suddenly he turned towards Ashley and the silent women, stamped an apoplectic foot, punched the air and started a chant. One he'd obviously committed to memory for the occasion. 'Burnet! Burnet! Burnet!'

I felt a mounting sense of dread. He didn't look like a man who came in peace. The huddle joined in, timidly at first, then increasing in confidence and volume. 'Burnet! Burnet! Burnet!'

Ashley's name again.

The women turned and watched, prepared to hold their ground.

But wait!

What was this?!

He whipped a canister from his bulging shorts.

The bulge settled down.

> *'Hold it there. You'll need a name for him, Een.'*
> *'Mr. Bulgy Pants?'*
> *'The Bulge?'*
> *'Wait. I'm getting someting. Bulgy Man.'*
> *'That's the one. And that jacket! It makes him look oddly expectatious.'*
> *'Pregnant, Een. Plus it's far too small. He probably wore it for his Holy Communion.'*
> *'Wash your mout out, Dorrie. He's never a Holy Roman Katlick. Observe the top of his shorts. Union Jack undies.'*

They were right too.

He held the canister up and whipped a lighter from the breast pocket of his smoking jacket. Ah. I got it now. Lighter fuel! Not Burnet! *Burn* it!

Burn it! Burn it! Burn it!!!

There was an aggression building. A strong sense of impending conflict. I was on high alert. At the same time, I was hoping against hope that Bulgy Man would calm down or, more likely given the veins on his bulging eyeballs, explode. But no, he was advancing along the street, his tribe following angrily in his wake, the chant of Burn it! Burn it! growing louder, when Blaise picked a book off the table, walked calmly up to him, stopped, and held it out in her sweet, disarming way.

Now I am not a violent man, but I'm always ready to die in a good cause. Not that it had happened yet, but *theoretically*. And Blaise was, almost literally, playing with fire. She stood there, sweet, disarming, calm. But would Bulgy Man see her the same way? I somehow doubted it. I moved closer and clenched my fists in readiness. Bulgy Man's whole body was now a clenched fist.

> *'We're on tenterhooks, Een. It's like one of those bang bang fillums from a bygone era. The big showdown.'*
>
> *'All you need is the hats. And the bang bangs.'*
>
> *'But we're deflating the tenshion wit our dotty oul lady witterings.'*
>
> *'We bet John Wayne never had to put up wit this sort of ting in his fillums. A wonderful lover, Een, aldough he was known to poke your eye out wit his ever-present fagarette at the climax of proceedings.'*
>
> *'Sorry about this, by the way. Maybe cut it for the final draft. Where were we?'*
>
> *'Bulgy Man, Een. Clenched.'*

He was primed for violence. Face-smashing, skull-shattering violence. Then? A flicker of doubt in the vein-bulging eyes. This is not what he'd expected. He'd expected conflict. He'd *hoped* for conflict. But this? Sweet, disarming Blaise? This was – this was cheating.

And maybe it was, but whatever it was it worked. He grabbed the book from Blaise's outstretched hand, his face less apoplectic now than sulky, and stared at the plain white cover. I could see it from where I stood, blank.

Totally blank. As blank as the first blank poster.

As if sensing my unspoken need, one of the women walked over and handed me a copy of the book. I nodded thanks and opened it as he was opening his. Flicked through it like a card sharp. Blank. Blank from start to finish. White-on-White blank. I looked up. Bulgy Man's face was a petulant picture. That is so *unfair*! He didn't say it, but if he'd been six he certainly would have.

> *'Plus his jacket would have fitted, Een. But we digress. Do carry on. We're riveted!'*

As Blaise calmly turned and made her way back to the women, his apoplexy returned as if it had never been away. He tossed the book in the gutter, strode over to the builders' skip, and grabbed a cement-encrusted terracotta brick from the rubble. I let out an involuntary '*Oi!*' The women at the table moved almost imperceptibly back. Ashley Burnet sat regally still. I braced myself for action but before I had a chance to charge towards him he took aim, let out a low growl for effect, and fired the brick at the poster covering the *Qwe(e)rtyuiop* window, past an astonishingly unflustered Ashley, with all the force of his pent-up rage. A poisonous cocktail of ego, steroids and dodgy genes.

The window smashed.

Ashley Burnet stood slowly up, walked over to him equally slowly, and surveyed the shattered glass sparkling like ice on the pavement.

'Are you, perhaps, au fait with football terminology?' she asked, her voice stupefyingly calm. 'Because that's what I believe is referred to as a match-deciding own fucking goal.'

The camera, meanwhile, whirred on.

Bulgy Man left almost immediately, his apoplexy slightly compromised by his mental confusion, most of his fellow protestors following in his wake like a ragged troupe of circus extras.

What is it about men of a certain shape? I merely ask.

A small gaggle of his co-protesters remained, muttering among itself. I watched as Blaise calmly approached a young teen with long hair, wearing a tie-dyed sundress and standing quietly on the outskirts of the group. Less worried about her safety this time, I followed discreetly behind.

She spoke in a low, empathetic voice. 'Kyle?'

Kyle stared at the ground, embarrassed, and muttered softly. 'It's – Sophie.'

'Oh. Right. Sophie. How's your mum? I've not seen her in quite a while.'

Sophie shuffled from foot to foot, head still down.

Blaise waited.

Sophie shrugged.

Blaise smiled softly. 'Well, tell her I said hello.'

The trestle table was packed away in the back of a small van, and we were just heading off, when legendary comedienne Senga Mingin of *See Ma Fucken Show!* fame charged round the corner.

'Yon Ashley Burnet, is a pure dead cunt!' she roared, all spit and fury.

'Oh, thank you so much,' smiled Ashley as we passed. 'Pure dead,' she gushed. 'I guess that means 'stroppy' in Scots.'

Senga looked confused. 'Whit'd ah fucken say?' she said. 'Whit'd ah fucken – where the fuck *is* everyone?!'

We left her ranting at the empty space, the early morning sunlight shining on splinters of broken glass in front of *Qwe(e)rtyuiop Book*s like the final scene of an apocalyptic, low-budget film. And I couldn't help thinking, as the volume increased to a self-pitying roar behind us –

She'd make a magnificent Lear.

29

Ash was delighted with her launch. The camerawoman, apparently, had captured everything for whatever she had in mind – she wasn't saying – so it was a relaxed and buoyant Blaise and Ash who celebrated with a coffee-fuelled critique back at the flat. After the motorbike incident, and the block of ice near miss, a period of calm and recovery was called for.

Not that calm and Ashley Burnet necessarily went together. Two coffees in, they parted company. Ash got positively skittish. Blaise had just popped to the toilet when Ashley started wandering around the deep pile rug giggling quietly to herself. Then, without warning, she was off.

> *'Now, young lady, you put yourself in a very precarious position back there. It could have gone eider way. Fortunously, however, Een was there to ride to the rescue –'*
> *'If called upon.'*
> *'Exackly. On his magnificent, albeit metaphorical, white charger.'*
> *'There will be furder challenges ahead, Een, seemingly insurmountuous.'*
> *'Some physical, some mental.'*
> *'We're tinking here of your fortcoming extravaganza, Book Snuff.'*
> *'Det: The Final Frontier.'*
> *'Frontier? Insult more like. But you, like the ancient heroes of old, will rise to the seemingly – what was the word again?'*
> Insurmountuous, ladies. The word was insurmountuous.
> *'Just checking you were tuned in, Een. Passed wit honours. Well done.'*
> *'That you will rise to the seemingly insurmountuous challenges, like the ancient heroes of old.'*
> *'Or maybe not. Put it this way. We haven't decided yet.'*

Ashley turned to me with what looked like six tiny, nonagenarian eyes, smiled impishly and bowed from the waist.

Things settled down after that, and several hours passed peacefully. Just as well, because *Book Snuff* was on the following night. After lunch, while Ash appeared to be meditating on the sofa in front of the window, Blaise gave me her undivided attention at the kitchen table as I talked her through the structure of the evening. Running order. Hilarious ideas to use, others to jettison as they might not be hilarious to others. Outfit to wear.

Blaise nodded her appreciation. Made suggestions where needed. Was generally a much-needed calming influence. With a final 'Don't forget to pat your hair down', my cue to open a bottle of wine.

At which point, Blaise, who has suffered more than anyone for my art –

'You included, Een.'

– opened her laptop and settled down to a relaxing me-free break.

But no sooner had the cork popped out of the bottle with a pleasing thlump than – 'Fucking hell!' The phrase was pure Ashley, the speaker was Blaise.

Ashley snapped out of her reverie. 'What is it? You okay?'

Blaise pointed at the laptop. 'It's Karima. She's been taken off the plane at Karachi.'

'Cunts.' Not me. Ashley.

'Taken off?' I said. 'What do you mean? Why?'

Blaise gesticulated angry at the laptop screen. 'The authorities said she's a flight risk.'

'What's she done?' I said. 'I mean, that doesn't make sense. There must be a reason.'

'She's a woman,' said Ashley.

'Disseminating propaganda,' said Blaise, reading from the screen.

'They searched her luggage and found a copy of her latest. *The Chattel Market*. Told her to go home and –'

'– look after her fucking husband,' snapped Ash.

'This is serious,' I said, and I'm ashamed of what I was about to say next, '*Book Snuff* is looming and I'm now missing an act.' Fortunately, I stopped myself on time. Well, Ashley did.

'You're spot on it's fucking serious,' she exploded.

She was right, and I'll be the first to admit that Karima's situation was far more pressing than mine. At the same time, I *had* a situation. Thousands of authors in Edinburgh and, with no Karima, all I had booked at this late stage were two. Attracta Boyle. Chuck Weill. Was *Book Snuff* jinxed? Maybe, maybe not, but as Karima couldn't make it, even if she got on a flight in the next twenty-four hours, I needed another author. And fast. Preferably one who, at some point in their life, had said something funny. Time was of the essence. *Book Snuff* was –

> '*Immulent. August tirty first. According to our ancient timepieces, that's tomorrow.*'
> '*So festina lente, Een. But witout the lente.*'

Less than a day to go. No Karima. Replacement needed forthwith! I now had my token man, Chuck Weill, which put Val Muldoonican back in the frame. Torquil had been very keen until I let slip that Val was a woman. An excellent one too. I've always loved her stuff. Her latest collection, *Perhaps the Finest Limerick Ever Written About Newtownmountkennedy and Other Poems*, was suggested by a simple but beautiful thought. As explained in the introduction.

"The limerick, most pleasing of all poetic forms, has shamefully neglected the multi-syllable place name in favour of Dundee. Muldoonican has made it her life's work to redress the balance. She is proud to share the first fruits of her labour."

> A young Wicklow woman named Liz,
> Who travelled by mule to Cadiz,
> Has put it in writing:
> 'It's not as exciting
> As Newtownmountkennedy is.

Wouldn't you just know it, though. I checked her out. First thing that came up? Poetry Spat. Two words that seem destined to inhabit the same sentence. So what was it this time? Welsh poet Angharad Llewelyn Pryce, also at the Book Festival, had made an explosive claim. Her limerick, *There was a young fellow named Gwyn*, referenced, according to Angharad, Llanfairpwllgwyngyllgogerychwyrndrobwllllantysiliogogogoch. Under wraps at the moment, "awaiting my next collection". But you see the problem? Ask Val to do *Book Snuff*, Angharad pops along 'to show her support', *aka* 'have it out'. My place name is longer than yours. Two poets, one room. It wouldn't end well.

Of course, there was always my old pal, Abe Altman. He'd said something funny. He was also alive. And sprightly enough to do a round of golf as his daily constitutional. Late eighties, as previously mentioned, but perhaps Abe could be persuaded to come out of retirement for one last outing. A big request, and I didn't want to upset him with the memory of past glories, but I was desperate. I'd hold out the offer of Blaise's matzo balls, and accept his decision either way with grace and dignity.

I had his number from way back. Big, old mobile. He'd had it for years so, if the battery hadn't run out or it now proved too heavy to carry, I might still be in business. I found the number, pressed call and waited. A click. Then the sound of a musical instrument in the background.

'Abraham Altman is currently glockenspieling, but accepts your call as a gesture of solidarity between our two great nations. Now you.'

'Excellent intro, Abe,' I said. 'But that's no glockenspiel.'

'Indeed not,' said Abe. 'That's Ephraim Kishon, the celebrated bandleader, on jazz clarinet. We're rehearsing.'

'Rehearsing? Where exactly *are* you?'

'The Chelsea Hotel.'

'As in New York?

'Indeed. I'm in the *Chuck Weill* room. The band popped round ahead of our performance.'

'Performance? You never mentioned this.'

'Ah. Perhaps the mind was on higher things. How is Blaise, by the way?'

'Relentless, Abe. I'm matzo-balled out.'

'Lucky man. Ah. Got to go. Lift to venue pending.'

Venue? Performance? I gave myself a moment to settle my head. 'So,' I said. 'This – performance.'

'Ah yes. The Klezmer Orchestra of Yonkers have adapted my humble glockenspiel voicings for a ninetieth birthday celebration. Radio City Music Hall tonight, then we tour the States and – subject to regime change in the interim – Uzbekistan. But enough about me. Was there some reason for this charming, if ill-timed, call?'

'To wish you luck, Abe. I must have sensed something.'

'You've always been a most considerate friend. But hark, I hear the sound of distant car horns. Or is it Eimear Kreitman, tuning her flageolet?'

'Two points, Abe. The flageolet is not a Klezmer instrument. And you don't tune it.'

'Try telling that to Eimear. But hark encore! Leonora Daiches is about to massage her bagpipes. Time, perhaps, to wind our little chat down.'

Interesting choice of words because, far from winding things down, this had precisely the opposite effect. It fired me up. If Abe was heading off for a tour of the States at ninety, I was still very much in the game. I was years younger than him. Blaise had suggested I do one final search of the festival brochure. By far the easiest way to check who was there on the 31st, she said. She'd plonked one on the sideboard from a recent trip out, so I flicked through it for that elusive final act like a man reborn. I was, however, running out of time and, if my search was anything to go by, I was also running out of talent. Lucky escape with Rory Stagg, though. To complement his sell-out show he'd written, it seems, a tie-in bestseller book. *How To Beat Your Wife*.

> *A ****ing stonker'* – Sun
> *'Had me pissing myself and I wasn't even reading it'* – Lad

What if his wife and business manager, Amelia More, had said yes? Thinking of Rory brought me back to Dorian Wilde and my George Square phone call with Torquil. Dorian had seemed pretty keen then, and Torquil was obviously keen, so maybe I'd have to learn to love him. Attracta Boyle? Dorian Wilde? Was this what Ireland had come to? Still, Attracta was a draw, Dorian *aka* Foetus O'Flaherty seemed to be back on top and, as previously mentioned, *Book Snuff* was drawing ever closer. The more I thought about it, the more I realised it would be an excellent career move. For me, that is. For me. Because a successful *Book Snuff* would put me right back on top.

Speaking of which, back to Dorian. I wasn't aware of a book, but he must have written one. His ego wouldn't allow him not to. As a standup he'd just captured the Misery Mirth market. Now was his chance to use *Book Snuff* to sweet-talk a leading publisher. There were bound to be some in attendance given Torquil's reputation. One problem, I didn't have Dorian's number. *The Vulvas*, however, did. They must have, they'd booked him for their show.

I didn't have a contact for them either, but a quick call to their venue sorted that. They frequented a local café near *The Church of the Holy Rude* most afternoons, so I set off, and sure enough there they were. Outdoor seats. Hooting at some private joke – possibly me. After I'd convinced them I hadn't taken a waiting job till things looked up – 'which, face it, Macker, they probably won't at your age' – they didn't give me Dorian Wilde's number. No. They phoned him for me. Not what I had in mind, but they insisted. Something about a code of ethics or, put it another way, a chance to have some harmless fun at my expense.

'Dorian? Howaya. That's great news whatever it is. Listen, you remember we told you about *Book Snuff*? Your nemesis, yeh. We've got him right here. He'd like to offer you a shot at suicide. Tell you what. Passing him over now. You'll know it's him by the deep, gravelly voice.'

'Dorian. Me, by the way. Normal voice.' Gritted teeth. 'Great talking to you and congrats on the Beckett thing.'

'Good man Sam,' said Dorian smugly, his ego loud and clear over the phone. 'He might be dead but he still has great taste. Speaking of taste, pal, your so-called novel. What's it called again?'

'*Sloot*. What about it?'

'Spotted it in a hospice charity shop. 50p? Bit pricey, so I left it.'

'Your point?'

'I'm told I'm in there as Foetus O'Flattery.'

'Flaherty,' I said. 'He's an amalgam.'

'What, me and me? So fair enough, Flaherty. Not very flattering but, hoh? Foetus? Not much of a part either, by the sound of it.'

'You haven't read it.'

'More of a Beckett man, moi.'

Yeh, right. Pop-up Beckett. I kept that line to myself.

'Well okay,' I said. 'Small part, and he's very young – a prodigy if you will – but he really comes into his own in *Hewbris*.'

'That so? What happens? Hold on. Let me guess. He gets offered *Book Snuff* by a loser on the make. Wins. Tops himself for real. Everyone laughs because he doesn't have a book out. No book deal, just dead. Close?' Dorian's version certainly had its merits as a storyline, but I was getting desperate. I was on the verge of debasing myself and appealing to his overweening vanity, his monstrous sense of self, the fact that he'd been begging for the booking before he won the Beckett thing, when he spared me the indignity.

'Thing is, you see, it might work for Foetus, it doesn't work for me. So how's about this for a rewrite? He gets offered *Book Snuff* over the phone.'

'By the loser on the make.'

'The very man. Hollywood agent on the other line. *Far Side of Funny*, Dore? Genius. Big career choice here. Adulation. Spondulicks. Pick of the LA bird life. That's choice A. Choice B? Your pathetic little gig. Thoughts?'

'Well,' I said, 'it all depends if you're into ornithology.' I don't think he caught that bit. Call on the other line. He was gone. I handed the mobile back. 'I don't suppose you lot could co-write a novel overnight? No? That's a relief.'

I grabbed a free seat and squeezed in beside them. 'You're just too damned entertaining. You'd *swamp* it.' Interesting. I'd been turned down by Dorian Wilde, but I was feeling a bit trippy. Relief trippy. 'Weird,' I said. 'I've just been turned down by our mutual friend there' – I gestured at the phone – 'but I feel fantastic! Why?'

'You feel fantastic, Macker, *because* you were turned down by' – a dismissive gesture at the mobile – 'our mutual friend there.'

'Brilliant,' I said. 'Who needs therapy? The coffees are on me.' I turned to the hovering waiter. 'Whatever everyone is having,' I said. 'And while we're at it – you haven't by any chance written a book?'

He had. I promised to read it. Bad move. I got away without offering him *Book Snuff*, though, so there was that.

On the way home, however, negative thoughts started creeping back in. I was a good deal younger than Abe Altman. I still had a healthy career ahead of me. Theoretically. But what if *Book Snuff* crashed and burned?

Experience of how panels worked told me I needed at least three authors or it would be an uphill struggle. This was a great opportunity to shift my career up several gears, but not if I couldn't even book the final act. There were literally thousands of writers in Edinburgh, particularly if you included novel-writing waiters. In fact, was there anyone in Edinburgh who *hadn't* written a book? Unlikely, yet there I was, stuck on two.

As luck would have it, I bumped into Robin on the way back to the flat, resplendent as always, this time in a grey herringbone two-piece with lime-green waistcoat. Any chance he could negotiate with Robyn, maybe do a one-off swap? 'I am so, so sorry, man. My people would never forgive me. My fans would never forgive me. History itself –' He stopped himself there. The point had been made. 'Besides,' he shrugged, 'Robyn would never agree to it anyway. It would upset her training regime.' He lowered his voice to an excited stage whisper. 'Bit hush hush at the moment, but she's been chosen to represent Wales at next year's Commonwealth Games. Women's 10k. I am so, so proud!'

That was a lot to take in. The Women's bit for starters, but I went for the soft option. 'I didn't know Robyn was Welsh.'

'Lawks, Mr. MacP! Where have you *been*?!'

Where indeed? I had no answer to that, so there we left it.

I arrived back at the Grassmarket, mounted the winding steps, paused for a quick breather at the top, and entered the flat. Freya yawned, stretched on Ashley's hat and greeted me in cat-speak. Blaise looked up from the book she was reading. 'Karima replacement,' she said. 'Any luck?' Straight to the point.

'In a word,' I replied, 'no.'

'I believe your show is immulent,' said Blaise. 'Correct?'

'Tomorrow,' I sighed. '6pm.'

Blaise winced. 'Can't get more immulent than that,' she said. 'Added to which, I know what you're like. You'll agonise. You'll pace. You really think

Fraser's floor can take that level of angst?'

Good question. But I didn't have an answer.

Blaise closed her book with a decisive thwack. 'Ash will do it.'

What?! Ashley Burnet? *Book Snuff*?

They'd obviously discussed the matter, but I didn't respond immediately. I was visualising, at incalculable and possibly irreversible cost to my mental health and well-being, the nightmare scenario. Ashley Burnet/Chuck Weill. Or vice versa. Chuck hated Ashley, Ashley hated Chuck. Seconds out.

Blaise may have sensed the toll on my fragile psyche. 'Besides,' she said, 'There's a bonus. Ashley's book has a whole chapter devoted to Karima.'

'Not *Stroppy Cunt*,' said Ashley, who'd just come into the room. 'Before you sully the reputation of an inspirational woman.'

'Mngiaow.'

I was about to be outvoted here, so I had to get out of this. And fast. Ah! 'Point of information,' I said to Ashley. 'What about you and Chuck Weill? Seems to me you've got previous. Anything I should know about?'

'Chuck's a sweetie,' said Ash. 'Well, apart from murdering anyone stupid enough to marry the trigger-happy fuck.'

'Hold on though,' I said. 'I thought you were flying back to Sydney.'

'One a.m. After the show. Plenty of time. I'll book a cab for the airport.'

'Any chance of an earlier flight?'

Ash laughed. I hadn't meant it as a joke, but accepted her response with a fatalistic shrug. And it was at that precise moment I realised I was holding the US President. Tapping him against my palm. No idea how that happened. Nerves? I put the president down, resigned to my tragic fate.

Book Snuff was only a day away.

I'd have to live with Ash.

Midnight. Blaise and Ash were busying themselves with the growing *Free Karima From The Shackles Of An Arranged Fucking Marriage** movement. I was standing by the window looking down on the drunken revellers. The spot by the Covenanters' Memorial where Dan always stood was bathed in melancholy. The melancholy of his absence. The spirit of Dan in the midnight hour, his sad moustache, his long, long face and tragic eyes, seemed almost more real than the physical, corporeal Dan. I felt terrible. I'd neglected my oldest, dearest friend. Not even taken him a coffee. And yet, his absent face didn't admonish me. In its inexpressible sorrow it seemed to understand, to empathise and, ultimately, to forgive.

Which made it even worse.

I was about to turn away when I heard the music. Boom boom. Boom boom boom. In the absence of anything else to occupy my time – I may have been suffering from performance nerves – I thought I'd nip down to the Grassmarket. See if I could locate the source of this nightly abomination. I skipped down the stone steps and out onto the crowded pavement.

Last weekend of the festival. Beautiful night.

The moon. The stars.

The noise. The bars.

The vomit.

I hurried across the road, dodging the traffic and, safely on Grassmarket Square, turned to look up at the buildings opposite. And in that moment I spotted, in the brightly-lit second floor window next to Fraser's flat, the beautifully framed figure of DCI Strang, gyrating woozily and playing air guitar. Strang! A closet heavy metal air-guitarist! I was almost amused. Over the weeks, the regular late-night music had merged with the sound soup of the festival until I almost didn't notice it; but now that I knew it was Strang? That was a different matter entirely. He was supposed to be upholding the law, not flouting it.

---

* Ash's title. Shortened to *Free Karima* for the mainstream media.

I strode across to the front door and studied the flat numbers. Three floors. One two three. Simple enough. Had to be the one in the middle. I pressed it, pressed again, then yet again. I heard the click of the receiver, the increased volume of the boom boom booms through the intercom. Before he could say anything, I hit him with my best schoolboy Latin. 'Quis custodiet ipsos custodes?'

Hah. That would give him something to think about. His response, however, was not what I expected. 'The custodes, my dear Juvenal,' he slurred amiably, 'are perfectly capable of custodying themselves.'

I was thrown. Juvenal? Strang a Latin scholar? The music, I noted, had also stopped. A scholar and a gentleman? I stood on the late-night pavement and thought this through. Then I bade him a peaceful and, I believe I used the word silent, night and headed next door to Fraser's.

But wait. Above the sound of the drunken revellers I heard a plaintive cry. 'Attenshun musht ashuredly be paid!' What? Chuck Weill's partner, Lorrie, out on the town? The cry rang out again. And through the revellers young Byron came staggering forth. Streeling home from some pub or other in a state of extreme pissedness. Worth following again? He was certainly a fascinating subject matter, for me at least. Take the *ashuredly*. It's exactly the word I would have used had I been his age and – ah! the memory of drink. 'Attenshun mush hondootedly be paid!' There he went again. Interesting that his version of undoubtedly had been delivered in a faux-Scottish accent. Exactly, I'm afraid, as I would have done myself. At his age. In similar circumstances. I assumed he was howling at the night sky, but no. I then spotted Chuck and Lorrie, heading down from Victoria Street, past the *Naked Munch*, and turning left towards the Cowgate. Lorrie was carrying a small knapsack, Chuck marching along beside her in positively spritely fashion for a man his age, in step with his own internal drum. A man with a mission. I paused for a moment in reflective admiration and, as they disappeared along the Cowgate, I turned back towards Fraser's flat and the hope of a peaceful night's sleep.

30

Dawn. August 31st. *Book Snuff* day.

Light through a gap in the curtains. The sweet sound of early morning birdsong. I'd been awake for most of the night. No way I was going to sleep now, so I slipped out of bed, donned Blaise's kimono, crept out of the bedroom, greeted Freya with a silent wave, fed her with an ease born of practice, and brewed a cup of coffee. Long day ahead, but the adrenalin would keep me going. Not to mention a second coffee, and possibly even a third.

Coffee in hand, I opened my laptop and went online. An ad appeared at the side of the screen, flashing dementedly. 'We at Previous Day Delivery promise to deliver your order before you've even thought of buying it – or your money back!' Obviously a scam. I ignored it.

Back to the internet search. Ashley Burnet's *White Ink* launch had of course been posted online. And gone viral. And there I was, about to add to the virus. I clicked on it. The viewing figures swam before my eyes. It had only been up for three hours, but all those noughts! And the video itself: selected highlights, edited for dramatic effect. The bookshop. The table. The books. Ashley Burnet, tall, dignified, striking, ripping the black tape from her mouth. Bulgy Man, bloodshot eyes bulging, in startling, lip-curling close-up. The terracotta brick through the window.

Cut.

Technically excellent. Perfect structure: beginning, middle, end. But… Ashley Burnet in Edinburgh! Ashley Burnet doing *Book Snuff*! I still had to break this to Torquil. My mobile phone trembled in my hand. I don't even know how it got there.

Text Torquil. Break the news. Or phone Torquil, deal with the fallout. Text? Phone? I dithered. I swithered. This was – how to put it? –

> *'An entralling conundrum, Een. To text or to phone? Might we suggest a tird option?'*
> *'Displacement terapy. Have you, for instance, checked your estimable podcast listening figures recently? We merely ask.'*
> *'Wit the festival and everyting else going on, they might have shot troo the roof.'*

Not a bad idea. And no, I hadn't. I was immediately on it. Shot through the roof? I very much doubted it, but the festival might have bumped them up a bit. I typed the title in. *Hardly a Fit Subject for Levity.* Click. *Did you mean…* No, dammit. Whatever it was about to suggest, I meant *Hardly a Fit Subject for Levity*. I tried again.

Did you mean… *Too Old to Die?*

What?! No, I bloody didn't. I typed that in. 'No, I bloody didn't.' I was about to type the "I meant" part – but hold on. Could it possibly be – no, surely not.

This was chilling. I froze. Then? I clicked affirmative and there it was. *Too Old to Die.* One episode. Publicity shot of – I can hardly bring myself to write this – not me, but the three nonagenarian, bane-of-my-fictional-life aunts! Had someone nicked my idea? This was intolerable!

> *'Not a bad idea indeed, Een. We'll get straight, if we may, to the point.'*

I couldn't believe it. The three aunts to the life. But I hadn't written this. I hadn't recorded it. Hold on. It wasn't –

> *'Don't interrupt, Een, albeit mentally. And no, it wasn't Ashley Burnet in ludic mode.'*

But –

> '*Bold boy. Learn how to listen. It will serve you well in the munts and years ahead.*'
> '*As we were trying to say, you didn't write us, Een. We wrote you. The podcast. This book. Which, by the way, is entirely fictual.*'

But – but –

> '*What's wit the buts, Een? Try finishing a sentence, then maybe you can try your hand at sustained narrative.*'

But – this is absurd.

> '*Well done. Beginning, middle, end. Transitive verb. But is it, dough? Sit down there for a minyute and stop pacing. It's doing our tree Hydracious heads in.*'
> '*Tanks. Now. Are you sitting comfortably? Then we'll begin. This whole Edinburgh ting. You should have known it was makey uppy, Een.*'
> '*Fiction all the way and here's the proof. Ready?*'
> '*The Church of the Holy Rude is in Stirling. We planted that for the more alert reader. It suggests, sublimulously perhaps, that the Edinburgh of this particular book is indeed a place of the mind. Wit us so far?*'
> '*We also planted the estimable Professor Emeritus Stern – a fictual character we tink you'll agree. From our estimable novel Sloot as we recall.*'

Our?! Our?!

> '*Exactly. Also from Sloot, Mad Doc McGregor. Certifiably bonkeroonius –?*'
> '*– or the finest flowering of the Scottish Enlightenment?*'
> '*Or, assertably, bote?*'
> '*When we sell the fillum rights to this bewke, Een, you could play him on cellulite. You've got the wild, staring eyeballs. All you'd need is the fright wig.*'
> '*To proceed. Polyamóry in a decidedly non-fictual town in County Cork? There's no way the Vulva ladies could have known about that in advance. Well spotted.*'

'Which brings us to the Sewer launch scene wit the bould Chuckademus Weill.'

'If you'd written it? One sip of naughty juice and you'd be off on the razzle for the durayshing.'

'aka the rest of the bewke!'

'We didn't want you ending up wit the bongo player from the Juicy Crones in a brotel in old Amsterdam wit no recollection of the picaresque journey from one historic city to the udder.'

'Besides, you're married to the lovely Blaise in reel life, so hold off on the whores. To coin a phrase. A beautiful lady, Een, and unashamedly monogulous.'

'In spite of her many Sapphic friends battering down the metaphorical door.'

'To proceed. You'd never have tought of the lovely Robin/Robyn by yourself, now be honest. Sure no-one like that exists in reel life.'

'Did you know he's the only woman to win the hundred-yard dash –

' – in the history of forever –'

' – signing autographs along the way?'

No. I didn't.

'You're not alone, Een, because neider did we. Till now.'

'We refer to him her them as The Estranged Twins, the way you never see them in the same room togedder. Come to tink of it, they're the exact opposite of us. The Conjoined Aunts.'

'And as you know, Een, we have existed since before time immemorial.'

'Same wit Robin/Robyn, apparently, aldough we must say we never met them at the time.'

'Them, Een. Isn't that gas? Bit like tree persons in the one God.'

'All they need is the Holy Ghost for a full house.'

'Where were we? Ah, yes. Isabella. Break it gently to Blaise, Een, but she's buried in Glasgow Necropolis. Photo at the side there.'

Glasgow Necropolis? But isn't that –'

'In Glasgow. Well spotted. We stuck it into the narrative to give you someting to do.'

> 'Moving swiftly on. Ah, yes. Dorian Wilde. We had great fun wit that one. Was he born of woman or discovered in a frame in the attic?'
>
> 'We also trew the odd word like contentuous into the main body of the text, as it were, to alert the more alert reader.'
>
> 'Oh, and those lovely Vulva ladies saying Een. Mind you, that was a typographical doodah.'
>
> 'It should have read Macker.'
>
> 'But we digress. Our teesis? We, the tree aunts, are the autors, the onlie begetters, of the narrative you now find yourself narrating.'
>
> 'Beautifully, if we may make so bold.'
>
> 'Which, being as how we wrote it, might come across as us complimenting ourselves.'
>
> 'You're a very good boy, by the way. Mentally polite all this time as we've laid out the case for the tree aunts. To wit, us.'
>
> 'Convinced yet?'

Don't be ridic –

> 'Didn't tink so. Which is why we've kept the final proof till last.'
>
> 'If you'd written the book, Een, it would have been derailed by a certing minor character.'
>
> 'Care to guess?'

No. I didn't care to guess. But I think I knew already.

> 'Of course you do, Een, the certing minor character in question being Byron.'
>
> 'Was that the über-sexy younger version of yourself you were tinking of?'
>
> 'Don't answer that. If you'd written the book, the whole ting would have been about you and Byron. Down the wynd. Into the eighteent century.'
>
> 'Plague and pestilence. The haar in from the sea.'
>
> 'Confessions of a Justified Doppelgänger. Very avant garde.'
>
> 'That's French, Een. For avant garde.

I know it's bloody French for –

> 'We know you know. We were just trying to lighten tings up. Le point est, you must be sorely chagrined. On the plus side, however, the book has landed an excellent publishing deal. Six figure advance.'

Hah. That is total nonsense. I haven't even finished it yet.

> 'No, but we have. Six figure advance, option on the next book. Which we've already started, so relax. It's about –'
> 'Don't tell him, Dorrie. He'll only nick it.'
> 'Oh, and one final ting. We weren't sure wedder to have you as narrator. We were toying wit making you younger and calling you Declan.'

That was it. The final indignity. I simply couldn't take it anymore. So I switched them off. 'Thank you, ladies!' Click. I shut the laptop. With malice aforethought. 'And that's your lot.'*

I hadn't noticed till now, but Ashley was standing behind me. Hooting. 'That is fucking brilliant!' she said. 'Declan.'

No it wasn't. Nothing I could do about it, though. I didn't remember writing any of this. It was all pretty scary. *Book Snuff* was now only hours away and my mind, not for the first time, seemed to be whirring out of control. I'd have to talk it over with my ther – hold on, I don't have a therapist, so I busied myself with pacing, sighing, feeding Freya twice by mistake, over-dosing on yet more coffee and checking my scripted quips. I also thought of a nice opening line. 'My one regret as a performer? I've never seen myself live. I was always working at the time.' I jotted it down, showered, shaved twice to be on the safe side, may have fed Freya again, re-opened the laptop and

---

* *'Very masterful, Een, but we'll be the judge of that.'*

treble checked the quips.

At which point the doorbell rang. I made my way down the stone steps and opened up.

'Tried it through the letter-box, pal,' said a genial delivery man. 'Here you go.'

'Thanks a lot,' I said, and took the flat, rectangular parcel.

He winked in a friendly way, hopped on his motorbike and sped off. I glanced at his high-vis vest. PDD. PDD? Hold on. It couldn't be. Previous Day Delivery? This was insane! Standing in the doorway I ripped the parcel open. A paperback novel.

IN THE
MADNESS
OF
TIME

This was – this was beyond mental! I opened it at page one. 'According to my therapist –' I stopped there and flicked through the rest of the book. Until, that is, I came to this bit. The bit, that is, that reads 'Until, that is, I came to this bit.'

I turned the page to Chapter 29. 'Several hours later,' I read, 'we set off for George Square.'

My hand was trembling uncontrollably. Obviously a psychotic episode. I marched upstairs, tossed the accursed thing on the sideboard and went to bed for a very long lie down.

31

Several hours later we set off for George Square. Up Candlemaker Row, along Chambers Street and over to the venue via Nicholson Street. Blaise in her summer dress, Ashley in her wide-brimmed hat and tinted glasses, trademark hair tucked discreetly out of the way, wheeling her portable suitcase for the flight back to Sydney. She looked like Cindy, she strutted like Ash.

We were about to take the turn-off at West Nicholson Street for George Square when I heard it. A raucous chant that chilled my blood.

'Burn It! Burn It! Burn It!'

It was like some kind of nightmare.

'It is some kind of nightmare, Een.'

Shut up.

'Now now. Not nice.'

Okay, okay. But come on!

Was this my imagination on overdrive? No, because when we turned the corner we saw them. A large, concentrated group, brandishing multi-coloured flags, flapping banners, all massed outside *Qwe(e)rtyuiop Books*, chanting.

'Burn It! Burn It! Burn It!'

At the head of the group, Bulgy Man, his sweat-drenched beard bristling with purpose. No paisley pattern jacket, but baggy shorts and an off-white t-shirt not quite meeting at the belly. Just back from a baseball knockabout on the Meadows if the bat he was brandishing was anything to go by.

'Burn It! Burn It! Burn It!' screamed the mob, while Senga Mingin roared repeatedly at the top of her voice. 'Ashley Burnet is a pure dead cunt! Ashley Burnet is a pure dead cunt!'

This was indeed the nightmare scenario. It flashed before my eyes. *Book Snuff* cancelled. George Square in flames. Ashley burned at the stake. I was about to point out, bitterly, that the second two would get the headlines, when Ashley stopped in mid-stride and turned to me.

'Relax,' she said. 'All will be revealed –'

'In the madness of bloody time,' I pretty well snapped.

Blaise placed her hand on Ashley's arm. 'Tell him,' she said. 'The madness of time is now.'

'You're right,' said Ashley. 'The endgame is fucking nigh.' She grabbed me and pulled me into a doorway as the chants reached burst-eardrum level. 'Double relax,' she shouted over the din. 'I'm Cindy, remember? They have no interest in Cindy. Plus, and here's the crucial piece of information I had to withhold in case it got into the wrong hands.'

'This,' I hissed, 'had better be good.'

'It is,' said 'Cindy'. 'While I was holed up in the Blue Hills proof-reading *White Ink*, the University of Edinburgh invited me to deliver this year's prestigious Betsy Fry Memorial Lecture.'

This bit I knew, but I said nothing.

'Betsy was big on 19th century prison reform,' explained Blaise. 'Particularly women's.'

'Good to know,' I shouted over the din.

Back to Ashley. 'Date agreed, Surgeon's Hall booked for the gig, I set about the lecture with gusto. Next thing? We're terribly sorry, but due to an administrative error – well, you can fill the rest in yourself. They'd booked someone else in my place. So I thought, administrative error my Great-aunt Grizelda's left fucking testicle.'

The chanters, by this stage, had worked themselves into a frenzy. Ashley whipped her mobile out. 'According to this fake press release, which I put online this morning, the guest speaker cancelled due to mental health doodahs. And the university –' she read from the screen '"– is delighted to announce leading feminist Ashley Burnet as a last-minute replacement".' Ashley pocketed her mobile. 'Total bollocks,' she concluded, pointing at the irate hordes, 'but try telling *them* that.'

As if on cue, the marchers set off from their meeting place at *Qwe-(e)rtyuiop Books* towards Nicholson Street. Wrong direction for *Book Snuff* and George Square. Past me, Blaise and, thankfully, Cindy, who raised her fist in solidarity.

'Go get 'em, comrades!' she yelled. A resounding cheer in response. The marchers reached the corner and, column by unruly column, disappeared from sight en route to Surgeon's Hall.

'Burn It! Burn It! Burn It!'
'Burn It! Burn It! Burn It!'
'Burn it! Burn It! Burn It!'
'Burn It! Burn It! Burn It!'

'Ashley Burnet is a pure dead cunt!'
'Ashley Burnet is a pure dead cunt!'
'Ashley Burnet is a pure dead cunt!'
'Ashley Burnet is a pure dead cunt!'

Ashley squealed with righteous pleasure. 'That should keep 'em busy for a while.'

And off she marched in the opposite direction.

Towards George Square and *Book Snuff*.

32

The square itself was teeming. Book lovers as far as the eye could see. Chatting, milling amiably, relaxing in deckchairs on the fake grass. A laid-back, late summer atmosphere. As we entered the main gate I spotted an anxious-looking Torquil. I hadn't yet told him that Karima couldn't make it. Ashley moved discreetly off with Blaise as I headed, trepidatiously, towards him. I was strangely touched to see all three *Vulvas* springing over the fake grass towards the *Salon Littéraire* tent. With celebrity friend. They saw me and came over.

'We finished on Saturday, Macker,' shouted Nose Ring *Vulva*. 'This is the fag end of the festival.'

'Only joshing,' said Head Girl *Vulva*. 'You'll kill 'em. By the way, this is our new best buddy, Jake Fedora. He's looking for an Irish guy to play his oul fella in his next movie. It's a non-speaking part. The coffin scene.'

'So why does he have to be Irish?' I said.

'Method shit,' said Jake. He did that framing thing with his fingers.

'Great face,' he said. 'Can you do dead?'

'Not,' I said, 'at present.'

Back to the *Vulvas*. 'Blow 'em away, pops.'

Jake gave me a what-can-you-do look as they headed off. I was about to move further towards Torquil when Robyn, of Robin/Robyn fame, spotted me. Spangly mauve mini-skirt. Generous bosom in a low-cut, tight-fitting top. Luminous pink stilettos wobbling over the fake grass, absently signing autographs on the way.

'Robin is so, so sorry,' she said. 'Great news, though. He's found his perfect movie project. Family of four, okay? Mom. Dad.'

'Sounds great,' I said. 'And thanks a lot for coming. Speaking of which –' I clicked my fingers in the general direction of the performance tent.

'Jeezo, man,' said Robyn, sounding strangely like Robin. 'Get in there. We are with you. Me in person. Robin – well, not in person. Can't have both.'

'Yet,' I said. 'Wonders of modern science. Congrats on the Welsh thing, by the way.'

'Oh, that,' said Robyn. 'I'm just so –'

She was lost for words. I wasn't helping her out. But I was still curious.

'Thing is,' I said, 'I thought you were from Westcliff-on-sea.'

'I was. You know? As in was. Not am.'

'Past tense. I see. So where are you from now?'

She fluttered her extra-long scarlet extension fingernails at me. 'The world, my dear! The world!' She signed another couple of autographs and dropped her voice. 'Speaking of which, we've just been offered Life Presidency of *Narcissists Anonymous*. Great honour. But – *Anonymous*? I mean, I mean, what does it even *mean*?' She waved a dismissive hand. 'But hey, this is not about us. You get in there. Slay 'em.'

Kill 'em. Slay 'em. Blow 'em away. I was getting a bit worried about the steadily mounting murder metaphors as I left Robyn to The fans! The fans! and moved closer to my goal.

'There you are,' said Torquil when, finally, I stood in front of him. 'Well done! Total sell-out. Great line-up.'

I steeled myself. 'Slight tweak on the author front,' I said. 'No Karima.'

He blanched visibly. 'I see.'

I took this as my cue to expand. 'Bit of a problem with passport control at Karachi airport.' I didn't embellish. Get it over with. Hit him with Ashley Burnet. Deal with the fallout. 'But I thought it would be good to have her here in spirit. So to speak.' I hadn't thought that, but I thought it now. It gave an explanation of sorts for my – well, technically Blaise's – choice of replacement. Torquil, I could see, was mentally bracing himself.

'Who?' It was quite a deep-voiced who. For Torquil. In other circumstances I would have been impressed.

'Who?' I repeated the question. To give me time, I suppose. I wasn't looking forward to his reaction.

'Yes,' he said. 'Who?'

'Ashley Burnet?' I posed it as a question to soften the blow.

Which it didn't. As if it was negotiable. Which it wasn't.

Torquil Pittock started to palpitate. I was keen to explain the steps which had led up to my decision, by which I mean Blaise's decision, but opted to let him have his heart attack first.

'What?!' Ah. He'd opened a dialogue. Good.

'Ashl –'

'Are you insane?!'

Just then, a tall man who'd been hovering nearby, tentatively tapped Torquil's shoulder. He gave me a sympathetic look. 'Sorry to interrupt,' he said. 'Timmy, son, your mother and I –'

Torquil turned on him. 'What have I told you about visiting me at work, Dad,' he hissed. 'It upsets the dominant narrative.'

'Sorry, son. It's just –'

Torquil lowered his hiss. 'It's just nothing.'

I may have been staring at him. His hiss turned into a whimper. 'Not now, Dad. Please.'

Torquil, *aka* Timmy, became the little boy he once was. Dad, a kindly-looking man, half-smiled in my direction, then walked away. Over to a woman of similar age. Brief interchange, sad look from Mum and they moved slowly off together. I watched them till they'd disappeared in the crowd, then turned back to Torquil. He was back to the hiss. To himself this time. Sotto voce.

'I have no mother!'

I wasn't going there again. Quick change of subject.

'Why don't you want her on?'

'Sorry?'

'Ashley Burnet. Why don't you want –'

'Are you insane?' Repetition. He really was upset. 'Have you *read* her stuff? *Woman*?! *Stroppy Vagina*?! She's – she's – she's toxic!'

Fair point, but the audience was already filing in. *Book Snuff* beckoned. Nothing Torquil could do at this stage. He needed an author, she was an author, the only one he was going to get, so he moued piquely* and left it there.

The pressure was now slightly off on DCI Strang's murder theory. 'This is Edinburgh,' he'd said. 'It's sure to end in murder.'

It was pretty obvious Torquil wasn't going to murder Ashley. So who was going to murder who? Ashley murder Chuck? Chuck Ashley? Bit melodramatic. So who? Ah. I murder Attracta. Now there was a thought. Not necessarily in my best interest, though. Book sales through the roof for dead Attracta, His Majesty's Pleasure for murderer me. Maybe, just maybe, nobody was going to murder anyone. With this reassuring thought in mind, I managed to relax slightly, which boded well for the evening ahead. Fame beckoned, yet again, and this time I was ready to embrace it.

The stage was all set up for the event. Four velveteen tub chairs – black, white, pink, blue – with clip-on mics at the ready. A stand mic stood stage right. The sound man raced around, the way sound men do, checking last minute cables. I moved up to the side of the stage and turned to survey the theatre space. The seats were slowly filling up. No sign yet of Attracta. Ashley, still in her glasses and hat, was chatting animatedly to Blaise. Enter Chuck Weill on his own. He looked slightly lost without Lorrie. Probably off buying a megaphone for her "Attention must be paid!" riff. Not a bad idea come to think of it. Excellent comedy moment. I'd have a word with her

---

* With apologies to Toby Smyrke.

when she arrived. Just let rip when you feel the time is right. I found myself laughing inwardly at the thought.

Yes. The evening was starting to shape up very nicely. The mood of impending doom was lifting. Nothing Torquil could do about Ashley Burnet at this stage, so all I had to do was confine Chuck and Ash to an acceptable level of badinage and all would be well. Their last meeting had, after all, been a quarter of a century ago. They were older now. Not necessarily wiser, granted, but the prospect of Chuck leaping across the stage to strangle Ash, or vice versa, had doubtless diminished with the passing years. A few salty barbs wouldn't do the *Book Snuff* brand any harm, and as for Ashley Burnet's filthy tongue, Blaise was probably right – great for the ratings. Touch of showbiz posturing about their earlier encounter, perhaps? Still no sign of Attracta, but what could you do? Cometh the hour, cometh the star turn. Besides, I had my "late Attracta Boyle" ad lib. Shame to have to waste it.

I was about to go over and help Chuck into his chair – he looked as if he needed it – but Ashley got in there before me. Still in disguise, she went over to him, linked arms, heaved him up the couple of steps and guided him towards the pink chair. He sat creakily down. Ashley let go of his arm, helped the sound guy fix his clip-on mic to his jacket lapel, then plonked down beside him on the blue chair and, clipping her own mic on, she then removed her hat and glasses, and gave him a winning smile. 'Hi, Chuck. Guess fucking who?'

Chuck smiled wanly. He looked a bit washed out, to be honest. The audience had now settled in. And it was quite a gathering. Torquil. Robyn but not, sadly, Robin. Cheroot-smoking Cyd but no Sinéad. All three *Vulvas*. Jake Fedora. Blaise. A few low murmurs rippled round the room as some of them recognised Ashley, but nothing hostile. A mature, sophisticated response. Ashley was happy. At least they recognised her.

I'd just fitted my own mic on, and was about to wave to Blaise in the audience, when I noticed she was patting her head. Hair alert! Ashley's hair suited her wild, mine didn't.

'Well said, Een.'
'And wit reference to playing the mad doctor on cellulite, forget the fright wig.'

I patted it down and blew Blaise a silent kiss. Head sorted. The music faded, the stage lights went up, Torquil strode towards the stand mic. A burst of applause from the now full marquee. Showtime!

Torquil started proceedings off. May have been minutes, seemed like hours. I had a quick look through my notes while he grandstanded grandiloquently. I'd included a couple of choice cuts from my standup days, all good for what we in the comedy business call a laugh. Ready when you are, Torquil. Get off while you still have some dignity left. I didn't say that, but what if he waffled till Christmas?

'But enough about my own personal journey.' The line I'd been waiting for. I set my notebook aside and sat up. 'I'd like to introduce you to a man, ladies and gentlemen, a man who, many years ago at a performance right here in this wonderful, this vibrant city –'

He had my full attention. His hand was vaguely waving in my direction. I braced myself for my own introductory spiel. At this point, however, he seemed to falter.

'– this wonderful, this vibrant –'

He was now repeating himself and, although I couldn't see his face, his whole body seemed to have seized up. I looked towards the tent flap and, strolling through as if he owned the place, DCI Fulton Strang, with two uniformed officers. The audience murmured, heads turned. I watched, bemused, as he flashed his badge and strode up the centre aisle, flanked by his two subordinates. Big fan of Chuck Weill. That was my first thought. Ringside seat. Torquil, however, seemed to have other ideas. I could only see him from the back, but it was almost as if he expected to be arrested. But wait! Forget ringside seat.

Strang by-passed a startled Torquil, took his microphone off its stand in passing, and nodded me a greeting. Here was a man in full control of his own narrative. I didn't know what that narrative was. Neither, I assumed, did my fellow guests. As for the audience, they thought it was part of the show, which it wasn't, so they didn't know either.

Torquil stepped back, still startled, like a man who expects the worst. DCI Fulton Strang turned towards the row of tub chairs. Ash, Chuck, the empty chair where Attracta Boyle should be. He paused. Walked slowly round the side of the blue tub. Moved beyond blue. Stopped at pink. The Chuck Weill chair. He paused again. Placed a firm hand on Chuck's shoulder.

'Charlton "Chuck" Weill, I'm arresting you for the first-degree murder of Lorrie Muller,' he boomed into the mic.

What?! This was – this was totally crazy! Was it really happening? Or was it my brain, off again on one of its psychotic trips? I made eye contact with Blaise. She looked shocked and upset. Ashley simply grimaced, as if she expected nothing less. Difficult to say with Torquil, but possibly relief. The audience? A short, stunned pause was followed by a murmur of confusion. Was Strang a genuine cop or was he part of the show?

Strang waited till the murmur died down. 'On the night of August 31st, on Salisbury Crags,' he continued. Then, in a lower voice as if he'd suddenly remembered, 'You are not obliged to say anything, but anything you do say will be included in my forthcoming memoir and will remain copyright of the author.'

The audience applauded, still thinking it must be a set-up.

Strang was in his element. This, his whole demeanour seemed to say, was what I was born for. Chuck? He didn't look too perturbed. He had previous. Maybe he thought he'd wisecrack his way out of this one too. Who knows, maybe he would.

Strang turned to the audience. His audience. 'We got the call early this a.m.,' he said. 'Murder victim at Salisbury Crags. Female. No facial recognition. Don't ask. Thought I'd seen the outfit somewhere before. Beige trousers. Beige jacket. Both blood-splattered. Body close to the cliff edge. Unmarked haggis with traces of gunpowder found at the foot of the drop. All the hallmarks of a Chuck Weill hit. Haggis must have rolled off her head when the bullet missed it and plummeted –' He stopped. Too painful. Strang lowered his microphone and motioned to the two officers. 'Okay, lads. Take him away.'

Chuck raised an aged, blue-veined hand. He was coming quietly. Strang nodded to the cops to let him be. Chuck stood laboriously, creakily up. He glanced over at me and reached for his inside breast pocket. Strang was on it.

'Hold it right there, old timer,' he said.

Chuck smiled ruefully. 'What're you expecting, bud?' he croaked. 'The murder weapon? Five bullets left?' He ignored Strang, withdrew a plastic-covered sheet of paper, and waved it weakly in my direction.

Strang gave me an almost admiring look. 'Looks like he'll talk to you,' he said. 'Ask him why.'

I wasn't expecting this, but there was something almost pleading in the way Chuck made eye contact. 'My mother's teenage diary,' he wheezed, his clip-on mic crackling as he moved towards me. 'I've carried it around for years. Kinda looking forward to reading it again.'

'Maybe hold off on that for now,' I said. 'Simple question. Why?'

'Well,' he croaked, 'the melon incident was Cuba.' He thought for a moment. 'Lemme work back here. Pineapple?'

'Hawaii,' snarled Ash. 'You shot your second wife in Hawaii.'

The audience gasped. Chuck nodded weakly. 'Thanks, missy. Appreciate that. Cuba, melon. Hawaii, pineapple. Greece, olive. Big mistake that one. Couldn't see the goddam thing. So I thought, Scotland? It's got to be haggis. Fourth time lucky.' The audience gasp was louder this time. Chuck's face took on a plaintive look.

'Missed again.' Blaise, who had been commendably restrained until now, couldn't help herself. 'With Chuck,' she said in a quiet but audible voice, 'the bullet always misses.'

Total silence from the audience. This was heavy stuff.

Ashley leaned towards him with a look of derision. 'Or maybe, you twisted old fuck,' she drawled ironically, 'you just hate women.'

He seemed to rally slightly at this. As if he was giving it his earnest consideration. 'You know,' he said, 'I never thought of it that way. So you're saying – my aim was pretty good. I was just looking at it from the wrong angle.' He smiled an almost beatific smile, 'Well shoot now, that is *most* reassuring.'

He waved the sheet of paper again, still smiling, removed it from the plastic cover, opened it out and read. In character. Bit like a female Chuck.

> '"I didn't want the kid."
>
> "Okay," says the goddam cleric, "so you didn't want the kid. Well here it is anyways. Care to give it a name?"
>
> "Leave me alone for Chrissakes, will ya? Just chuck it in the garbage."
>
> "Whoa now. You're pro-life, lady."
>
> "Goddam it to hell, so I am. Hnh. Think I'll call it Chuck."
>
> "Like, Charlton?"'

Chuck chuckled wryly at the punchline.

> '"Hell, no. Just Chuck."'

He then slumped forward, gurgling gently, and passed peacefully away. A troubled murmur ran round the audience. Blaise lowered her head into her hands and Ashley let out an exasperated "fuck". The sheet of paper fell from Chuck's cold, dead hand. I was about to pick it up when DCI Strang strode forward and clicked his fingers.

'Give.' I gave. Strang folded the sheet. 'Evidence,' he said.

'What?' I said. 'Mitigating circumstances?'

Strang smiled enigmatically. 'Hell, no. Chuck Weill wrote this himself.'

'I'm afraid you're ahead of me there,' I said.

Strang composed himself. 'Okay,' he said. 'Chuck was born – what? – 1939? 40? Mother pro-life? Let's say she was a bit ahead of her time on that one.' He had a point, but Strang wasn't finished. 'His mother,' he said, addressing the audience, holding the mic like a pro, 'was a real peach by all accounts. Shot by an intruder when the deceased here was six. Except maybe it wasn't an intruder after all.' He paused, I'm tempted to say meditatively. 'The mother/son relationship,' he said. 'Very complex.' Torquil may have squeaked. Strang ignored it, and seemed to take a moment to think about what he'd just said. 'Makes sense, I suppose. Our friend here had to start somewhere.'

With that, Strang took a packet of *Lucky Strike* from his jacket pocket, turned to the audience and eased towards the mic for the confidential payoff. The killer punchline.

'Well, folks,' drawled Ash before he could speak. 'Looks like you've got your winner.'

Strang looked crestfallen. That, his face seemed to say, was my line.

33

Strang and his team swiftly removed Chuck from the stage, exiting through a side flap. The audience looked perplexed. Was that it? No *Book Snuff*? Or was it, perhaps, a postmodern subversion of the panel game format? I looked around for Torquil, but he'd disappeared. Up to me then to take control. I removed the clip-on mic and was heading towards the more imposing stand mic, which Strang had thoughtfully replaced, when Robyn, with a frantic wave and accompanying feminine bellow, tottered forward in her zingy pink eight-inch-high stilettos and clambered onto the stage.

'Listen up, people!' she roared. 'Big shout-out to Mr. MacP! Minimalism, Maestro! You haven't lost it!'

Hard to know how to take that. I accepted the smattering of applause and was moving towards the mic to say Thank You and Good Night, when Robyn, reaching it first, grabbed it from its stand like a long-lost love.

'She sucked up all the ego in the room, Een. Stand well back.'

I stood very well back. And Robyn, bestriding the stage with narcissistic joy, was off. 'We, to wit both of us, Robin et Robyn s'il vous plaît, have some Very. Exciting. News! We have our movie!' Applause. Not a smattering this time. The applause of release. The tension around Chuck had lifted. Now was Robyn time! 'Settle down, meine ausgezeichnete Freunde!' The audience settled down. 'Okay. *Straight Swap*. Mum. Dad. Two kids. Wrong bodies. They play swappies. Boy girl, girl boy. Mum Dad, Dad Mum. Happy ever after. Hands up! Questions!' She pointed at Jake Fedora, whose hands were nowhere in sight. 'Yes! Jake!'

Jake Fedora shrugged. 'Okay. Obvious question. Which one are you playing?'

'One? One? A teensy tiny clarification, Señor Fedora, if you will. No thespian I. Robin is the act*or*, I a mere athlete, although I have been chosen to stand for The Scottish National Party at the next parliamentary elections and, before you ask, Auchtermuchtie Central. Big, big challenge. The noo, however, I maun awa. Il me faut partir. Prior engagement. Oh, and Robin is playing Dad.' Pause. 'Mum.' Pause. 'Both kids. The lovely doctor who performs the snippy things. The evil lady who tries to put a stop to proceedings on ideological grounds and ends up in a prison hospital for the criminally insane. Other parts played by members of the cast. Yay! Catch y'all at the Oscars!'

With a flutter of his magenta fingernails Robyn teetered away from the mic stand. As if guided by a higher power beyond my control, I strode towards it.

'Higher power indeed, Een. Compliment duly accepted.'
'Oh, and before we forget' – giggle giggle giggle – 'knock 'em dead.'

Mic out of stand, finger pointed at Robyn. 'Give it up for Robyn!' I hollered. Total cliché, but I'd long since lost control of my own narrative. 'Robyn!' I repeated. 'Of Robin/Robyn fame! Soon to be honoured with a knighthood! And a damehood!'

'And the Order of the Garter, Een.'
'Don't forget the Most Noble Order of the Garter.'

'For their undying service to humanity! Their unstinting work in relieving poverty worldwide! Bringing peace to the Middle East! And, perhaps most importantly for the future of the entire cosmos, averting climate change catastrophe with their bare hands!'

I had no idea where all this was coming from, and to my astonishment I hadn't finished yet. 'Not to mention their unstinting work promoting National Lactation Month!'

Ashley, still seated in her blue tub chair at the far side of the stage, raised a clenched fist. 'National Lactation Month! Fucking Yay, Maestro!'

Lactation? I didn't even know what it meant.*

'Just deliver the text, Een. Leave the rest to us.'
'Well done udderwise, dough. You'd be mega on the evangelical circuit. That face.'
'But pray proceed.'

So I did. 'Robyn/Robin also, and this is possibly their most beautiful, selfless act of all, ordered a new-born baby from an impoverished surrogate in Dunfanaghy, because – wait for it – "we've been so blessed in our countless humble endeavours, we truly felt we had to give something back."'

A stunned and expectant hush from the audience. How would Robyn react? Would she accuse me of degrading ridicule in the service of cheap laughs and burst into heart-rending tears? Or say something witty and amusing in response – a killer quip to put me in my place and round the evening off?

Neither, as it turned out.

She looked at me. Her eyes glistened. A thin trail of mascara trickled down one cheek. An exceptionally long, exceptionally pregnant, pause.

Then?

'That was so, so *beautiful*. But –' tiny trembly voice '– how did you know?'

She moved closer and put her hand over the mic. 'Our great sadness,' she confided, her voice tinier still. 'we couldn't have a child together.'

'Of course not,' I confided tinily back. 'Incest.'

---

* I looked it up later. Details, for those interested in such matters, in *Suckers and Suckling*.

She puzzled over this for a moment. 'Hadn't thought of that.' Unhanded the mic, tottered emotionally down from the stage and made her way, fulsome bosom bouncing, discarded tissues littering her glittery path, towards her next, historic, all-important triumph. Signing, signing, signing all the way.

The audience started to file out, still unsure of what had just taken place. Fortunately, the *Guardian* critic was in. He'd tell them what to think.

Ashley, meanwhile, whipped off her clip-on mic, grabbed her wheelie suitcase from behind the blue tub chair, blew me a theatrical kiss and headed towards the tent flap where Blaise was waiting for her.

I thanked the sound guy and looked around for Torquil. Still no sign, which was understandable really. Outed by his own father as Timmy, *Book Snuff* snuffed out. Difficult to see how either could feed his ego. My own ego had taken a battering too, but the life of the performer is littered with disappointments .

I hopped offstage and hurried to join Blaise and Ash. 'I maun a-fuckin-wa, Jimmy,' Ashley dead-panned. 'Blaise has ordered a taxi to take me to the airport. I am so out of this fucking nut-house.'

As the tent emptied I spotted the quietly departing Stagg Nighters. No T-shirts. No ribald banter. I was strangely touched. I hadn't even known they were in. The *Vulvas*, meanwhile, were heading off with Jake Fedora. They called over for me to join them. I declined. I needed therapy, not ribald banter, and the prospect of playing Jake's father's corpse had somehow lost its appeal.

Ashley's taxi stood waiting as we left the main gate. Warm hugs all round. Affectionate swearing from Ash. She'd just grabbed her suitcase and was about to hoick it onto the back seat when Robyn tottered over and scrambled

---

* See Sterne's excellent essay on the subject: *After The First Death There Are Seven Others*.

in ahead of it.

'To the Surgeon's Hall an't please you, my good man,' she cried, ignoring the skimpy micro-skirt that had slipped dangerously northwards up her thighs. 'And an extra sovereign if you break the speed limit.'

The cab driver stared straight ahead. 'Your name Cindy, pal? Thought not. Out.'

Robyn pouted and held her ground. 'To the Surgeon's Hall, I repeat,' she pretty well boomed. 'There to deliver the inaugural and highly prestigious Betsy Fry Memorial Lecture.'

The cab driver was unimpressed. 'Something to do with chocolate is it, pal? Never touch the stuff. Out.'

Ashley looked as if she was about to hoick Robyn out by her cleavage, but exploded in laughter instead. 'Betsy Fry's Chocolate-fucking-Cream,' she hooted, and then, to Robyn, 'Do as the man says, mister. Out!'

Robyn, furious, super-pouted but did as she was told.

Ashley sighed a philosophical sigh and hugged us both. 'Thanks for the book, guys,' she said, patting her tote bag. 'Great inscription.'

'Book?' said Blaise. 'What book?'

Ashley opened the clutch bag and whipped it out. The Previous Day Delivery book I hadn't written yet! She opened it and passed it over to Blaise. Blaise laughed. I looked over her shoulder. The inscription? In my handwriting! '*Haste ye fucking back!*'

Ashley hugged us both again. 'I certainly fucking will.'

As she got in the cab she glanced over at Robyn and grimaced wearily. 'Take me now, Lord. Take me fucking now.'

The cab driver chuckled.

'Lord? Wrong surname, Miss Ash. Airport, wasn't it?' And with one last, fond farewell from Ashley, they were off.

I was about to dwell on the book inscription as another psychotic episode –

'Perhaps life is a psychotic episode between two periods of calm, Een.'
'Ever tought of that?'

– when Robyn snapped me out of it. 'Gotta grab me a cab,' she wailed, whipping her luminous pink stiletto-matching mobile out just as it started buzzing like an apoplectic hornet. She tapped to answer. 'Hi, it is I.' Pause. 'Sorry, what do you mean it's – I'm due onstage in – a – a brick through the window? A mob? But, but – *cancelled*? It can't be cancelled. Does it know who we are?! We are Robin! We are Robyn! We are Robin/Robyn!'

Robyn plunged her mobile into her clutch bag, and stamped her tiny foot.* An irate stiletto heel snapped. So did Robyn. 'Shit!' she spat, her Adam's apple rigid with righteous ire. 'Who'd be a fucking woman?!'

'Well, I would for one,' replied Blaise sweetly. 'Trouble is, you need to start young.'

'How young?' I asked as we walked off, while Robyn staggered furiously into the traffic to hail a passing cab.

'Moment of conception young.'

Which possibly ruled Robyn out.

As we walked away we passed a relaxed-looking Attracta Boyle, strolling lazily towards her customary look-at-me late arrival. I waved a cheery farewell with my Blaise-free hand and off we slipped, alone together at last.

Or were we? Blaise let out a suppressed 'Uh, oh.' Walking towards us in the distance, staring at his mobile and lost in his own thoughts, cross-generational doppelgänger Byron. As he approached, Blaise's hand stiffened in mine. Byron looked up from his mobile directly at me. Slightly puzzled frown. He then went back to his mobile. Repeat. Mobile, frown, me. Blaise walked faster, almost dragging me along in her wake. Byron looked up as we approached, stopped, and stared straight at me. He wheeled around as

---

* Literary licence. Size ten.

we passed. I wheeled around too and there we were. Older me, younger me. Eyeball to eyeball.

'You,' he said, 'are the spit of my dear old da.'

He held the mobile phone out. I glanced at the image on the screen.

'Can't see it myself,' I said. 'Wrong eyes. Different jaw. No beard. Hold on. Who's the lady?'

'That,' he said, 'is the beloved mammy. Why?'

'Thought so. Right eyes.' They weren't. 'Same jaw.' It wasn't. 'No beard. Now that,' I said, 'I can see.'

Byron punched me playfully on the shoulder. 'You remind me of myself in thirty years,' he said.

'Twenty-five,' I said. 'I'll accept twenty-five.'

'Done.'

And off he went, laughing, as it seemed to passers-by, for no reason. A wide berth laugh.

'Well that's a relief,' said Blaise, as we walked on.

'What is?'

'You. Byron. You know. Even the name. It's such a *you* name.'

'What? Like, pretentious?' I stopped in mid-stride. 'Hold on. You thought he might be my – Jesus! Are you suggesting I'd be unfaithful?'

'I think you'll find he was conceived before we met,' said Blaise.

'You think I'd be pre-emptively unfaithful?' I thought about it for a moment. 'It is weird, though.'

'What is?'

'He'd be perfect to play younger me in the film.'

'What film? Hold on. The hagiography.'

'The very same.' We walked on in companionable silence. We'd do a post mortem on *Book Snuff*. Blaise knew that. But not now. Now was for lovers. Now, in a word, was for us.

34

Fiction can be yanked into whatever shape you want. Life, on the other hand, isn't so biddable. There remained a few loose strands to tie up. We strolled towards the end of the festival and Fraser's flat, loose strands dangling behind us in the softly fading light.

'You know *Visconti's*?' said Blaise. 'Up on Victoria Terrace?'

'I do,' I said. First time I'd used that precise phrasing since our nuptials, which may have added to the romantic charge of the moment. I stopped, turned towards her, and fell into the deep pools of her beautiful brown eyes. Mountain stream brown. Has to be pools, though. For the shape.

'Funny you should mention *Visconti's*,' I said, 'because here's a thought. Why don't you and I go there for a celebratory nightcap.'

'There's an idea,' said Blaise. 'Now why didn't I think of that myself? But celebrating what?'

'Our undying love,' I said. 'Thanks for the feed line.'

35

Things were winding towards their natural, drama-free end as we sat holding hands across the intimate two-seat table in *Visconti's* window. Okay, *Book Snuff* had been a disaster –

'Unmitigated, Een. We were hoping you didn't notice.'

Having said that, I still had a few years to go before I caught up with Abe. Uzbekistan at 90? You simply never knew. For now, though? Just Blaise and me.

'You're smiling,' she said.

'Am I?'

Blaise said nothing. Just smiled back.

'I was thinking,' I said. 'Time to put all this madness behind us.'

As I was about to elaborate, a Lambretta screeched to a halt outside. A sky-blue Lambretta. Guido, the proprietor, muttered a string of something in Italian. The door flew open and a tall young man in black leathers and motorbike helmet charged through. Guido muttered to a halt.

'Quick translation,' he said, gesticulating expressively. 'Why me? Why does it always have to be me? Did you see that? Did you see that? The boy's mama sends him over for the summer. Look after my little boy, Guido, you're his beloved uncle. Little? He was that size when he got here. What can I do? I phone his mama. "Salvatore," I say, "will finish his days on the end of a rope." "Negativo," she says. "No death penalty in Scotland. You think I didn't check?" "Sylvia," I say, "forget the death penalty. There's a terrace outside. Railings. Big drop. I, Guido Visconti, will supply the rope." "You touch a hair of my little boy's head," she says, "sell up, leave town, because know this. I have the contacts."' Guido sighed. 'Her six beloved brothers. My beloved brothers too.'

I was about to interject with some soothing words, but he was off again.

'And you know my majestic ice sculpture? It used to sit right there, displayed in its special freezer? *The Leaning Tower of Pisa*? My pride and joy! *Mussolini's Penis* he called it, what can I say? But worse! Worse! Il stupido takes it out after we close. Stands it on the railings for a – what do you call them?' he gestured with his hands.

'Selfie,' said Blaise.

'Grazie. Off it slides – Splat! Distrutto. Totalmente!' He flapped a hand as I reached in my pocket for my wallet. 'Put that away. Therapy. You can't put a price on it. Grazie encore. Have a beautiful night.'

The make love bit was unspoken, but I like to think it was there.

Back at Fraser's I opened the front door and waved Blaise in. She walked ahead of me up the winding stone steps. But as we approached the door to the flat, I sensed something not quite right. Probably those few loose strands troubling my subconscious. The mysterious note on the door had been resolved. And the Lambretta, and the ice block too. Which left the headless Frida and one envelope with blank sheet. Both pranks? Possibly. But possibly, also, not. That blank sheet, for example. A coded reference to *White Ink*? Pretty chilling if it was.

I knew Ashley was headed back to Sydney, but did the possible perp?

I whispered to Blaise to hold on, stepped in front of her and opened the flat door quietly. Not a sound. In. Still nothing. I crept along the hall to the living room.

And who should be standing there but Torquil Pittock! Clutching the statue of the President of The United States of America!

'What the – Torquil?' I blurted.

He gripped the President tighter, his knuckles whitening as if ready to lash out, a mad glint behind his spectacles.

Keep talking, I thought. Isn't that what you're supposed to do?

'How did you get in this time?' Questions. Good move. Start a conversation.

'He's got in before?' Blaise gasped.

Bad move. Blaise had brought attention to herself. This seemed to upset the president and, by implication, the man clutching his legs.

Torquil Pittock. The president of the United States of America. I was transfixed by both. One deranged, one a lethal weapon. Both highly dangerous. I was about to step in front of Blaise* to fend off both of them, when the back window suddenly yanked up.

'I think I can explain that,' said Sinéad, clambering nimbly in. 'But first, Sir,' – she addressed the now palpitating Torquil – 'put the President down. He's caused enough damage already.' Probably referring to American foreign policy, but she certainly succeeded in confusing Torquil. He plonked it down by Blaise's laptop. 'Now, step away from the table.'

He stepped away, out of grabbing distance of the President, and glowered at the floor like a naughty boy caught in the act. I felt a twinge of pity, but this was serious. 'You climbed in the window,' I said.

'The front door was shut,' he whimpered.

'Oh well,' I said, 'so that's all right then.'

I was working out a way to avoid mentioning the unlocked front door on his previous visit when the downstairs buzzer buzzed. Angrily.

'Ah,' said Sinéad. 'That will be DCI Strang. I said I'd let him in.'

'I'll get it,' said Blaise.

I kept an eye fixed on Torquil while DCI Strang coughed and wheezed his way up the stone steps. Cigarettes. Booze. Retirement pending. I could see why he hadn't clambered through the window. He wanted to cash in

---

* *'On your white charger, Een. Our hero.'*

his pension. Blaise ushered him in. We waited politely till Strang's rasping cough subsided. Then down to business. I removed the X-note from the drawer and waved it in front of Torquil.

'I swear it wasn't me,' he whined.

I moved closer. 'I know,' I said. 'But what made you think I thought it was? Guilty conscience, perhaps?'

This was by way of being a softening up exercise. Torquil said nothing, but I could see he was rattled. I moved closer.

'Which brings us to the beheaded Frida Kahlo.'

Blaise folded her arms. 'Torquil?'

He did a thing with his hands. And his face. What? *Me*?

'What's this about a beheaded Frida Kahlo?' said Strang. 'I thought she died years ago.'

'I think we'll find it's a doll, Sir,' said Sinéad. 'On sale at the *Naked Munch*.'

'Exactly,' I said. 'It was shoved through the letterbox with malice aforethought.'

'Malice aforethought, eh?' said Strang. 'Do we have a body? Failing that, a head.'

My turn to look sheepish. 'I'm afraid they might have got thrown out with the rubbish,' I said.

'In that case,' said Torquil, with a hint of a smirk, 'I have nothing to say.'

Okay, I thought. My mistake. Next time, bag the evidence. I was about to bring up the blank note posted through the letterbox when Freya appeared from a gap between the sideboard and the wall, playing with the small, circular, battered head of Frida Kahlo. As if waiting for this very moment. Torquil Pittock froze. He looked incredibly guilty, and he knew it.

'Darned cat,' he muttered. Freya hopped on the table, turned to face him and gave him both eyes. The inscrutable cat stare. 'Oh, what the hell,' he snapped. 'I had my reasons.'

'We'll get to that,' said Strang. Then, to me, 'Anything else?'

'Indeed,' I said. 'This blank envelope.' I took it out of the sideboard drawer.

'A blank envelope,' said Strang. 'Intriguing. But what, in a word, was inside?'

'A blank sheet.'

Blaise sighed. 'Writer's block?'

This infuriated Torquil. 'No,' he snapped. 'I put the wrong sheet in. This –' He whipped a second sheet from his breast pocket – 'was the one I meant to send. You might as well read it now.' He thrust it at –

'Me?!' said Blaise.

'Of course you,' he spat. 'Who else? Written, mark you, in the author's very own blood.'

'Give it here, young man,' said Strang, snatching it from Torquil's outstretched hand. 'Evidence.'

Strang read it silently. He looked at Blaise. 'I don't think you want to read it,' he said. 'As for you,' – he turned back to Torquil – 'it's murderous not murdorous –'

'I'm dyslexic,' snarled Pittock. 'So?'

'Neurodiverguous, Een. It's all the rage wit the tirty sometings'.
'But do go on, Inspector. This is all most illuminacious.'

'And I think you'll find –' Strang passed the note to Sinéad.

She glanced at it. Then put it to her nose and sniffed. 'Lamb's liver?'

'Not human blood. There's a subtle difference. You're a good cop, Sinéad. I hope you get my job.'

Sinéad looked flustered, but in a good way. I, on the other hand, was totally flummoxed. 'But – why?'

'Glad you brought that up,' said Strang. 'Sinéad?'

'We've had our eye on Torquil Pittock for a good while now,' said

Sinéad, turning towards him. 'Not your first time is it?' She counted them off on her fingers. 'Incident at Moniack Mhor with a creative writing tutor. Exclusion order at St. Andrew's University. In both cases an unhealthy fixation on a father figure. Both hushed up.'

'Oh, for God's sake,' spat Torquil Pittock. 'There are no dead bodies.'

'I had wondered,' I said. 'No corpse, Detective Inspector. So why the sudden interest?'

Strang mulled this over. 'Fair point. Thing is, you, Sir, lead us, albeit inadvertently, to solving a heinous crime perped by an icon of American letters. Charlton "Chuck" Weill. Collared by DCI Fulton Strang, of Scotland's finest, as he was about to pass away. We felt we owed you. Besides, this young man has been a person of interest to us for some time. A most disturbing case. Quite fascinating from the purely psychological angle.'

'How so?' I said. 'We still don't know exactly what he's being charged with here.'

'Well, stick around,' sneered Torquil. 'The great detective is about to elucidate.'

'Elucidate,' said Strang. 'Good word.' He winked at Torquil. 'One L, C not S.' He crossed the room, stood behind the accused, and put an almost paternal hand on his shoulder. 'Sinéad has already touched on it, but young Master Pittock here –'

'I'm twenty-nine-and-a-half!'

'– had developed yet another fixation, this time on,' – he pointed a dramatic finger at me – 'you. Moniack. St. Andrew's. Edinburgh. In all three cases, older male author, much younger wife.'

'Excuse me?' I was two years older than Blaise. '*Much?*'

'Precisely. Fifteen years? Twenty? Ball park figure. To return to the subject, I'm a keen student of psychology, as Sinéad here will attest –'

'I didn't know that, but always happy to attest.'

'– and this particular case reflects a growing trend among the current generation of young males.'

'Of the species,' I said.

'Just so. The desire to kill the mother, metaphorically in this case it has to be said, and sleep, also possibly metaphorically, with the father.' The whole room was stunned. Strang shrugged modestly. 'Just a theory.' He squeezed Torquil's shoulder gently. 'And now, Sir, perhaps you could accompany us to the station to discuss the matter further.'

36

What an unfortunate time to not have a therapist.

That line came to me as I opened the shutters on this first of September Edinburgh morning. A light snowfall caressed the window. A well-fed Freya was purring quietly on Ashley's fairy fort hat. I went over to the bedroom door. Opened it gently, looked in. Blaise was still asleep. I'd like to blame our hot night of passion, but I'd hit the pillow the previous night with a thud. 'Busy day,' she'd said. 'Perfectly understandable. It's what I get for taking up with a much older man.' She'd snuggled in at that point. 'Much Schmutch. Besides, we've got the rest of the week to ourselves. No festival, no *Book Snuff,* no Ashley. No anything. Just us.'

First, though, I'd take a solitary stroll in the melancholy autumn morn. I closed the bedroom door gently, put my inappropriately light summer jacket on, waved to the softly purring Freya, and headed, in a contemplative frame of mind, out of the flat and down the winding steps. I opened the main door and stepped outside. Snowflakes kissed my face. A bitter chill in the air. I wasn't dressed for it, but what the hell. I was a free man in – Dan? Still here? But – why? The festival was over. *Straight Swap* had been packed away. His kids? Probably off being fêted around the world.

> *'The next generation's Robin/Robyn'*
> Guardian

And Dan? Had they forgotten him? Because there he stood, a solitary figure at the Covenanter's Memorial, with not a passerby in sight. Still with that look of inexpressible sorrow on his inexpressibly sorrowful face, still holding out a *Straight Swap* leaflet in the chilly autumn air. I waited for a break in the traffic and hurried over.

'Dan,' I said.

He nodded. No change of expression. 'I read your book,' he said.

'Great.' I didn't know what else to say.

'Guess who my favourite character was?'

I paused before answering. 'Dan?' I said.

He nodded slowly, as if giving the matter some thought. 'Dan,' he said. 'Dan the man.'

I thought about the madness of the festival. The Ashley Burnet and Torquil Pittock and *Book Snuffness* of it all. I thought of Blaise waking up. No festival, no Ashley, no Torquil, no *Book Snuff*, no anything. Just us.

And then?

'Dan the man,' I said, and I put my arm round his shoulder and eased him gently back towards the flat.

'The book is ended, Een. Go fort in peace.'